MORE THAN MEETS THE INK

Elle Aycart

Loose Id®

ISBN 13: 978-1-62300-021-9
MORE THAN MEETS THE INK

Originally released in e-book format in June 2011

Cover Art by Anne Cain
Cover Layout and Design by Scott Carpenter

Printed in the U.S.A. by
Lightning Source, Inc.
1246 Heil Quaker Blvd
La Vergne TN 37086
www.lightningsource.com

CHAPTER ONE

"Mom, this is insane! What the hell makes you think Mr. Bowen killed Amy?" Tate muttered as she spat a piece of wet grass from her mouth. Damn, someone had been watering the lawn. Her white top was going to suffer big-time.

"Watch your language! And I know he did. Now keep quiet and crawl or you'll get us caught," her mom said while elbowing her way through the part of the backyard that connected her condo with Mr. Bowen's as swiftly and efficiently as if the fifty-eight-year-old woman did this for a living.

"I'm sure Mr. Bowen has everything to do with it," she continued in a whisper. "Amy hasn't come home for a week, and the police won't do anything."

The police were doing nothing? No shit!

"It's up to us."

"Up to us?" Tate all but shrieked. "There is no 'us' here, Mom. There's just you bullying me into making an ass of myself."

As her mother's back immediately went stiff, Tate winced in regret and softened her attitude, trying her damnedest to keep her voice low and her tone conciliatory. "Amy's an independent cat, Mom. She probably just took a vacation."

Away from this Florida Eternal Sun Resort insanity, she thought to herself. Living in this senior complex was like being stuck on a very demanding, never-ending, hyperactive vacation hell, with bingo nights, afternoon salsa lessons, and morning gardening. Not to mention hula classes, self-improvement workshops, feng shui instruction, writing seminars, bonsai pruning, painting lessons, yoga, meditation exercises, pet training courses, tai chi, and other activities sane people only engaged in once a year during their two-week vacation and then spent the rest of the year recuperating from. Tate had only been here for a couple of days and was already exhausted—mentally and physically. No wonder her mom was cracking up. Big-time. Still, it was one thing to understand her mom's weird "coping mechanisms," another very different matter to condone them or take part in them, even if only grudgingly.

She should at least try to make her realize all this was silly. "Let's be reasonable here. Did you see him kill her?"

"Nope," her mom answered.

"Well, did Mr. Bowen tell you he killed her?"

"No, he didn't say he killed Amy, but neither did he deny it," she explained, turning to Tate and giving her a conspiratorial look that froze her daughter in place.

Tate stared incredulously at her mother. "Did you ask him?"

"No, I didn't."

Oh God, this was even worse. "Sooo, how on earth can he deny the accusations if you don't even ask? Really, Mom, we need to find you another place to live. This one obviously isn't agreeing with you," she muttered, shaking her head.

"Good morning, ladies. Mind if I ask what you're doing crawling out there?"

Tate cringed at the sound of those words. Damn, busted.

She tilted her head up, surely sporting a monumental deer-in-the-headlights look on her face. Despite the fact that the sun was in her eyes and silhouetting the imposing figure nearby, she had no doubt it wasn't her mom's neighbor. If for nothing else than because the senior complex only accepted residents from fifty-five years old and up, and the man in front of her was in the prime of his youth—all tight muscles and broad shoulders.

Oh boy, she'd known this was a very bad idea. Furiously blushing, she hurried to stand up and then moved to help her mother, only to realize she was already on her feet and glaring at the man.

"And who might you be?" her mom asked, arms crossed over her chest, one foot tapping the grass impatiently.

Jeez, leave it to her to get caught with her hand in the proverbial cookie jar and force the other person to justify himself. Had she been born in another time, Tate had no doubt whatsoever that her mom would have made it to inquisitor general in no time.

The man chuckled, amused, obviously not that impressed. "I'm James Bowen, ma'am. My father happens to live here. And who are you? The resident SWAT team?"

"Ha-ha. Very funny, young man. No, I'm Mrs. Cooper from condo A4. Next door actually."

James kept silent, probably waiting to hear why they'd been crawling through the lawn, but she didn't offer any more explanations, and Tate knew she wouldn't.

She nervously wiped her palms on her cutoffs to clean off the blades of grass and the dirt still attached to them, and then extended her hand, offering the young man a tentative smile. "Hello, I'm Tate. Sorry for"—she searched for a word that would describe the situation, but soon gave up—"*this*, but my mother seems to think your father…um…uh…killed our cat," she said, mortified, her voice getting lower and lower as she reached the end of the sentence.

To the man's silence and baffled expression, Tate answered by shrugging, her smile apologetic.

"Or at the very least kidnapped her," her mom crisply added. "Or maybe that horrible saber tooth of yours has eaten her. He had her totally terrorized. Ugly, ugly beast."

"I see," James said, unsuccessfully stifling a laugh. "And what were you doing? Engaging in a covert operation behind enemy lines hoping to make an extraction, dead or alive?"

Tate had avoided staring straight into his face, partly because the sun was blinding her and partly because she was too embarrassed to make eye contact after her mom's wacky stunt, but his obvious amusement at their expense and his flippant remarks had her gaze darting up, her lips pursed in a tight line. With the sun right behind him, she still couldn't see him clearly, so she shaded her eyes with her hand and faced the jerk.

The jerk was gorgeous.

Tall. Imposing. His dark blond hair was short but on the shaggy side, honey waves framing a devilishly handsome face with sharp masculine features. He took his shades off, his hazel eyes sparkling with amusement. *My*. Beautifully thick, blond lashes. He looked rugged and sexy. Sinfully yummy with his five o'clock shadow and that cocky smirk on his lips.

"Don't get smart with me, young man." The elder woman scowled at him. "Just give us Amy or tell us where she is, and we'll be on our way."

For a second, he looked startled and turned toward Tate. "Amy?"

She threw her hands up in defeat and sighed. "The cat."

"That's right, the cat," he repeated, barely holding his laughter.

"Your father never liked her crossing over his lawn...even made a couple of nasty remarks. She's missing, so either your father killed her or he's keeping her prisoner."

James's stance was relaxed, playful even, with his bulging arms crossed over his broad, hard chest. "I just came this morning and haven't been debriefed yet about the status of our latest prisoners. As a matter of fact, I'd barely stepped inside," he explained, a hint of mockery in his tone. "I guess you understand I'll have to talk to my CO before pardoning anyone. Dad?" he called toward the patio doors, his eyes never leaving Tate and her mom, his crooked smile showing off his sparkling white teeth. Or maybe they seemed so white because the man had that glorious suntan, the one Tate never got. Exposed to the sun, she always went from paper white to crispy red, no intermediaries.

It was a pity her mother wasn't as impressed with him and wasn't willing to wait outside; she narrowed her eyes on him defiantly and then darted inside the house through the open patio door.

"Mom, please..." Tate mumbled as she tried without much success to stop the determined lady. She threw a pleading glance at James and, letting out a harsh groan of annoyance, followed her mother. Thank God he was finding the whole situation amusing enough not to call the cops—so far.

This was so not happening. Not fair. Her life was shitty enough as it was; she had enough trouble with Rosita's crumbling down on her and her own private stalker e-mailing her to death. Her peace of mind couldn't afford her mom going bonkers on top of that. They'd all gone through enough, dammit; she didn't need any more crap right now.

After stepping into the house, a shorter and older version of

James intercepted them.

"What do you want now, Ann?" the man asked, his tone resigned. As he glanced at his son, a huge smile broke across his face. "Hello, Jimmy boy, you came early!"

"Just in time to intercept the invasion, it seems."

"Ha! I knew it," Ann said, ignoring everyone else and lunging for the kitchen, where a faint meow could be heard.

"I've done nothing to your cat," Mr. Bowen said, trying to placate her.

When Tate reached the kitchen, she saw Amy in a cardboard box, curled around what looked to be five or six of the ugliest kittens she'd ever seen. Nothing like the aristocratic, full-blooded, cream-colored, short-nosed Persian Amy was. The kittens, despite being just days old, had pointed ears, already too-long noses, and were three or four different shades of badly mismatching colors.

Her mom was so going to freak. She'd been saving Amy's reproductive capabilities for last year's European champion. Pity the sheltered pussycat had had other arrangements in mind and gone swinging.

Her mother shrieked.

"Now, Ann, don't be upset. She just started popping them out under my kitchen table. What was I supposed to do? I warned you she was not just getting fat. You just didn't want to hear it."

Yeah, that pretty much sounded like her mom, self-denial until the very end.

That was too much. Tate turned around and, dragging her feet, went to sit on the wooden deck of the patio. She didn't need to be ringside to witness her mother's meltdown. No, thank you very much, the backyard would be quite close enough.

JAMES DROPPED HIS duffel on the floor of the kitchen and, leaving his father to deal with the kitten situation, followed that sexy piece of ass currently wiggling its way out of the condo. All and all, the sexiest commando chick he'd ever had the pleasure to intercept. She was nicely curvy where it mattered, her cutoffs riding low on her hips, hugging her cute behind, the huge, crazy knot of hair at the back of her head bouncing with each step, threatening to unravel at any second, especially as she was shaking her head vigorously. He was about to yell for her to wait when he realized she wasn't running away. The girl harrumphed in exasperation, sat at the far edge of the wooden deck, bent her knees up, propped her elbows on them, lowered her head, and placed her palms on the nape of her neck. She was muttering something much resembling a blue streak any sailor would be proud of in between clenched teeth.

James grinned. Nice new neighbors—a bit weird, but nice. And they were new, he was sure of it; such a luscious behind wouldn't have passed unnoticed. Not that he was on the make. He wasn't, especially not here, but this place was always crawling with visiting granddaughters, daughters, and nieces, and he was, in one way or another, acquainted with all of them. Not personally or by choice, but old folks loved to play at matchmaking, and introducing all the eligible women in their families under thirty-five to him seemed to be the number one sport around here. He tried to dodge as many as he could without insulting anyone, but apparently decent sons-in-law were scarce. Or so he'd heard repeatedly since his father had moved down here.

He sat beside her. She smelled nice. Sweet and fresh. Like rain. Like pine and grass. Maybe all the wet grass smeared on her arms and stuck to her chest had something to do with it. For a while he sat just there, hearing her swearing under her breath, until curiosity got the better of him.

"Upset about the kittens?"

She stopped muttering, looked up at him, and smiled, her whole face lighting up with that small gesture. *Whoa.* He almost choked on the breath he was taking. She was even prettier than he'd thought: huge eyes the color of a Siberian husky's, soft pink mouth, dark hair, mischief in her smile, a deep sadness in her gaze.

"No, those are some ugly kittens all right, but I couldn't care less about their pedigree or lack thereof. I gather your saber tooth is multicolored, right?"

James nodded. "It's not ours though; he just drops by quite often."

She shook her head and chuckled silently. "Fantastic, an alley cat. Getting better and better."

Ann's words interrupted his daughter's as they carried from the kitchen. "Oh, but I can and I will! I'm blaming this on you, mister; after all, you're the one who was always—"

"You know," Tate said, turning to James, cutting into the voices coming from the house. "I blame myself. I should've insisted on her moving to a residential complex for seniors in Alaska, not in Florida."

Her pale blue eyes were so mesmerizing and her sweet voice so captivating that for a moment they blocked the whole world. His dad and Ann could be torching the place, and James wouldn't have given a fuck. And that was weird because she wasn't his type—at all. He tended to gravitate toward another kind of beauty—the more overt, sexually wicked one. Lots of makeup, in-your-face women. Exuberant, sophisticated, glamorous, a bit artificial too. Aggressive, sexually and otherwise. Real-looking women seemed to fly below his radar. Not this one, though. He'd noticed her right away; she was adorable with those huge, beautiful, husky's eyes and her chocolate hair trying to escape the confinement of the twist it had at some point been pulled into. No makeup on her, none that he could notice anyway. And no strong, expensive cologne searing his nostrils, which was usually the case with his dates. When he used to date, back in the Stone Age.

He saw her lips moving but couldn't catch a word. "Come again?" James asked, confused. All his blood supply was en route somewhere much farther south than his head; it made him a bit distracted. And twitchy.

"I said this heat is melting my mom's brains. A complete neurological meltdown. I take full responsibility."

He chuckled. "Nah, she's just new here, and this place is quite overwhelming at the beginning. Take it from me. My dad's been here for five years, and I still get intimidated every time I come to visit."

She smiled at him, and for some reason he felt that smile all the way down to his toes.

"Sorry for this scene," Tate said, gesturing toward the house. "And for almost breaking and entering. I'm sure by the time she was forcing your lock with her credit card, I'd have found a way to get her to see the light. Even if it doesn't look that way, we are good people. Normal. Neighborly."

"Are you telling me that apart from crawling guerrilla-style, your mom also busts locks with credit cards? Whoa, I'm going to have to watch out for her. Too much of a bad influence for my father."

She fought it for a couple of seconds but then burst into laughter. An earthy and unrestrained laugh that had her shaking uncontrollably while all the tension seemed to seep out of her body.

Jesus, she was beautiful. And sweet. And she was making him hot, here on his dad's patio, just by laughing. Go figure. Spontaneity was something else he wasn't accustomed to. His dates were always more restrained in their emotions. Uncontrolled outbursts of any kind, besides lust, weren't first on their to-do list.

He'd bet this girl wouldn't do restrained in any form. The twist at the back of her head had all but given out, and James realized she had tons of hair, spilling in an unruly fashion all over her shoulders, swallowing her, falling over her face as she doubled over laughing. Nothing like Faith, his last on-and-off-sex-without-strings partner, with her platinum blonde, straight, chin-length hair. Faith had kept her hair back and out of her face, even used a fixing gel for it. Restrained, sexually aggressive, and artificial. Tate was anything but artificial. She was damn spontaneous. The sweet, what-you-see-is-what-you-get girl next door. That white-picket-fence, happily ever after sort of woman he normally avoided like the plague.

Holding her stomach, she drew a deep breath and tried to stop laughing. It took a while before she succeeded. "Sorry…this is hysterical laughing… Can't help it. I'm just worried sick."

He remained silent, curiously observing her. Her snug, white tank top was covered in green stains and pieces of grass. He felt like dusting them away. Sure, like groping her tits on his dad's patio was going to go over well with her, even if his intentions weren't all that sleazy; he was neat to a fault, and the blades of grass and those smears on her top were badly messing with his conception of the world. To avoid giving in to temptation and getting his ass kicked, James shrugged off his jacket. As long as his hands were busy, they wouldn't dart toward Sweet Tits here and start feeling her up. And he was sweating. From having her so close by or from the Florida heat, he wasn't sure. Probably the former, not that he was ready to admit to anything.

The second he took his jacket off, she lifted her eyes to the tattoo on his arm, wrinkled her nose, and flinched in distaste. Her smile froze on her face. Man, spectacular shut down. She wasn't sweet and relaxed anymore. Stiff as a board was more like it.

"Nice," she said, pointing at the visible part of his dragon under his short sleeve. If her expression was anything to go by, then in her world, nice double-teamed with repugnant and disgusting. He looked at his arm, half expecting to find God only knew what there that would explain her reaction, but no, it was just his tattoo, nothing more.

There was a story there, but he was so not getting into that; too early in the morning. He ignored her reaction and plunged forward.

"Tate, right?"

She peeled her eyes from his tattoo and nodded.

"Are you down here visiting your mother? I haven't seen you around before."

"Yeah." She sighed and looked up into the open sky. "She moved here five months ago. This is my first visit. I've been busy at home."

"Where's home?"

"Boston."

"No shit! We're also from the greater Boston area. From Alden, a thirty-minute drive from the city. What a coincidence."

She shrugged a bit uncomfortably. "Actually it isn't. A coincidence, I mean."

His eyes narrowed on her. "Not only intrusive tendencies, but stalking ones too?"

She sighed again, her eyes still fixed on the sky. "Not exactly. When my mom moved here, there were several condos free in the area assigned for her age group. I asked if there was anybody from Boston or the greater Boston area, and your dad's name came up. The Nicholsons too, but there was no available condo near them. So you got us."

"Lucky us."

Tate grimaced. "Yeah, lucky you. I thought she wouldn't feel so disconnected from home this way. Needless to say, I didn't foresee her behaving like a...lunatic. She's been going through a rough patch, and she's developed some freaky tendencies."

He'd seen that. Maybe it would be in everyone's best interest to help her adapt before her "tendencies" escalated into full-blown, trigger-happy ones and the whole Eternal Sun Resort ended up on the five o'clock news. "Listen, why don't you come to the common area tonight? Country music and line dancing exhibition."

"Line dancing? Country music?" She shook her head. "I don't think so. Not my thing."

"Come on. It'll be fun. It's pretty simple stuff. As you might've noticed, the average age here is sixty-five, not an age to go swinging too much or doing risky steps. Bring your mother; it'll take her mind off other matters."

Someone stomped out to the patio, and they turned around.

"Help me with this," Ann said while juggling the box with the cats in her arms. "We're taking Amy and the little ones home. Hopefully those kittens will grow lots of fur to hide behind. We'll keep them until somehow they improve and we can give them away, or until they grow into us, whichever comes first. And we're so having a word with that vet and the damn birth-control shots he was giving her. And you," she continued, now staring at Mr. Bowen, "you better keep that misfit of a cat away from us. There's no joint custody here."

Tate choked on the breath she was drawing in and turned to James, a grimace on her face. "On the other hand, I think we'll take you up on your offer. Socializing and going out for a while might be a good idea."

CHAPTER TWO

Damn. James was sexy.

For the first time in her life, Tate understood Elle's hopeless crush on infamous bad boys.

This was so not good. She was the levelheaded one, the responsible, reliable baby sister, difficult to impress, not the one prone to lose it after a tight ass and a crooked smile. But despite her mental pep talks, she couldn't deny seeing James line dancing was making her stomach do funny things—triple somersaults without a safety net actually.

He was stunning. James looked spectacular; nicely worn-out jeans, cowboy boots, long, muscled legs, and a black T-shirt that clung perfectly to his roped chest. To say he was easy on the eyes was a gross understatement. The man belonged on the front cover of a firefighters' calendar, for God's sake, not in the common area of a senior community skyrocketing everybody's blood pressure to the moon. He should come with a warning from the health department: *Handle with extreme caution and use at your own peril. Looking will cause palpitations, dizziness, and hyperventilation.* She knew, for she was having all of those and then some.

He was definitely too much for her undersexed body to handle, his whole self flaunting so many sex vibes it was breathtaking. All those hard muscles flexing rhythmically to the country music, laughing with Mrs. Samuels on his right and some perky grandma on his left, not taking himself that seriously. Definitely too much mojo on the man. Add that to his rugged looks, his wicked and funny comments, and his warm hazel eyes, and Tate felt overwhelmed. Which didn't make any sense—her sister was the sucker for bad boys, not her. And he was a bad boy, no doubt about it. He had the act down to the letter—tattoos included. As far as she could see, he sported only one, but it was a huge Japanese-style dragon covering his entire right arm. Space wise, it amounted to four tats at the very least. Thank God it wasn't the tasteless, homemade-looking ones some of Elle's friends had. She'd despised all those guys, even the somehow nicer, mellower specimens. So why she was now drooling over James was beyond her.

From across the dance floor, he signaled her to join him, but she vigorously refused. No way. She was dead on her feet; those seniors had more energy than she did. Besides, she could salivate over him much better from a distance, thank you very much, where she didn't have to worry about the steps and the turns, or about feeling mortified to be caught staring. And she'd done plenty of those things, the staring and the getting caught. He'd smiled wickedly every time, but thank God he hadn't said a word about it.

It seemed that she'd done nothing but run into James the whole day. And it had been good. He was...compelling and damn distracting. Charming and funny, a shade of mischief in his eyes all the time, a ready smile on his lips. It wasn't only easy to talk to him, but he also had a knack for making her laugh. Such a sucker-punch combination. It'd been confusing in the morning, but now, while dancing, it was lethal. No wonder she was unable to put two and two together.

James had walked her through the steps, joked with her, all while his big capable hands glided over her, gripping her waist, directing her body, making her hot and flushed with just a slight brush, with no more than a look. His actions seemed casual, but she'd have bet anything he knew damn well the effect he had on women. Probably reveled in it. That knowledge was in his bottomless eyes, in the way his lips curled up every time she blushed. Here was a man used to leading, a take-charge kind of male. And thank God for it because she'd been unable to put one foot in front of the other without tripping over or stepping on him. He must have thought she was musically challenged or terminally stupid, but the truth was her ears had been roaring so badly she'd barely heard the music, let alone any instructions he may have given her.

She would do well to remember guys like James were bad news, each and every one of them. Fun for a while, but soon their devil-may-care attitude got old. And she should also keep in mind that her last boyfriend—a responsible, well-mannered man—had bailed on her when she'd needed him the most, but not before claiming that her being a drag was a huge turnoff for him. He accused her of getting all needy and clingy too, suffocating him. Well, it wasn't half his family that had just been buried or his family business going down the drain. Sorry if she was stressed-out, needy, and clingy, unable to be witty and entertaining or put him and his needs first. She didn't have that luxury; she had responsibilities, even if Aidan hadn't wanted to share them with her.

And that was a reliable man, basically a good man. Relationship material. She didn't want to think what a bad boy would have done.

As the band took a break, James approached her, all easy smiles and laid-back playfulness, and pulled her out of her mental divagations.

"Here's the gorgeous girl that bailed out on me and left me to dance all by myself."

"I'm done; no more dancing for me."

"I'm done too, dear," Mrs. Samuels said with a huff as she reached them. "I'm off now. You'll come by tomorrow to take down the curtains in my living room, yeah?"

James nodded. "I'll be there, Mrs. Samuels; don't worry. And have some of that delicious strawberry pie of yours ready. The last one you gave me I took to the guys in Boston, and they didn't leave me a crumb."

The old lady smiled, obviously pleased. "Yeah, yeah, just let me know when you're heading back north, and I'll bake a couple for you. And call me Violet, for Christ's sake." She stared at him for a second and then slowly shook her head. "I hope you'll let me introduce you to my granddaughter. She's a beauty; she'd make you a great wife."

"Oh no no. I told you already, you're the only one for me," he said as he grinned at her.

Violet, easily seventy-five years old, slapped him on the chest and turned to leave. "Flattering rascal," she murmured while walking away. "Don't think I'll let you off the hook with all that nonsense. Next time Tessa comes to visit, I'm hunting you down, do you hear me?"

Laughing, he turned to Tate. "Mrs. Samuels makes one hell of a strawberry pie. You have to try it."

"You're popular around here," Tate said, impressed. This place must have an endless supply of granddaughters coming and going. He probably had a revolving door in his bedroom and a mile-long line at the entrance.

He winked at her. "Well, it's nothing personal. Having the ability to climb a staircase without dislodging your pelvis will make you extremely popular around here."

Tate melted into laughter. How he did that to her, she didn't know. She hadn't laughed for so long she'd feared her facial muscles had forgotten how. Apparently not; she'd known the guy less than twenty-four hours, and her face was already sore from the extra exercise.

"I've worked up an appetite with so much dancing. Let's go for some burritos. What do you say, dance partner, interested? There's this place I know nearby."

She was famished, but she was going to decline. Or try to anyway, just on principle, but before she even got her mouth open, her stomach began rumbling, which, if his grin was anything to go by, he heard loud and clear.

"Okay, burritos it is." She was having fun. Why not indulge a bit longer? And besides, if her body insisted on melting at the very sight of him, then the least she could do was suffer the humiliation with a full stomach.

"My pickup is this way."

A pickup? That took Tate by surprise. "Where's your Harley? Bad boys ride Harleys, not pickups. You know, the whole tough-assed biker dude attitude."

He threw an amused look her way and placed his warm hand on the small of her back, gently directing her toward the parking lot. The heat seeping into her through his palm was overwhelming; liquid need rushed down to further dampen her core, and her already hard nipples hardened even more, making the beaded tips rasp wickedly against her bra, adding to her general state of twitchiness. Shit, this was embarrassing; he'd just invited her to eat burritos, not to fuck him under the stars.

"Bikes are fine, but I prefer pickup trucks," she heard him say.

Her gaze followed his to a shiny black monster pickup, which of course fit his image perfectly.

"Well, I can see the appeal of it myself." Tate knew nothing about pickups, but what was in front of her was definitely a badass's ride. Elle would be sooo impressed.

Before she could climb up the passenger side, James lifted her from her waist and settled her on the seat. He even buckled her up, ripping a surprised gasp out of her when he loomed over her to do it. Oh boy, too much sensory data. He smelled so nice, like sun, soap, and man. If she left a wet spot on the seat, she was going to die of embarrassment.

He offered her a wicked smile before walking to the driver's side, and after the engine roared to life, he maneuvered them out of the parking lot.

Unwilling to analyze her overloaded senses further, she groped around for something to talk about, anything at all that would divert her attention from the annoying way her body tingled. "Do you drive down here?"

He nodded. "I fly if I have to, but I love taking road trips, disappearing for a while. Nothing on my calendar, just miles and miles of road ahead. It's liberating."

She rolled her eyes. Of course he loved road trips; of course it was liberating. *Let's hit the road, fling responsibilities out the window, and let others take care of the tedious business of making money and keeping the boat afloat.* Didn't she know all about his kind!

"Do you take anyone along on those trips, or is it an all-by-yourself, solo thing?" she found herself asking.

He smiled knowingly. "Is that your subtle way of finding out if I have a girlfriend?"

"No," she answered crisply. Wait, or was it? she thought, horrified.

"No, it isn't your way to find out if I have a girlfriend? Or no, it isn't subtle at all?"

She frowned at him, ready to snap and say neither, but before she got to answer, he continued, "No girlfriend."

Duh. What was she thinking asking such a stupid question? Of course no girlfriend. These guys never had girlfriends; they had babes, bootie calls, fuck buddies. Or deluded girls like Elle thinking they could change them. Not happening. It was a sure thing, as sure as death and taxes. Men like him entered your life, put you through the wringer, and dumped your minced remains the second you stop being amusing.

He turned to her with a questioning expression. "By the way, what made you think I'm a bad boy?"

Hello? What didn't? She snorted. "Apart from the rogue looks, the macho attitude, the tattoos, and the ride? Not much really."

"Don't let appearances fool you. In essence, I'm a good guy. Golden."

He offered her a cocky smirk, and Tate reciprocated with a well-rehearsed yeah-right look.

"Sure." She chuckled and crossed her legs. Damn, the vibrations from the motor were so not helping. "Aren't you all? Down to the last scout and choirboy."

"I was never a scout, but I was a choirboy. Here, I can prove you've got me all wrong; one, I don't own a Harley, and two, every one of my tattoos has been done by pros in reputable establishments while being totally sober. Both me and the tattoo artist."

Tattoos? As in plural? Gosh, she should have known. She lifted her eyebrows in faked surprise. "No shit. And here I was thinking you got them in jail."

James looked amused. "No jail tattoos; hell, no jail at all. I'm as clean as a newborn baby. Well, maybe a bit harder and bigger all over, but otherwise sparkling clean to my angelical Catholic soul. And let me tell you, I'm very selective with my tattoos. I have three, and all of them have a very special meaning, mark a certain point in my life." He rolled up his short sleeve and showed her the dragon that swirled from his shoulder down around his arm in full. "I got that baby from a Japanese artist when I got my second black belt. I have another tattoo for when I came home after the military, and—"

"Let me guess, you got 'Born to Kill' tattooed on you for your army time?"

He barked out a laugh, surprise visible in his eyes. "Close enough. It says, 'Hard to Kill,' and that one I got after my divorce, not after the army. For that I got a group of Oriental signs that celebrates balance."

"So if 'Hard to Kill' was the tattoo of choice for your divorce, which one did you get for your marriage?"

He shrugged. "None. I told you, I only have three."

An uncomfortable silence followed his words and filled the cabin. Was it something she said? After all, she was quite rusty on bad boys etiquette. Then it dawned on her; mentioning marriage was probably a big no-no. Well, too late to take it back now. Turning to the window, she pondered what he'd said; three tattoos for three pivotal moments of his life—proficiency in martial arts, getting a divorce, and coming back from the army. Boy, was that self-explanatory or what? She should be already running for the hills.

"Um...thanks for dragging me and my mom out tonight to the line dancing," she began, hoping to engage him again. Despite everything, she liked his company and regretted the charged silence. "She did seem to enjoy herself, made some friends. A lady invited us to a barbecue."

His eyes glinted in knowledge. "Mrs. Nicholson. I know. I asked her to."

"Did you now? Why?"

"Just broadening your friend base. Hoping you'd have other people to stalk." He teased with that sexy smile of his.

"True." Despite her light tone, it bothered her more than she'd ever admit that her mom hadn't made any friends during her time in Florida. What had she been doing these past five months? Hiding at home? Bitching at James's father about his cat? "We know how to make a fine first impression, don't we? I guess you're already considering moving your father to another condo on the other side of the complex before my mom loses it and takes out the big guns."

"Oh, I don't know; I think my father can manage just fine. And as far as I'm concerned, that was a five-star first impression. Meeting a sexy girl for the first time while she's on her hands and knees with her cute ass pointing to the skies is a personal fantasy of mine."

Her face was instantly on fire. In just one second the man had efficiently stunned her into silence, although her body had the reverse reaction. Everything that had been tingling before was now throbbing like hell. Damn mortifying. When had she turned into a ticking sex bomb? If he did as much as brush his arm against hers, she was going to spontaneously orgasm in his car—at the very least.

He threw a fast glance her way and chuckled, amused at what she was sure was a panicked expression. Or maybe he was just jerking her around; God knew she didn't have the looks or the experience to hold the attention of such a specimen.

"Is it just the two of you, you and your mom?"

This subject was even worse; it'd get her weepy. "There's my sister too." She cleared her throat. "My dad and my brother died in a car accident a year ago."

"I'm sorry," he said, looking at her.

For a moment, Tate was afraid he'd press for details about the accident, like everyone else did out of morbid curiosity or wrongfully assuming she needed to talk. *Talk? Please, give me a break*! But James didn't ask her anything.

"Mom and Dad had always talked about coming to Florida to spend their retirement years, so after the funeral, Mom decided to move down here. I guess staying home was too painful. My sis transferred from BU down here so she could keep an eye on her while I'm in Boston." Yeah, because Tate was too damn busy trying to keep Rosita's afloat to bother herself to come visit her mom more often than once every five months. It shamed her to her bones, but she could do nothing about it. Well, she could, but she wasn't going to sell out, no matter how much her sister and her mother insisted.

"Anyways, Mom is just not herself right now, and Amy is very important to her. That's why she freaked out so badly today. She needs to feel she controls something, you know? Even if it's only a cat."

He nodded. "She'll be fine. Those kittens will improve, you'll see."

Tate burst into giggles. This guy was dangerous; even with her feelings in the gutter, he made her laugh again and again.

"I surely hope so. She has me worried." She sighed and smiled, unwilling to let the incapacitating sadness take a hold of her. She'd been down that road, and it wasn't pretty. "What about your father?"

"Dad? Solid as a rock. He got tired of waiting for grandchildren, says he isn't coming back until we make him some of those. But he likes it here, plays golf, takes salsa classes, drives the ladies crazy with his slick moves," he said, winking at her. "Me and my brothers come to visit as often as we can. Here we go," he said, parking the car and turning the engine off. "Best burritos in town. Never mind the shabby surroundings."

"Nice," she said when they reached the burrito stand.

Out of the four tables, only one was available, and he directed her toward it. All the women sitting at the other tables turned their appreciative gazes toward him, their eyes intently on his back or his front or whatever part of him was in their field of view. He didn't seem to notice, or if he did, he chose to ignore it.

"Nice? Specify for me, do you mean nice-nice, or nice-repugnant?"

She looked at him in confusion. "What do you mean?"

"I'm trying to get the nuances of your language down right," he explained while they sat down. "This morning when we met and you glimpsed the dragon on my arm, you also used the same 'nice,' but your face said otherwise. Your nose wrinkled as if you'd smelled something offensive."

Ah, that. She'd forgotten how embarrassingly expressive her face could be sometimes. Aidan used to say she couldn't lie worth a damn. And he should know; he *was* a lawyer, after all. "I see.

Well, don't worry, this 'nice' is a genuine, honest-to-God one."

After they had given their order, Tate continued, "And for the record, the 'nice' from this morning wasn't exactly a nice repugnant. Me wrinkling my nose was more like...a reflex."

His brows furrowed.

As he ran his hand through his hair, she found herself staring, wondering how soft his sun-bleached waves would feel between her fingers. Shaking her head in dismay at her utter lack of common sense, she forced herself to concentrate on the matter at hand.

"Disliking tattoos is like a Pavlovian reflex for me."

"So you see a tattoo and you automatically dislike the person that wears it? Is that it?"

Said like that, it sounded hypocritical, judgmental and ridiculous, snotty and conceited, but it didn't make it less true—for her at least. "Kind of. It's innate already," she hurried to explain; suddenly the idea of James thinking she was an uppity bitch was not appealing at all. And why Tate would care what he thought, she didn't have a clue.

"You see, my sister has the reverse impulse. I've spent my whole life seeing her heartbroken, cleaning up the messes those guys leave in their wake. They're like magnets to her; she sees a tat and there she goes, headfirst. It never fails. And trust me, I've come to learn most of those men aren't worth her time." Or her tears or her money, as it always was. "Every boyfriend she's ever had was in the bad boy category. Motorcycles, tattoos," she added making a point of looking at his. "Fun to be with, charming in their own Neanderthal way. Exciting with their rogue and wild attitude, but at the end of the day, completely unreliable. Loners at best, at worst low-life thugs with long rap sheets and a highly developed taste for all illegal things. All of them Peter Pans unwilling to grow up or take any responsibilities. They claim they need to be free. They need space...puhleeze! This is BS code for you having to deal with all the realities of life—groceries and rent included. They can't be bothered to keep their checkbook balanced or to remember birthdays or appointments. Or, God forbid, try to hold down a steady job. Too conventional for them, too boring. They're bad boys, they're above human laws," she said, rolling her eyes. "They're so full of it, it makes me puke."

He looked terribly amused. "Whoa, you seem to have given it quite some thought. Do you really see *all* that in a tattoo?"

A snort escaped her. "No, I see more; you just caught me off guard so I answered off the top of my head. Give me a couple of days, and I can write a dissertation about this."

"Bigoted, much?" He flashed her a cocky smirk. Jeez, even while making fun of her, the bastard looked sexy. So unfair. "Come on, Tate, getting inked is quite common nowadays, lots of people doing it. Nothing so horrifying."

"Not horrifying? Ha! Wait until all of them are in their eighties, dragging their blurred, sagging tattoos all over the place. Let's talk then about horrifying."

James threw his head back and laughed so hard she couldn't keep her face straight.

Tate was well aware that tattoos were entering the mainstream. There were plenty of reality shows about it, plenty of middle-aged, pudgy housewives getting them too, but that didn't sway her. It wasn't those housewives breaking her sister's heart every other day with their inarticulate, immature behavior and moronities. Although James was surprising her. He was sexy *and* articulate; who'd have guessed? And she was definitely enjoying herself in his company...too much, in fact.

"Now seriously," she said, trying to explain. "I don't see all that in a tattoo, but it seems that nine times out of ten, tattoos are an unmistakable marker for the whole bad-boy, I-am-above-all-that-mundane-shit style of life. So like Pavlov's dogs, I learned—tattooed men are evil." Then she looked at his dragon and winced at her words' implications. "Sorry, I didn't mean to insult you. I don't really know you, so you may be the one out of the ten that defies the rule."

He lifted his eyebrows in mock surprise. "Is that a compliment I'm hearing? Be still my heart. God forbid I'll get the impression you like me."

"I know I'm a bit...prejudiced," she said, blushing furiously. At his incredulous look, she corrected her words. "Okay, I admit it, a lot. I'm a lot prejudiced, I'm something of a tattoo hater, but believe me, it is a learned response; you wouldn't believe the lowlifes my sister fell for. All of them tattooed men, I might add."

"You're judging me by another book's cover, sweetheart."

"Maybe, maybe not. I know your type."

"My type?"

"The charming bad boy. You see, there are two types of bad boys: the brooding ones and the charmers. The antiestablishment, angry-with-the-world, brooding, temperamental type. Silent, arrogant, moody. And then there are the charming, funny ones with their lighthearted humor and fast wit. That's a facade; they're just as intense, they're just undercover, full-conceal mode 24-7. My sis gravitates toward the brooding, silent type. She hooked up with one charmer though. Total devastation. They're just as dangerous, if not worse. You're one of those. Both types only good for one thing."

He narrowed his hazel eyes on her, his thick, dark blond lashes framing them, a slow grin spreading on his lips. The guy was gorgeous. "Which is?"

Yeah right, like she was going to say it out loud. "Never mind. The charmers are that much more dangerous because of their goofy smiles and playful attitude. They like to dance, to party. They're fun to be around, treat you like a queen, but before you get your defenses up, they've hooked you and your life goes down the drain. They're like a black hole wrapped up in fancy, frilly gift wrap."

He laughed. "You've got to be kidding me. Are you a shrink?"

"Nope."

"Thank God. If your day job was anything to do with analyzing people, you'd die of starvation."

She shrugged. "I run a restaurant; dying of starvation is not an option."

"Good. Because you've got me all wrong."

"I don't think so," she murmured, giving him a once-over. She knew she was doing that disparaging thing with her nose again, wrinkling it. She moved to cover it, and he reached for her, brushing the tip of her nose with his finger.

"I am not that…disagreeable, am I?"

No, actually he wasn't. He had her insides sizzling, and her outside too. Very unfortunate for her. Every time he narrowed his eyes on her, everything inside went warm and itchy. Fuzzy. Her nipples were almost tenting her top, and her pussy was working overtime, flexing and pulsing in preparation, flooding her sensitive folds. Damned treacherous hormones. That was what you got for being celibate for more than half a year. They had her so worked up it was all she could do not to grab him, put her tail up, and rub herself against his leg like a damn horny kitty.

"No, you aren't. You're quite likable. I haven't decided yet if that's a good or a bad thing. Probably bad." After all, her sis always found them extremely likable, and look at the result.

Yes, she was too prejudiced, but with good reason. Bad boys were only good for sex—hot, wet, nasty, grinding, all-night sex if James and what looking at him did to her rioting hormones was anything to go by. Well, on the flip side, maybe this was her chance to experience some of that phenomenal fucking her sister talked so much about. It might wash off the dull taste of once-a-week—twice tops in high season—one-orgasm-per-session, usually his, of course, missionary-style vanilla sex Aidan had been so fond of. Besides, she had the feeling James packed more punch in one kiss than Aidan had in all his sex repertoire.

"Extremely likable," she found herself blurting.

And he was. The thought began forming in her head. James could be a great candidate for a purely sexual, no-strings holiday fling. After all, she was going to be out of there in no time. How much damage could he really do in that time? None, she wouldn't let it get that far. She had no expectations aside from great sex. She'd be safe from his bad-boy magic. Expectations. That was Elle's mistake over and over again. She expected so much from them, too much really. With those guys, any expectation, no matter how small, was one too many. They symbolized carpe diem at its very finest, at its most dangerous. Making any emotional demands on them was a lost cause, as was asking for commitment. Hell, they couldn't be trusted to water your plants or feed your cat when you were out of town; what else was there to say? It wasn't too clever to hand them your bleeding heart. Your throbbing body, on the other hand...

Her divagations must have been written all over her face,

for he offered her a cocky grin. "Ah, so I still have hope to get inside your defenses?"

"You mean inside my pants, right?" she said before she could censor herself. Damn her own mouth, no filter whatsoever.

"That too. A guy has to have his priorities straight. After all, I just discovered I have a reputation as a black hole to live up to. I should get every possible girl sucked in."

Well, he made sense. Kind of.

Thank God food came to her rescue before she thought and said any more stupidities. She was going to stuff her mouth full and shut up. Comfort food. Sex substitute.

He didn't seem to mind her sudden embarrassment and grinned when the food arrived. "Great. I'm starving; I used too much energy on the dance floor."

She welcomed the change of subject. "Yeah, you dance pretty well."

"Lots of practice. My wife loved to dance, dragged me with her all the time."

As the word "wife" computed in her head, so did the word "loved." Loved? As in past tense?

He noticed her sudden stillness and broke into a laugh. "No, no, don't get me wrong. She's fine and well, still *loves* to dance, but now she's my ex-wife and doesn't get to drag me anywhere. Hence the past tense."

That brought to mind the awkward silence in the car. "Listen, about the tattoo for your marriage... I'm sorry. I didn't mean to intrude."

"Nah, it's okay," he said after taking another bite of his burrito. "It was a fiasco. We were married for three years before she had the good sense to dump me."

"If it was such a fiasco, why didn't you walk out on her before that?" she said before she could stop herself.

His face hardened. She didn't mean it as an insult, but he sure looked as if she'd slapped him. He snorted in disdain. "Despite whatever despicable character flaws my tats are a sign of, at least in your eyes, I don't bail out when things get rough. And when she left me, even if I knew it was for the best, it stung. I don't like failing, and my marriage was a huge failure."

"Sorry, I didn't mean to insult you. Or imply you're a quitter." Which, of course, she was implying big-time. After all, bad boys were quitters in her experience; nothing was ever quite important enough to fight for, except for their own freedom, that is. For that, the insufferable fools fought tooth and nail, as if the women in their lives were there to rob them of it.

Hell if he knew why he'd talked to her about his marriage, failed or otherwise. Not her business. Besides, it had been ages since his divorce—water under the bridge. So why the fuck did he suddenly feel the need to justify himself? It wasn't like he was an unemployed bum. He might not be the most conventional guy on earth, but come on, he was hardly the worst. He was reliable, remembered birthdays, kept his checkbook balanced, ran his own business—successfully, he might add. He wasn't a loser because he had a couple of tattoos. It didn't make him a user either. The nine-to-five scene wasn't for him, but that was hardly a punishable offense, was it?

Despite all her badly misguided comments, he liked her. He liked listening to her talk. She had the oddest notions and misconceptions, but she was damn fun to be around, and the way she blushed and shook her head after catching herself staring at him got him every time. She was being judgmental, yes, but in an innocent sort of way. The girl was pretty much straightforward, called it as she saw it, no agendas. Her inquisitive eyes were continuously sizing him up, sometimes appraisingly, most times, though, disapprovingly. She was dead wrong about him, but hell, who was he to contradict her? A charmer, a bad boy, that's what she'd called him. A black hole wrapped up in frilly gift paper. He shook his head. Really, where did chicks get all those fancy terms and classifications?

They ate burritos and chitchatted. The girl had no problem eating like a trooper, and that was good, because he hated women unable to swallow anything but carrots and celery. She didn't ask him what he did for a living, probably assumed he was unemployed or up to no good, and he hadn't felt like offering details; after all, she thought she had him figured out, and he didn't feel like bursting her bubble. They briefly talked about her job, how she ran the little Italian family restaurant. Although she didn't say much about it, he had her pinned down on the spot. Oh yeah, the poor thing had overachiever written all over her. Overachiever and high maintenance, like his ex-wife. The ex that had, for over three years, accused him of being a slacker and drilled him about his lack of goals. He was extremely clever and gifted, she'd claimed, just too much of a lazy dumb-ass to climb up the ladder of success. Now that he recalled, she'd also hated his tattoos, had a cow when she saw the dragon, complained that no one would ever hire him. Suits and dragon drawings didn't mix, and he was self-limiting his own future, and hers by extension. Elaine had been dead right about that; but the point she was missing was that there wasn't a chance in hell he'd end up being a suit working sixty hours a week for some stinking company. That wasn't him, dragon or no dragon. He'd worked damn hard anyways and hadn't appreciated being put down. Still didn't. But this little minx here wasn't his wife, and he didn't have to justify himself or his choices.

Since this morning's incident at his dad's, he'd made a point of running into her. And each and every time, his body had instantly reacted, which was a surprise because lately he'd been quite uninterested in sex, tired of the empty feeling those physical encounters left him with. Not with Tate, though; she smiled at him and he got hot—hell, she frowned at him and he got hot too. He liked her, a lot. She wasn't only gorgeous and outspoken, but there was something in the strength and vulnerability he glimpsed inside her that called to him. She worked hard trying to hide the latter, but he saw through all the smoke screens; she was hurting and stubbornly refusing to let it show. That was why he enjoyed making her laugh; she probably hadn't done much of that lately with the sudden death of her dad and brother. James couldn't even imagine going through something like that. No wonder her mom was losing it. But Tate was a fighter; he could see it in the stubborn tilt of her nose and chin, in the way she narrowed her astonishing eyes before snapping at him. She was *not* going down.

By the time they were driving back to the Eternal Sun Resort, James was hot and painfully hard, pretty much dying to get to know her better—intimately. Her proximity played havoc with his senses, her body broadcasting a do-me vibe that was driving him totally insane. Although she tried to appear unaffected and even indifferent, she was flustered and twitchy, and her brights were so totally on his fingers itched with the need to reach out and pinch them. Not to mention, the way her thighs tensed and her breath caught slightly at every bump in the road were making his cock pound and ache in agony. Her brain might not want to admit it, but she was so ready to be fucked she was glowing.

He looked at her out of the corner of his eye, wondering which kind of panties she was wearing under those snug jeans. Whether they'd match the white lace bra he could glimpse under her white top. He wanted to lavish attention on her perky tits, spread her open, and fuck her senseless, see if her pale blue eyes got all smoky and glazed with passion, find out if she screamed when she came. Oh yeah, he'd bet his truck and then some that she was a screamer, he decided as he stole another peek at her. How would she taste? Salty or sweet? Curly hair? Dark or light? Trimmed? Shaved? Raspberry nipples or brown ones? Oh hell, all this fantasizing was giving him a dizzy spell.

In spite of what she thought of him, would she let him close? Could he get her so hot and bothered that her desire would override her prejudices? He wasn't sure, but his cock surely hoped so because with every passing second, it was more and more difficult for him to ignore his reaction to her.

He parked the car, and as she fumbled with the belt, they sat in silence.

"Well, thanks for a great night," she said when she finally got free.

For the longest moment, neither of them moved. They just sat there, a vortex of shiny, flirtatious energy swirling around them, growing thicker and sweeter, engulfing them.

He turned to her. "Great enough to grant me a kiss?"

She wasn't answering, but neither was she screaming *uncle*. And what the fuck, since when was it his modus operandi to ask verbal permission for a kiss? He reached for her and brushed his lips against hers. Softly, nothing scary. Fuck, she was sweet, and hot. And not pushing him away.

"I've been dying to do this all night," he said, after nibbling at her lower lip. "Actually I've been thinking about it since this morning."

She smiled. "Was it worth your wait?"

"Very." He scooped her up and placed her on his lap.

"Hey." She squeaked in surprise. "What are you doing?"

"You were too far away. I wanted to see if you're as breathtakingly pretty up close."

And hell if she wasn't. Her mane of hair had started the night loosely pulled back in a thick, long braid, but now it fell free over her shoulders, framing her beautiful face, with those huge silver blue eyes, so pale they looked like a husky's eyes. She had delicate features, with high cheekbones and a cute, small nose. And those pouty lips, soft and pink and warm, calling to him. He lifted his hand and traced her lips with the pad of his thumb, unable to stop imagining how that pretty mouth would look stretched around his cock, sucking him in. How that sweet little tongue of hers would feel swirling around his crown. Man, he had to put a lid on his dirty mind right now or his hard-on would burst from his jeans and scare the hell out of the poor girl.

"You're trying to charm me, mister." She scowled at him without much intensity, her gaze straying to his mouth.

"Yes, ma'am, I am. Is it working?"

Her breath was shallow and urgent, her pupils dilated, and the pulse at the base of her neck was speeding madly. Yeah, despite all the red flags his so-called "kind" raised in her, she was melting for him.

Her gaze glued to his mouth, she finally nodded, nervously licking her lips, her tongue accidentally brushing his thumb. Oh fuck, that little tiny lick went straight down to his groin, his cock jerking like a motherfucker. He cupped the back of her head and fell upon her. The second her lips tentatively opened for him, he pushed his tongue in and took charge immediately, owning the kiss, letting her taste explode in his mouth and in his head. She tasted sweet and a bit spicy from the Mexican food, and he couldn't get enough of her.

Her small hands reached up to his neck, her delicate fingers caressing him, and the kiss grew amazingly hot amazingly fast, catching James by surprise.

Without breaking contact, he rearranged her in his lap, getting her to straddle him. She sat on his throbbing dick, opening her legs wide enough to accommodate him in just the right place. Fuck, that felt too good. Her hot mound against his hard-on—beautiful.

"God, you're gorgeous," he mumbled into her mouth. "And you're turning me on big-time." He glided his hands to her breasts, brushing his knuckles over her hard nipples. He swallowed her gasps, and as he cupped her tits, her body quivered and she arched her back, begging for his touch. Although her boobs were not too big, they were cute and soft and filled his hands nicely. As he rolled his fingers over a nipple, she jerked so badly in his arms he almost lost it, especially as she whimpered and breathed a ragged "yes" against his lips while her hips ground into him.

Unable to stop himself, he moved his other hand to her ass, pushing her against his aching hard-on, pressing his shaft through her open folds, adding more fuel to the fire burning in his loins. She began riding him, her hips rolling against him, her pussy going up and down the length of his painfully hard dick.

"Jesus, Tate, you're so hot you're burning me alive. So responsive." Even through his jeans and hers, he could feel her heat branding his cock.

Her hands sank into his hair while she continued wantonly rubbing herself against him. Her movements felt so good he could almost feel the head of his erection nudging at her clit. He redoubled his efforts on her nipples and urged her on. With every tug on the hard buds, she seemed to go wilder, her breath getting more labored. He was dying to have his mouth on them, but there was so much he wanted to do to her he didn't know where to start. He kissed her jaw, her throat, nipped at her neck, licked her where her pulse beat erratically; then his lips slid back up to her ear. She tasted so damn good he wanted to devour her.

Her hands moved to his chest, her short nails raking it, her hips sinuously rolling against him while she kissed him with sensuous abandon. Gritting his teeth, he roughly surged into her, giving her and his cock more friction. Man, she was driving him out of his mind. She was letting out the most adorable, gasping moans. She looked so sexy, her eyes glazed, her breath ragged. Suddenly her body tensed, her back bowed, and she choked out a soft scream as she went over. Despite the pain his poor shaft was in, he had to smile. A screamer, as he'd suspected. Just the way he liked it.

He closed his eyes, trying to regain control. Fuck, he was breathing hard. Dry fucking had never been so intense for him; he was more than ready to explode. Making love to her was going to knock the wind out of him.

As she came down from her orgasm, her dazzled eyes opened slowly. "Whoa," she mumbled, seemingly in awe. "I've never gone off like that before."

He grinned. "You know, for all your utter lack of coordination out there on the dance floor, you sure know how to roll your hips to maximum advantage."

She silently chuckled and lowered her head, shying away from him, engulfing them both in that curtain of hair of hers, making it all that much more intimate. He reached for her, trailing his thumb over her lips softly, feeling her hot breath searing his skin. As his gaze lifted to hers, he recognized the same restless awareness in them he was feeling inside. She was far from done.

"I want you," he said, dragging her face to his. "Can I have you?"

She took her lower lip in between her teeth, chewing at it. He could see the dilemma in her eyes. "This is just sex, right?"

"Great sex," he corrected her.

"Just a hot vacation fling. Nothing more," she repeated as if trying very hard to convince herself. "I'll be gone in less than a week. End of the holidays, back to reality. Just sex and fun. No strings, no regrets, no commitments. No future."

He nodded. He had to leave in less than a week too. Not enough time for a relationship, not that he wanted one. Still, her thinking he wasn't good enough for anything else besides screwing rubbed him the wrong way. Fuck if he knew why; after all, he was the one always giving the I-am-not-available speech.

At the reassurance this was just sex, she let her guard down and licked her dry lips, her pink tongue now not accidentally but wickedly brushing his thumb. "Then yes, you can have me," she whispered to him. "Because I intend to have you too. If you're as good as you say you are, that is."

He offered her a cocky grin. "Oh, I am, sweetheart, I am."

She was on board; he could have her body, not her mind or her time, and that was great. Up until now, that had been the perfect scenario, the one he'd gone for with all his women. Now for some inexplicable reason, this win-win situation pissed him off. Whatever; he'd take what he could get. He didn't need a relationship either. That door had closed years ago, the day he signed the divorce papers, in fact.

He reached for her and dragged her face to his. He wanted to ravish her. Kiss her all over, make her come again, and then bury himself deep in her. Damn, this truck wasn't big enough for all the things he had in mind. As she placed her hand on his groin and palmed him, he groaned and ground his hips into her, his mind going completely blank. He was forgetting something, something damn important. Never mind. He gripped her ass, pushing himself against her and dipping into her mouth.

As she began working the zipper, she asked, "Um, do you have protection?"

Fuck, that's what he was forgetting, his damned no-sex-in-Florida rule. "I don't. Do you?"

She shook her head. Of course she didn't. Just his luck.

"You mean you don't have condoms right here with you, or you don't have them at all?" she questioned him.

Not here, not at his dad's condo. The closest condom was a ten-minute ride away. Hell! "Not at all. I never bring condoms when I come to visit my dad," he said, breathing hard, throwing his head back and trying to run away from her enticing smell. He could barely think as it was. With a huge effort, he peeled his fingers from her. Damn his stupid no-sex-in-Eternal Sun Resort rule. Who knew it would come back to bite him on the ass.

Tate stared at him suspiciously, one eyebrow cocking up. "How come you don't bring condoms when you come to visit? Or is it that your kind doesn't use latex at all?"

His kind? Which kind was that, the brain-dead one? That ticked him off. "Come on, how stupid do you really think I am, uh? Of course I use protection; I'm quite fanatical about it."

"Sorry. I didn't mean it that way." She looked contrite. Maybe she didn't think so little of him after all. "So then why don't you bring condoms along to Florida? You know, they are legal here..."

He rolled his eyes at her. "This is a senior community, Tate. The eligible women here are a bit outside my generation."

She laughed. "Well, I know that, but what about all those wonderful granddaughters like Tessa?"

He was shaking his head before she even got to finish the sentence. "No sex with them either. It's a rule of mine. My dad lives here; any involvement would be too complicated in the long run. Until now, I've been religiously avoiding complications."

"Until now?"

"Until now," he repeated. He didn't give a flying fuck about complications now. He needed to be inside her—the sooner the better. He wanted to charge to the next drugstore, but by the time they had the fucking condoms, the moment would be gone. Poof. Lost. Tate would build her barriers and leave him outside with his dick in his hand leaking like a pathetic motherfucker. Unable to resist her, he sank his hands into her hair and pulled her in for a kiss. He may not be able to fuck her, but damn if he couldn't work her up to another of those sexy orgasms.

As he began unbuttoning her jeans, she stiffened and grabbed his hands. "Forget it. We can't—"

"I know I can't take you. But that doesn't mean I can't pleasure you." He'd like that very much.

"And what about you?"

"What about me, babe? You let me worry about that."

She didn't look totally convinced but slowly let go of his wrists, and he finished unbuttoning her jeans. Her breathing quickened as he slid his hand down and delved his fingers under her panties.

Silky, soft skin. Bare.

"Fuck me," he said on a whoosh of breath, dick pounding in

desperation. "No hair."

She was bare there, soft and bare and delicate like a baby's butt.

"Brazilian wax," she whispered into his mouth. "Like it?"

"'Like' is too mild a word," he said with a deep growl and captured her lips, eating at her mouth, taking possession of her with his tongue. He wanted his fingers inside her, pushing into her as his tongue thrust in her mouth.

He ventured lower.

"Oh God, you've got to be kidding me." He hissed as he grazed something metallic. A clit ring. He was going to come in his pants. She was exceeding all his expectations by far, and those had been frigging high to begin with.

"You have a piercing on your clit?" he all but shouted out.

She laughed at his outraged tone. He didn't mean it as a reproach, but come on; she looked all sweet and soft on the outside, the perfect good girl. And then she turned her smoky eyes at him, and surprise, surprise, she was a she-wolf. A sex goddess. With a clit ring. And he was the one who was supposed to be a bad boy? Please.

"On the hood of my clit," she corrected him, clearly amused.

"If tats make me a bad boy, I'd like to know what that clit ring makes you, baby."

"Bored," she answered, shrugging, trying to sound nonchalant. He studied her for a second. She wasn't fooling him; she was far from unaffected. As he purposefully brushed the piece of metal with his fingertips and then caressed her swollen clit, shivers raked her body and she gripped his shoulders, her breathing labored.

"No, sweetheart. It makes you a wicked pirate princess. Now I'm in trouble. You're going to make me come in my pants like a fucking freshman."

"Hardly." She rolled her hips, offering herself to his touch. A ragged moan left her lips as he let his fingers wander south, sinking into her tender folds. She was hot and wet, her folds creaming, ready for him. Shit, getting her to come was going to be damn sweet torture for him.

"I'm going to love doing you with my tongue," he mumbled into her mouth. "Later, though. First I want you to explode around my fingers."

Her scent was all around him, making his mouth water, getting his hard-on to flex and pulse in agony, when suddenly someone knocked on the truck window.

"Hey, James, is that you?" he heard.

Pop. There went the bubble.

Tate screamed and jumped away from his lap, trying all at once to close her blouse and button her pants.

It took James a couple of seconds to reroute enough blood supply from his cock to his brain to be able to fully understand what was going on and get his bearings. They'd obviously been so busy with each other, panting like horny teenagers, the glass so steamed up that they hadn't seen anybody approaching. *Crap*. On second thought, thank God for the steamed-up glass…

"Wait here," he said to Tate as he rearranged himself and stepped outside, immediately closing the door behind him to give her privacy.

It was Norman, the security guard. Nice guy, horrible timing.

By the time he managed to shake him off, the moment was totally gone. Not for him—his boner was alive and well, didn't even notice the interruption—but for her. He peeked through the door. Yep, she was all buttoned up, already picking up her purse and scrambling out, looking as embarrassed as hell.

"I have to go." She hurried past him, avoiding looking at him.

He chuckled, grabbed her by the waist, and pulled her to him. No way was he going to let her go without getting to taste her again.

"A pity we got interrupted," he whispered. Cupping her by the nape of her neck, he took her mouth. Although a bit more reserved now, she licked at his tongue, allowing him access to her. He could smell her heat on his fingers, feel her nipples rasping at his chest, and it was all making him insane with need. His dick was screaming at him to drag Tate to a place where they could be intimate, but he knew there was no way she'd go for it now. Nothing to do but grit his teeth and beat the urge down.

"Good night there," someone called out to them.

The intrusion startled her into breaking the kiss. A couple, Mr. and Mrs. Thorncape if he was correct, was waving at them from afar. Damn, the normally deserted parking lot was worse than a fucking Fourth of July parade today.

Without breaking their embrace, he rested his forehead against hers, breathing hard. "You know how they say old people lose hearing and sight as they grow older?" She nodded in amusement. "A total lie, I assure you. Come on, sweetheart; I'll walk you home."

Tate offered him the sweetest of smiles as they fell quietly into step.

"So that you know, I am not giving up on you."

"You aren't?"

"No, I am not. You agreed to a hot fling, remember? That includes bouts of steamy sex. And I've never had a wicked pirate princess in my bed before. I can't wait to debauch her."

She snorted and rolled her eyes. "Yeah right, like I'm going to believe I'm your first waxed, pierced pussy."

God, she didn't say that. She didn't, did she? At her words, his cock got even harder, throbbing in agony, straining against his jeans, begging to be released. He'd have to beat it into submission if he intended to pee anytime this century. Concentrating on walking without injuring himself, he shook his head. "Yes, you are, at least with such an innocent face. I'm not as wild as you think. I'm pretty much a traditionalist."

She gave him another of those yeah-right looks but remained silent.

On her doorstep, he kissed her again, deep, making his point clear. Tomorrow he'd be better prepared, and she wasn't escaping him. Before he could finish, the porch light turned on, bathing them with bright light. Tate scurried away from him with an ironic smile on her lips as her mom harrumphed from the window.

Jesus Christ, this fucking community was damn hard on a guy's nerves, not to mention a guy's cock. This was going to be worse than being back in Catholic school.

CHAPTER THREE

The barbecue was delicious, the company great, and her mom was smiling. Well, she did frown every time her gaze strayed to Mr. Bowen, but other than that, she seemed to be having a great time. Tate sure was. James had pulled her to his side as soon as they'd arrived, and had that cat-eating-the-canary look on his face again. It was a bit unnerving. She wasn't escaping him today, that much was certain. Tate knew she'd been miraculously saved by the bell the other night, and yesterday too, as they'd had people tagging along all day, and during the night they'd got dragged into playing bingo until the wee hours. James had been a great sport about it all, ready to go along with any activity those crazy seniors pushed them into, always finding an opening to joke with her and touch her.

Today it was going to be another story altogether. That predatory glint in his eye was an unspoken promise. Scary too. And the worst thing was she could hardly wait. After all the lectures she'd given Elle about her poor choices, about hooking up with the wrong men, here she was, salivating after that sexy piece of tattooed ass—rubbing her hands at the prospect of sampling it. How stupid was that? But this was different, she assured herself; there was no danger here, her heart was safely tucked away, she was after vacation fun and sex. No love, no commitment or long-term anything. James was...hormonal relief—fucking material.

She'd dressed for the occasion; a teeny-weeny summer dress that encased her boobs, making them look bigger, which, given their sad B-cup condition, was welcome. The skirt was short, well above her knees, and it was loose, floating all over her thighs and her not-so-small ass. She'd bought the dress because it was damn sexy in an innocent, understated sort of way. She'd worn it once, for a company dinner, but Aidan had hit the roof, accused her of going all sluttish in front of his bosses, which of course wasn't true. It didn't matter though; like a good, obedient girl, she'd never worn it again. She hadn't been sure whether a guy like James would appreciate the push and pulls of it, but from the expression on his face when he saw her, she realized he did. He liked it a lot.

Fortunately, he got drafted to barbecue duty right away, so she was in no imminent danger of being kidnapped and ravished on the spot. Although as soon as he took off his shirt and began taking care of the fire, she felt her jaw going slack, her libido kicking in, and began considering the advantages of the kidnapping and ravishing scenario. She'd been shooed away when she'd tried to help Mrs. Nicholson and her mom with the salad, so she just parked herself in a chair in Mr. Bowen's backyard, where the barbecue had been moved to at the last minute, and watched the show. Under the intense Florida sun, James looked like a damn pagan god. His muscles were glistening, his tattoo swirling around his shoulder and arm. The colors shiny. Damn sexy. Whoa, stop right there. Sexy tattoos? She fanned herself with her hand. That was something she'd never have thought of saying in her life. The Florida heat was starting to affect her; she was delirious already.

At the nape of his neck was that "Hard to Kill" inscription, partly covered by his shaggy hair, and right over his left hipbone, spreading upward, were the oriental symbols he'd got for his army years. The ones that celebrated balance. Compared to the huge Yakuza-style tattoo, the others were reasonably small and not that noticeable. Or disagreeable. Hell, not even the dragon was disagreeable; as a matter of fact, they looked damn good on him. Powerful and virile. Temperamental. Rough. Dangerously sexy.

Man, she was toast.

As her gaze swept over him, a sweet longing spread through her body, raising her temperature to the sky and firing her desire. She squeezed her thighs together as she remembered his touch, his kisses, that huge hard-on persistently pressing against her ass while they'd played bingo, Tate perched on his lap, his breath tickling her ear. As if on command, her clit engorged, the metallic ring pressing against it, creating friction, making her shiver in anticipation. *Oh come on*! One peek at him and she was ready to go, her mind running wild with thoughts and images of the man. The wicked pirate princess, as he'd called her, was working herself into a state just by looking at him and thinking of how she couldn't wait for the man to offer her his undivided attention. Having that dark blond-haired head buried between her thighs, his tongue feasting on her, was going to be a damn good memory to take back home. Certainly better than the stupid T-shirt Aidan had given her from their last trip together.

As if James could read her mind, he turned around and winked an eye at her. Oh hell, was she so obvious? Or maybe she'd been thinking aloud. A giggle bubbled up in her throat. She had to stop fantasizing before those images and the scorching sun of Florida transformed her into a human torch. Spontaneous combustion, how fitting.

Tate had never before felt such an out-of-control sexual attraction toward a man, much less toward one she'd just met. She didn't consider herself a sanctimonious prude, but she wasn't an easy lay either; she needed to know quite a bit more about a guy than his name before jumping on his lap and molesting him. Apparently not with James, which was weird because even if love at first sight wasn't something she believed in or lived by, neither was sex at first sight. The latter, though, she could better understand, especially when looking at a man like that; he'd hardly touched her today, yet she could already feel her damp panties clinging to her folds. Her core was hot and needy. Embarrassing as it may be, her body was itching, her nerve endings oversensitized and tender, longing for his touch.

Shaking her head, she closed her eyes and took a deep breath. It was time to calm down and regain some semblance of self-control, even if only on the surface. She couldn't believe how fast and how daring she'd gotten with him; it was so unlike her.

Elle had insisted she take this minivacation, said she needed to unplug, forget about everything for a while and let go, have some fun. Well, it looked like she'd taken it quite literally. The second she'd made up her mind about having James, a huge, bolted door had flung open, granting her the right to go for what she wanted just for the sheer pleasure of it, because it felt good. And damn if it hadn't felt good. That orgasm on his lap had taken her totally by surprise, hit her fast and strong. She didn't come that easily, ever, much less when there was another human being involved in the process. With James, it had felt so safe to let go; nothing had mattered but her body and the way he was making her feel. No restrictions or inhibitions. It was so weird she felt that way around him; after all, he'd caught her at her most vulnerable, with all the unwelcome changes in her life, with sicko Prince Charming making her feel two inches tall and Rosita's helping him along.

During these past months, she'd been so immersed in the restaurant she hadn't had time for anything. Not even Aidan dumping her had made a real impression. Oh sure, she'd been devastated at the time, but she was too intensely involved with Rosita's, too frantic, no time for boyfriends or for pondering the lack of them. She hadn't even missed sex all that much—not the kind Aidan had to offer anyway—until she'd stopped her frenetic rhythm, went on vacation, and, *ka-boom*! she'd become a nympho. She'd heard that after a very intense period of stress, running basically on pure adrenaline, you slow down, let your defenses down, and automatically become ill. What did she do? She went and got horny. Go figure that one.

When it came time to eat, James didn't worry about formalities. He grabbed her hand and dragged her to the table to sit beside him, where he could touch her. Between him, her hyperactive imagination, the heat, and Mr. Nicholson's spicy barbecue sauce, Tate was out of breath most of the time. Fortunately this crowd wasn't in any danger of running out of conversation anytime soon; they chattered nonstop, especially Mrs. Nicholson, who seemed to know everyone and everything that was going on in the place, so Tate just basically smiled and nodded through the meal. Then something caught her attention.

"How's business?" she heard Mr. Nicholson asking James.

"Busy as always."

Mrs. Nicholson, who'd been most amused the whole time James had been playing touchy-feely with Tate, caught her intrigued stare and smiled at her. "Hasn't James told you he runs his own business?"

James gave her a chastised look. "Now, Mrs. Nicholson, don't go breaking the enchantment. Tate thinks I'm an unemployed good-for-nothing bum/surfer/biker dude who charms girls out of their pants and drives them to perdition. I have to live up to that image. Don't ruin my reputation."

The Nicholsons and James's dad laughed earnestly. Tate just frowned.

Unemployed bum? She hadn't called him that, had she? Certainly not a surfer, anyway. "I don't think that of you."

He grinned. "Yes you do." He turned to the others. "She's convinced I'm a tattooed lowlife cashing in on my sexy aura. But she likes me anyway, don't you?"

Everyone looked expectantly at her, and Tate felt all the blood in her body rush to her face.

"You do?" her mom asked inquisitively.

Ignoring her mom, she turned to James. "Don't grin; it's unbecoming, mister," she muttered, mortified.

Mr. Nicholson cut in. "The unemployed bum here has a great thing going on."

"I've gotten some lucky breaks." He shrugged, absentmindedly caressing her arm. His touch was gentle, insistent.

Goose bumps prickled her skin. What was it about him that got to her? She didn't know. He was gorgeous, true, but it wasn't as if she'd never seen a gorgeous guy before. No, it was more; there was something about James she couldn't explain, something that called to her at a basic level, down there with primal emotions and primal needs. And at the same time, it felt so much more than just physical, like they connected in some way, which was totally crazy because they didn't really know each other that well. And what she knew wasn't that encouraging, except for that piece of news about him having a business. A legit one, anyway. That was a surprise, totally out of character for his type.

After eating, she went to lie down on the hammock. She was stuffed and needed to get away from James for a while, from that restless, needy feeling invading her every time he touched her. Breathing deeply, she closed her eyes and relaxed. She didn't pay too much attention to the chitchat around her; she just let go, enjoying herself.

It'd been so long since she'd rested, since Dad and Jonah died, really. First it'd been incredulity, then fierce grief. She'd have loved to lock herself away from the world and the pain, like her mom had done in a way, but she hadn't been granted that small mercy. Someone had to take over Rosita's. Since then there had been one crisis after another, not even time to draw a breath in between. She'd left her job, put her life on hold, and tried her damn best, but it seemed her best wasn't cutting it. She didn't have what it takes to make the restaurant work, not when everyone was against her, not when tears welled in her eyes every time she looked at the pictures hanging on the walls. And as if dealing with her staff acting out and her maître d' trying to bully her weren't enough, there was the sicko and his foul e-mails to deal with too. Man, what she'd give to find out who the asshole that had been sending her e-mails for the last six months was. Nasty ones, insulting and threatening, demanding she close the restaurant—sell it or else. She shuddered to think of the new ones in her in-box, unopened, waiting for her to get back to Boston and get sucked into its bile again. She shook those memories away. No, she wasn't going to let them ruin her short break. She'd deal with all that when she got back, not a second before.

She slowly opened her eyes to find James staring down at her, two bowls of ice cream in his hands. She sat up, feeling awkward and embarrassed, as if he could somehow read her thoughts and find out all that she was trying so hard to conceal.

"You seemed miles away." He sat down beside her. "What's up?"

She gave him an absentminded smile. "Nothing; just thinking about all the crap waiting for me back home."

"Such as?"

She opened her mouth but closed it again, shaking her head. "Nothing. I just hope they're managing in the restaurant."

"Didn't you close it down for the week?"

She shook her head again. Of course not, she couldn't afford it; she was already badly behind on her bills, playing catch up with her credit card.

"I see. Why wouldn't they manage?" James inquired.

She shrugged, blabbed some nonsense, and as she heard someone mention something about playing gin, she grabbed on to it for dear life. "Come on; let's play too."

James frowned but didn't push it, and boy was she grateful for it.

Unfortunately she sucked at gin and sucked at losing too, just as bad, if not worse. She pouted and cursed, and James laughed at her duck face. Soon he was eating her with his eyes though. Too bad she was busy frowning; losing with grace was definitely not one of her virtues.

After some rounds, things started to slow down—her mom and Mrs. Nicholson wandered from the table and went to check some flowers, while Mr. Bowen and Mr. Nicholson chattered about golf clubs. James took the chance to snatch her away.

"Come with me, Tate," he said while gripping her wrist and pulling her unceremoniously into his father's house. Luckily everyone else was distracted.

She didn't have to ask what for; it was written all over his sex-starved face. Nevertheless she indulged in it, just for fun. "Why? What for?"

His wicked smile made her skin prickle. "I thought I'd show you my room."

"Ah, I see." She chuckled. "Is that what they call it nowadays?"

He closed his father's front door and turned to kiss her—hard. She sank her hands in his soft, warm hair and gave herself over to the sensation, licking his tongue. She'd been hungering for him too, all through the barbecue, every time he smiled at her or touched her, which he did plenty, to everyone's astonishment. Hers the most.

"That dress is designed to send a grown man to his knees, it should be X-rated. It was cruel of you to wear it in public where I couldn't touch you."

She laughed. "You've been touching me, mister. For the last couple of hours, you've been caressing my arms and my neck. Feeding me on the hammock. Brushing my hair from my face. Everyone was staring, or didn't you notice?"

He shrugged. "I like touching you. And we *are* adults."

"Not to them we aren't."

James ignored her and led her to his room, closing the door behind her. "Well, here we are. My room."

She looked around, amused. The guest room looked quite nondescript, like hers at her mom's, but it smelled like him. Big plus. "I see. Now what?"

"I don't know. What should any self-respecting man do when he's got a beautiful but elusive woman alone in his room?"

"I don't know. Has the self-respecting man got protection this time?"

He grinned. "Lots of it; two drugstores worth of it."

"Maybe the beautiful but elusive woman would appreciate him getting on with it some other time, when there wasn't company downstairs in the backyard. Kind of embarrassing, don't you think?"

"They haven't even noticed we're gone. Besides, I've been dreaming about you all night, about that cute clit piercing in that sweet little pussy of yours. I want to see it."

Tate blushed. Talk about going straight to business.

"I want to play with my pirate princess," he said as he pulled off his shirt. He was huge, and beautiful, his chest an expansion of taut muscles. "I want to go down on you. Play with that ring, lap at your pussy, and make you come. For starters."

He walked toward her, forcing her to take a step back. Her calves made contact with the bed, and she tumbled onto it.

James was already on his knees, pulling up the skirt of her dress.

"James, wait a second." She giggled and twisted, trying to keep him from under her skirt. She doubted the others would miss them; she was fairly sure they hadn't noticed them sneaking in, but still. Flashing her mom and the neighbors wasn't something she was dying to do. Besides, having lovely but extremely nosy Mrs. Nicholson walk in on them was like handing the chatty, perky lady a microphone and giving her permission to broadcast the whole "event" to all the Eternal Sun Resort.

James didn't seem to care.

"No, no more waiting. I want to taste you. Now." He placed a hot kiss on her mound through her damp panties, and Tate screamed at the contact, the acute sensation sending a powerful jolt of electricity to her lower belly, making her womb spasm. In a second, he had stripped her of her panties and was parting her thighs wider. "Open up for me, babe.

"Fuck you're beautiful, all flushed and pink," he said with a growl, staring at her core, his fingers playing with the ring at the hood of her clit. "And this is the sexiest thing I've ever seen."

She wanted to say something but only managed to gasp. Finally she found her voice and her bravado. "Yeah? And what do you plan to do with it?"

"I'm going to lick every inch of this pretty pussy. All over until you come. Then I'll wrap your legs around my waist and fuck you until you scream. How does that sound for a plan?"

She felt embarrassed for about half a second, as long as it took him to fall upon her. Then everything was forgotten.

His fingers opened her carefully. "Damn, you're wet, babe." His mouth lapped at her folds, exploring every inch of her flesh, his tongue also caressing her entrance and then sliding up to her clit. He sucked at it and played with the little ball of the piercing while his fingers probed her. First one, then two.

"You're snug, baby, sucking at my fingers. I can't wait to get my cock in you. You're going to be as tight as a fist."

His expert mouth sucking at her clit and his fingers rocking inside her, pressing at her hot spots, were driving her mad with need. She writhed under him, her hand on his head, urging him on. He was taking his time, humming against her swollen clit, working his fingers inside her sheath, not thrusting hard enough.

Her pants grew louder. "James..."

"Yes, baby?"

"I need to come... Make me come, please."

"In a little bit." His voiced rumbled, the vibration making her jerk.

"No, now," she urged him, pressing his head to her, lifting her hips to him. Damn him! She just needed a little more friction. A little more and she'd fly apart. But he wasn't cooperating.

He chuckled, placed one hand over her stomach, and held her down, immobilizing her. "Soon, baby."

As far as Tate was concerned, soon didn't come soon enough, but when it did, it rocked her world. With his fingers steadily fucking her and his mouth sucking her clit, her womb began convulsing, sending jolts of pure energy all over her body, burning all her synapses. Her back bowed, her head dipped into the bed, and she felt herself split into a thousand pieces. Her mouth was already open when, at the last second, she somehow remembered there were people nearby, so she gripped the sheets hard and did her damn best not to break the windows with her shouts.

She came hard and long, James stroking her until he drew all the pleasure from her. When she floated back and opened her eyes, he was stark naked, rolling on a condom. She licked her dry lips as James pulled her to her feet.

"Come here, sweetheart, on your feet, and let's get this dress off you."

She obediently raised her arms and let him undress her. She chuckled. To his questioning stare, she shrugged, "This is my first nooner. So far I'm loving it."

"I surely hope so. You're gorgeous, and loud. And I fucking love it."

He kissed her, entangling his tongue with hers in a fierce, wet caress while his hands stroked her breasts and his fingers pinched her taut nipples.

Although he'd loved getting blowjobs, as if it were his God-given right, Aidan had rarely gone down on her, and when he had, he'd been very careful not to do a great job. God forbid she'd like it and start asking for more. Besides, Aidan didn't do fluids—too blue-collar for him. James was a totally different story; not only was he spectacular at oral sex, but he seemed to dig fluids; he'd wiped his mouth, but even then she could clearly taste herself on him, smell herself on him, on his chin, on his cheeks, in his mouth.

She moved her hands to his dick and palmed him, stroking him from tip to base and then back to tip. He jerked, a ragged growl escaping from him.

"Not now, babe, or it'll be over before it starts. I want you too much."

He lifted her by her ass, two steps, and he was on the bed, placing her on her back while he settled between her legs, probing her with his fingers, his mouth licking her neck.

"Damn, you're small. I should make you come a couple times more before fucking you, but the truth is I can't wait, princess. I'm big, but you're wet and soft from that orgasm, so it'll have to do. I'll go slow on you."

That was fine by her. She urged him with her hands, clutching at his shoulders. She couldn't wait either. She felt his blunt head sliding up and down her slit, spreading her wetness on him, and then nudging at her inner folds.

"You're so hot, baby. And tight. My dick is dying here." He reached down in between them and began gently rubbing her clit, building her desire. Of their own volition, her hips began swaying, lifting, granting him access for deeper penetration. "That's right, baby. Open up for me; let me in."

He'd worked the crown of his cock firmly in when a knock on the door made her heart somersault.

"James, you in there?"

Mr. Bowen.

Tate froze. From the corner of her eye, she saw the doorknob turning. Holy shit!

James's hand shot to the door, pressing his palm against it. "Don't come in!" he shouted. "I hmm... I'm changing."

"Well, get to it fast. Mr. Nicholson is waiting for us downstairs. Did you forget we have a time reserved for golf?"

"Now?" he asked with a strangled tone. "But..."

"Yeah, now."

James fixed his eyes on Tate. Such strength in them. "Give me five minutes."

"You only have two; we're running late."

As soon as Tate heard Mr. Bowen walking away, she let out a shaky breath, her first one since being interrupted. James seemed in horrible pain, poised in her entrance, the head of his dick stretching her. Damn, she was too old to get caught in such predicaments. Her heart was stampeding, and her ears were roaring so hard she wondered how Mr. Bowen hadn't heard her.

In spite of everything, she couldn't help but break into giggles. Judging by his expression and his curses, James didn't find the situation so funny.

"Give me five minutes?" she mocked him in a whisper. "I really hope that didn't mean you just need five minutes to fuck me. I'm not into light-speed wham bams. I kind of expected better from you."

"Oh come on!" he grumbled, his voice full of exasperation. "Of course I planned to fuck you for longer than that."

Her shoulders lifted. "Just checking."

"It's going to take me just that long to gather the strength to pull away from you. Shit, I am not going to survive this. I can't pull away from you now, babe." He exhaled as he tried to control himself.

"You have to," she whispered, afraid they'd be heard. In spite of her words and her fear of getting caught, her hands still clutched at his shoulders, not ready to let go.

"Just a second more." He took her mouth and pushed himself in half an inch. He was big; her muscles trembled and clasped around him, trying to accommodate him. The more her insides spasmed around the head of his cock, the more his body shook with barely restrained tension.

He pulled out a little and surged in another half an inch while she threw her head back and stifled a groan of pleasure.

"James?" She heard his father yell from the bottom of the stairs. "What's taking you so long? Come on!"

"Oh God." Tate giggled.

"Fuckcrapshit! This is not happening! I want you so much, princess, I'm dying here. If I start moving now, I won't be able to stop again." He hissed as he slowly pulled out of her. He was sweating, his muscles straining from the effort.

Tate was flushed, her core swollen. She needed him inside her, pounding at her, making her scream in pleasure, but one look at James made her realize she had nothing on him—if he'd looked in pain before, now he looked in pure agony. Two baby steps from hell.

He got rid of the condom and, still cursing under his breath, began hastily dressing while she sat on the bed and stared at him. His dick looked so painfully hard and so angrily red, bobbing in front of her, silently demanding retribution, she reached for it, encircling it with her hand.

He hissed, placing his hand over hers and squeezing so hard she felt his cock throbbing, blood madly pulsing through it. He stroked himself harshly, his head falling back.

"Let me take care of you," she whispered.

His warm eyes looked at her with such mixture of gentleness and hunger it startled her. "Baby, I'd love to, believe me, but we don't have the time," he said, letting her hand go, wincing as he tucked himself in, the zipper almost not making it all the way up. "Wait here until we leave. When you're sure the coast is clear, sneak out."

She laughed at the image her mind instantly conjured—her sneaking out his bedroom window. "Jesus, we've regressed to high school level."

"Tell me about it." He came down on her, forcing her to lay back. He planted his arms at the sides of her head and looked into her eyes. "As soon as I finish with the golf, I'll come for you," he said against her lips. Then he kissed her hard and left.

Once alone, Tate looked around and sighed. She'd known from the get-go James was trouble. It was written all over his gorgeous body and in his cocky grin. What she hadn't expected was to have so much fun unraveling that trouble. It seemed she'd misjudged him a bit; it took a great deal of discipline to run one's own business, especially to run it successfully, no time for being irresponsible. And to his benefit, she had to recognize he sounded nothing like Elle's losers. Not that she'd spent that much time talking to them—she'd always been quite hostile, but anyways, she'd never gotten more than a couple of grunts out of them, once a sleazy remark about landing the sister with the bigger boobs. Assholes. On the upside, Elle had heard that remark and broken up with him, after kicking him in the balls. Tate held that memory dear.

Maybe James was the exception that confirmed the rule. Maybe. She wouldn't hold her breath. That she'd been a bit off about him didn't mean he was a harmless pussycat, or relationship material, for that matter. There were intense vibes coming off the guy, definitely trouble. She could feel it deep inside, a certain awareness that rattled her every time he smiled at her, like he was casting an unseen web of traps around her and she was just too damn eager and stupid to realize it was insane to jump into them headfirst.

Or maybe that rattling feeling inside her was nothing more than her throbbing pussy begging for action. Too damn bad he wasn't getting any today, before or after the golf—she had to accompany her mom to the vet, and they'd agreed to stay in town for supper afterward, a girls' afternoon out. Tate didn't want to risk letting her go alone to the vet's appointment; someone might have to restrain her if the vet got cocky. Although her mom seemed better, more relaxed. Unfortunately now that she was less hysterical about Amy, her attention was turning to her. Tate sighed and reached for her dress; better start rolling. Sooner or later, she'd have to go and explain to her mom why her six-foot-four tattooed neighbor was fluttering around her daughter and she was letting him.

"I'm going to take a wild guess here and say the hard-on you've been sporting all afternoon is not on account of Mr. Nicholson continually bending over to pick up the golf balls, right?"

"For fuck's sake, Dad!" James cursed, looking horrified at his father, who just shrugged his shoulders at his son's shocked expression.

"Whaaat? Just making sure," he added, hardly hiding his amusement. "It's because of that cute spitfire, the Cooper girl, isn't?"

At the thought of Tate sprawled on his bed, her eyes drowsy, her arms held out to him, beckoning him, her core glistening from her release, ready to be taken, James's erection grew even harder. He shifted uncomfortably in his jeans. Damn, those denims were strangling his shaft.

"A hard-on girl." His father chuckled after a quick glance at James's lap. "How interesting."

"What?"

"A hard-on girl," he repeated. "The mere thought of her has you painfully standing in full salute."

James chose to look straight ahead, avoiding his father's scrutiny, awkwardly aware of his straining erection. They were sitting on a bench in the open air, waiting for Mr. Nicholson to come back from his bathroom break, the seaside breeze filling his nostrils, and all he could smell was her and the sex they'd almost had. His dick swelled some more. Damn, he was fucked; his father was going to use this to make fun of him until his very dying day.

"I love you, Dad, but let's change the subject; I'm not comfortable discussing this shit with you."

Laughter rumbled through the old guy. "Please, I had hard-ons long before you were even conceived; don't get prudish on me now."

"Hand me a beer, will you?" James held his hand out and drank half of it in one go. "A hard-on girl, Dad? Are we reading *Cosmo* now?"

He ignored his son and took a swig of his own beer. "I believe you only get one of those girls in your lifetime, so you better make the best of it."

I was making the best of it when you came knocking at my door, he was itching to say, but he bit his tongue. There was no fooling Dad though. He stared at him in surprise and then laughed. Loud.

"Oh God, that was what you were doing up in your room, right? Before I interrupted? I thought Tate had gone home. Now I understand your painful look. And stride."

"Drop it, Dad," James warned. His...whatever it was he had—or didn't have—with Tate wasn't up for discussion.

"You drop it," he said, snorting and pointing at his son's crotch. "Oh wait, you can't, can you?"

James growled in annoyance. Damn, the old man was having too much fun at his expenses. "A hard-on girl, remember? Nothing I can do about it."

"Yeah, I remember. Mine was your mother. We—"

"Oh no no. I'm so not listening to that. I'm too young for this—I don't want to end up in therapy, thank you very much.

Besides, we all know how that ended with Mom. Not the best of comparisons to make."

"True," his father said pensively. "Still, I just meant it's not every day you meet a girl who can keep you on your toes, literally and figuratively speaking. And she's good for you. I've seen you looking at her, laughing with her."

James chuckled. "Yeah, well, she seems to know how to press all my buttons." And he had the hard-on of the century to prove it.

His father shook his head and threw him a suspicious look. "It looks like more, son. For the past two days, she's been dragged to all the activities here at the resort, and you've tagged along. Happily, I might add. What's going on?"

"Nothing, believe me." And how true that statement was. He was ready to burst from lust at any second.

"Listen to me, Jimmy boy; after that bitch Elaine, that's all you allowed yourself to have: a fat lot of nothingness. You've fucked your share of women, but that's all you do, fuck and run. That's not good for you. You need to start thinking about your future; you need a wife. At your age, I had three sons, a wife, and a mortgage."

"Oh Jesus." Here it was again. "Why don't you do me a favor and concentrate on Cole? He's the oldest and still single. I tried that scene, remember? I'm divorced, didn't work well for me."

"I'll get to Cole, you don't need to worry about that, but for the moment I'll concentrate on you."

Just my luck, James thought. He lifted his eyes in time to see Mr. Nicholson approaching, huffing, golf club in one hand, more beer in the other. Man, this was going to be a long afternoon.

CHAPTER FOUR

Tate was drifting off to sleep when her cell phone rang. With her heart in her throat, she groped around in the dark. Please Lord, let it not be the police or anyone from the restaurant; she couldn't cope with any problems right now, she was too…unplugged for that.

Thank heavens, it was James.

He didn't waste any time with formalities. "Why do you think it is that you always get off and I don't? I'm going to spontaneously combust any moment now."

She stifled a laugh, relieved to hear his voice. Happy actually. "Maybe because you always start with me?"

"Well, those are the house rules, babe. Girls always get to come first, five or six times, as a matter of fact, so they're shiny and juicy and ready."

Show-off. "Is that so?"

"Yep. Girls' Happy Hour nonstop, that's me."

She snorted. "Well, then you've been cheating me, mister, orgasmwise, I mean."

His laughter rumbled through the phone. "Sorry, baby. The circumstances aren't the best; they keep interrupting us."

"True," she answered with a sigh. There was no way to have a hot vacation fling with half the continental US senior population running interference. At this rate, she had more chance of catching contagious dementia than getting laid anytime this century.

"Your phone call scared me," she admonished him. "Calls in the middle of the night aren't a good sign." The last two phone calls in the wee hours had come from the police; one informing her the restaurant was on fire, the other telling her Dad and Jonah were gone. Yep, phone calls in the middle of the night scared her. Badly.

"Sorry," he said sheepishly. "Who did you think it was?"

She cleared her throat. "Well, I don't know," she lied. "Probably Elle calling from San Francisco. She went there to visit some friends while I came to stay with Mom. With Elle on the loose, you never know."

Silence.

"I see." By his tone, he hadn't believed a word. "Were you sleeping?"

"I was trying to, but Mom's downstairs with two of her new friends, and they're too loud. What time is it, by the way?"

"Close to one a.m.," James answered unapologetically. "Can't sleep. I thought you could keep me company so I wouldn't feel so miserable. After all, it's your fault I can't sleep."

"My fault? How do you figure that?"

"Do you have any idea how long it takes to go through a nine-hole golf course with your dick so hard you could use it as a golf club?"

She laughed. "No, I can't say I do."

"It's torture. And all I could think of was you. It didn't help the situation at all. And then I come back, and you're gone."

"I had to go to the vet with my mom. Amy's nursing, so we had to go with the kittens. The golf might have been bad, but believe me, holding my mom while the stupid vet made the mistake of commenting on the kittens was no walk in the park either."

"That bad, uh?"

"Yeah, that bad." She sighed and left a long pause, not sure whether she wanted to talk about this or not. "You know, my mom had plans for her life; she was going to study archeology, uncover lost cities, pagan temples, forgotten kings' tombs. Hell, she had a map of all the dig sites in the world she was going to organize; my aunt showed it to me. But she met my dad and got derailed. Got married, started a family, and in a way gave up her dreams. They had the restaurant to run and three kids and a household to care for—not too much spare time. I don't think she regretted her choices; she was happy. But now she's alone. Half her family is gone, and she's running. That's what all this moving to Florida is; she can't stand to set a foot in Rosita's."

"What exactly happened to your dad and brother?"

She was giving him the short version. Details made her sick. "Drunk driver."

"I'm so sorry, princess."

Yeah, so was she, not that it changed a damned thing. "Thanks. Anyways, it was fun to spend time with my mom. It's been too long since we did that, with me working my ass off in the restaurant all the time."

"Is everything okay with the restaurant? You systematically avoid talking about it; I get a vibe something's wrong."

Ha, like she was going to unload her crappy life to her summer fling before getting properly laid. No way; it would be such a downer he might run away. Although lying there in the dark, talking to him, it felt so…intimate. It'd be such a relief to share her problems with him. That was what friends were for, right? But of course, that wasn't what was going on here.

An ironic chuckle bubbled up. "No, things are by far not okay at Rosita's, but I really don't want to talk about it. Or about my mother either. Please, let's talk about something else."

He was silent for a pregnant moment, then caved in. "What do you want to talk about?"

That was a no-brainer. "You. Let's talk about you, your life."

"Too broad a topic. Could you narrow it down a bit for me?"

"Okay, let me see," she said, taking her time. Where to start? "Tell me, if your tats signal pivotal moments in your life, why didn't you get one when you got married? I'd say getting married is a huge turning point in a man's life."

More silence. Leave it to her to choose the worst topic.

When Tate was almost convinced he wasn't going to answer, he began, "Elaine and I were high school sweethearts. After I came back from the military, we hooked up again, and she got pregnant. Despite our regular clashes, I insisted on marrying her. No child of mine was going to be raised without me; that was totally nonnegotiable. She miscarried in the fourth month, just before the wedding. Deep down I knew we weren't right for each other, but she was so devastated from losing the baby I didn't have the heart to call the whole thing off. And hell, I loved her, or so I thought. My subconscious knew better, though. It never felt right to celebrate with a tattoo, so I didn't. It turned out the pivotal moment wasn't the wedding, but the divorce. Life's a bitch sometimes. The tattoo is there to remind me of how royally I fucked up, just in case I ever feel like getting married again."

"Sorry."

"No need for sorrys; that's just the way things are. I wasn't what she wanted, so she cheated on me and dumped me. I believe she called it 'upgrading husbands.'"

"Ouch."

He chuckled. "Yeah, fucking ouch. At the time, though, it shattered my pride more than my heart."

She didn't say anything for a long while. What could she say? She'd been dumped too, several times actually, but never upgraded to a better model, at least not right away.

Well, now that they were on touchy ground...

"Where's your mom? Is she back in Boston?"

"Nope. Or maybe she is, I don't know," he answered matter-of-factly. "Never cared enough to go looking for her." She winced. Jeez, wasn't she a buzzkill today. "She bailed out on us when I was small."

"Sorry," she mumbled. "That must've been hard."

"Not really." She could almost hear the shrug in his voice. He didn't sound upset or uncomfortable with the subject. "She wasn't such a great mom to begin with. Pretty absent from what I recall. So I wouldn't say it was that hard when she left. I had a strong safety net behind me. Aunt Maggie, Dad's older sister, moved in with us to help, and between her and Dad, they managed quite well. Me and my bros turned out pretty fine." Yeah, you could see in the easy and self-confident way he carried himself and how he interacted with his father that James had emotionally lacked for nothing while growing up. "For the most part, I was cool with my mother's absence. Besides, it wasn't unexpected or as if we lost her all of a sudden. Yes, she left one day and didn't come back, but it was a long time coming."

Well, a sudden and unexpected loss was definitely worse, she could attest to that, at least as far as feeling abandoned and lost was concerned. Her safety net, as he called it, had disintegrated in a fraction of a second, leaving her scared, alone, and in free fall ever since. All she could think most days was how much longer she'd fall until she hit bottom. Her lower lip began trembling, but she shook her head. No way. No breaking down. No more pity parties. Enough drama. Change of subject.

She cleared her throat. "It looks like I owe you an apology."

"Uh?"

"About hinting that you were the type that couldn't hold down a job even if your life depended on it."

He laughed. "Ah, that."

Tate went for casual. "By the way, what is it that you do?"

"So we're curious now, uh?"

She shrugged, and when she realized he couldn't see her, she reluctantly added, "Maybe."

"When I came home from the army, I did some carpentry work in my dad's construction company. Then I went into the bounty hunter business and—"

"Bounty hunter?" she all but yelled. "With that goofy smile of yours?"

"Yeah, and believe it or not, this smile of mine has opened more doors than my fists."

Well, yeah, that she'd believe, no problem. She'd been right; he was a bad boy in full-conceal mode.

"Then I got tired of chasing after criminals and losers and went into business with Zack and Sean, two colleagues of mine. We set up a security installation firm; we provide security systems and other security ware for specialists. We have a long-term contract with city hall; plus we handle a lot of private business."

She was quiet for a while; Tate was not big on apologizing. "Well, in light of this new information, I have to recognize I might have been a bit rash in judging you."

"Might have been?" He was probably trying not to sound too cocky but was failing miserably.

"Don't push it, buddy. That you can actually hold a job down doesn't mean all the other attributes don't apply. There are the tattoos and the rogue looks to consider, not to mention your colorful career choices, macho pickup and arrogant attitude. You're bad news."

His voice was low, velvety rough, arousing her senses. "But it makes you hot."

She chuckled. "It shouldn't though. You aren't for me. Too dangerous."

"Ha. Says the wicked princess with a pierced clit."

"It's not the clit I have pierced, it's the clitoral hood; big difference."

"Whatever, honey. Tell me, what on earth made you get your pussy pierced? As long as I'm spilling my guts here, it's only fair you do the same."

"Do you really want to know?" She paused, toying with the idea of telling him. "Honestly? You'll think I'm a psycho."

"I already think you're a psycho, so you see, you have nothing to lose. Hit me," he pushed her.

She closed her eyes; there it went, something she'd never told anyone. "My clit is too small," she blurted so fast she wasn't even sure he understood.

Silence. Then a groan of disbelief. "No, it isn't."

"It is," she insisted. "That's why I put the piercing there, as a therapeutic device. I had trouble coming."

That last piece of info seemed to baffle him even more than her earlier admission. "Really? I'd never have guessed that."

No, she supposed he wouldn't, seeing how fast and loudly she exploded around him every time.

"Stop gloating; it isn't nice. I know it doesn't seem so now that you're around, and you get me all bothered with just one look, but until you came along I...struggled to orgasm." That was putting it mildly; sometimes she'd feared the guy was going to get a cramp in his hand. More than once she'd been tempted to offer him a drink hat so he could sip liquid and replenish his energy while he was at it. "I figured by putting a ring there, the whole area would get more...detailed attention."

He chuckled. "You mean you thought having a bouncing, shiny distraction on your clit would draw more attention to it? Like the baby toys adults swing in front of a baby to get a reaction, to get the infant to grope it, inspect it, lick it, and play with it?"

"Well, I didn't think of it in those terms, but yeah. It's my come-and-find-it to men." Not that it had worked that fabulously with anyone before.

Now he just laughed openly. "Sorry to inform you, but you've been having sex with morons."

No shit, she could have guessed that on her own. His cockiness rattled her, though, and an exasperated groan left her throat. "Well, you seem to like to play with it too, mister."

"I do, but I'm no child. I'm a man. I don't need any extra stimuli to go for what gives you pleasure. I'm not interested in the ring per se but in what's beneath it. And by the way, what's that bull about your clit being too small?"

She cleared her throat, not sure whether she should continue talking. She had to face the guy tomorrow, for crying out loud. "It is smallish, not very big, or in any way protruding, kind of insignificant. They tended to miss it when making love. I thought the piercing would help me. When I'm...um...aroused and my clit is hard, the contact to the cool metal ball is very exciting. And there's more friction during sex, bigger chance to get off. Plus it's sexy," she finished while blushing madly. She'd never been so overtly sincere with anyone.

"Yes, it is damn sexy, I'll give you that, but I don't know how you got it into your head that your clit is insignificant. It's bullshit. You have a beautiful clit. Big enough, very demanding, as a matter of fact. When it's throbbing with need, it flushes a crimson red. It's gorgeous. You're gorgeous, princess."

"Um...thanks." The piercing in the hood of her clit had also been a vain impulse to be naughty and wicked, to spice things up with Aidan, not that he'd really appreciated it. James had appreciated it. She smiled at the memory of his transfixed face that first day in his truck as he'd slid his fingers down and found her sex bare and pierced. Need and lust had roared in his eyes—and surprise—at the piercing and the lack of hair. It was like he hadn't expected her to be so daring. Waxing her pussy made her feel feminine, wanton. Plus she loved her folds bare, sensitive, and smooth. James had loved it too, if the appreciative sounds he'd made while going down on her were anything to go by

"If you weren't able to get off, as sure as hell it wasn't your fault or your clit's. It's the shit-for-brains dickheads you've been having sex with. Unskilled assholes. Let me come over, and I'll prove it to you. You'll come so many times you'll be limp by the time I'm done with you."

A nervous giggle bubbled up in her throat. She couldn't believe she was having this conversation with him. "Not a chance in hell, mister. We'll get caught. They're downstairs still; I can hear them. One near miss per day is enough, thank you very much. I'm too old for that shit." She hadn't recovered yet from the earlier fiasco, and she wasn't ready to give it a second go.

"Having you so close by and not being able to make love to you is killing me."

"Abstinence, self-control, and denial of the pleasures of the flesh is good for your soul, choirboy."

He chuckled softly. "Sorry, baby, never got into the whole Catholic self-denial thing." There was a thick silence charged with roaring need. "What do you have on, sweetheart?" The huskiness in his voice abraded her senses. His question thundered over her nerve endings, and she instantly broke out in goose bumps. Man, even his voice did it for her. How freaky was that?

She swallowed, not sure if she had the courage to utter the words. "A short camisole and panties, but—"

"But what, baby?" he asked hoarsely.

She closed her eyes and went for it; after all, this was her chance at being naughty with someone who'd appreciate it. "But my nipples are so hard and achy the brush of the material against them hurts." Which amazed her because they'd never been that responsive before. She'd always believed when her erogenous zones had been given, her boobs had totally missed out. But with

James around, her nipples were hard all the time, begging to be touched, and her boobs even felt bigger. "I may have to take the clothes off."

She heard a strangled curse from the other side of the line. "You're killing me here." He all but growled.

"Me?" she said with the most angelic voice she could muster. "What did I say now?"

"This is a classic scenario, the ultimate sex fantasy for Catholics: the temptress that whispers naughty things and uses the cover of night to seduce a poor bastard's virginal body. The all-time Catholic repressed dream."

"Virginal?" she choked out. "Yeah, right!" No matter how hard she tried, Tate could not reconcile that word with James.

"I've never had phone sex before; my Catholic, puritanical soul is immaculate in that respect."

She laughed. "There isn't an inch of immaculate in you. And I had no idea that was where this was leading."

"Hell yes. You started it, actually."

She chewed her bottom lip, uncertainty riding her hard. "I've never had phone sex; I don't really think I know how."

"I have some ideas."

No shit. "I bet you do."

"Put on your hands-free."

"Wait a sec," she said, fumbling around to get the small device.

"Do you have it on?"

She mumbled an assent.

"Good. First get comfortable, take the camisole off. Let's give some relief to those beautiful nipples."

She shuddered at his words, the sheer sexuality emanating from them searing her nerve endings and flooding her pussy. This was madness; she had no clue what she was doing, her hands were shaking, and her heart was speeding.

"Lick your fingers and gently rub your nipples with them. Pretend it's my tongue on them, soothing them."

She felt heat creeping up her face. He was turning her on,

there in the dark and quiet of her room, with her mom and guests downstairs. She'd have never said it'd work for her, but apparently it did; she could feel the moisture gathering in her flushed folds, the heated ache glowing in her core. She was needy, her flesh tender and sensitive and wet. Man, this was so naughty.

She did as he said. She licked the pads of her fingers and rubbed her nipples. The electrifying contact made her jerk, ripping a gasp out of her. She was so sensitized the cooler air on her fast-burning-up breasts was almost painful.

"Tell me what you're doing, princess, I want to hear. Are you touching yourself as I asked you to?"

Her mouth was dry, but she forced herself to form words. "Yeah, my nipples are tight and swollen. I'm stroking them with my wet fingers. They're darkening, hardening. They ache, James."

"For what?"

"For your touch, your mouth," she said as the scene unfolded in her head: James with her in her bed, kissing her breasts, caressing them. His mouth suckling at her nipples, his teeth gently nipping at them, his tongue flicking over her flesh. Nobody knocking at the door.

"You don't have to ache for my touch, babe; you have it, anytime you want. I'll worship your beautiful tits, touch that soft skin, kiss you all over. Forget where you are. Close your eyes and listen to my voice, feel me touching you. Take your panties off for me, princess."

She was so lost in her pleasure that she didn't understand his words at first. "Uh?"

"Panties off."

She laughed. "You're too bossy. Am I not supposed to be the temptress that sneaks into your bedroom to tempt and seduce your Catholic soul along with your body? I should be running the show."

"And you do, sweetheart. You don't have a clue how much you tempt me. I'd do anything now to please you."

"Are...are you naked?"

"I'm so hard for you I can't wear clothes. It feels like they're strangling my dick. I still remember how it felt to be inside you, so tight, so damn hot. I close my eyes and I'm back there, between your legs, driving inside you."

"Are you...?"

"Don't be shy, ask away."

"...touching yourself?"

"Do you want me to?" His low, sexy voice rumbled through her.

"Yes."

"Good, we're both on the same page then."

She imagined James stroking his cock, pearls of precum on the crown, and she felt her lower belly spasm, more heat rushing to her already saturated folds. "Next time I get the chance, it'll be Boys' Happy Hour. All for you." She'd lavish his cock, kiss and stroke it, bring him in her throat, and rake her teeth gently over his distended veins. "I want to see you lose control."

"Control? I don't have any control around you, haven't you realized that yet? Now take you panties off, sweetheart," he ordered in a rough voice, his breath shallow.

She shimmied out of her panties, trying not to sound out of breath.

"Are you wet?"

She was, sopping wet actually. "Yes."

"Good, I want you to slide your hand down, slowly, and touch yourself. Think of me fucking that pretty pussy. Pet your folds, your clit, tug at that wicked ring. And I want you to tell me all the time what you're doing."

"Um...okay. My panties were damp, James. So damp they even clung to my folds. I'm naked now. The ball in the piercing is on my clit, slightly pressing at it," she said as she circled it with the tip of her index finger. Her hips began to roll up of their own volition. "Maybe you're right, maybe my clit isn't so insignificant."

"Of course not, princess; it's perfect."

It was funny how much his acceptance meant to her. "My folds are wet and swollen. And I feel empty. I need you."

He groaned. "I want you to slide your fingers inside that juicy place. One finger. Now close your eyes and imagine how it's going to feel when it's my cock in there, pushing to get in, pumping you. I can't wait to feel your pussy clamping around me. I'll be in heaven. So tight. So good."

She pressed one finger in, rubbed her clit with the palm of her hand, and whimpered.

"Yes, like that, whimper a little more for me, baby. I can almost see you thrashing on that bed. Now slide in a second finger. There's so many things I want to do to you, so many ways I want to take you, you won't be able to walk properly for a couple of days after I get my hands on you."

"James..."

"And I'll fuck that pretty mouth too, come deep in your throat."

She whimpered again at that image, and her hips lifted to her hand. Her clit was throbbing with need, tension gathering behind it with unstoppable force. "James...I..."

His voice was hoarse. "Are you getting close, princess? I bet your thighs are tensing, your hips lifting up, searching for me. Yes, there are those sexy little moans you let out when you're getting ready to shout your release. Your back arched, your head thrown back, I can see you as if I were there. Let me have it, babe; come for me. I'm almost there too."

Her climax thundered through her with an intensity that surprised her. Who would have guessed, but James's voice was better than all the sex toys she had at home. Way better.

"James?" she called at him some time after, her voice drowsy, her body still glowing with residual pleasure, slow to float back to reality. "Are you still there?"

He was breathing hard. "Yeah, princess, I'm here."

"Sorry I was so fast..."

He chuckled. "Don't apologize for coming. I was hanging on by my last thread too. I exploded the second I heard you. You are loud; your mom is probably rushing up the stairs as we speak."

She rolled her eyes. "No, I'm not. And nobody heard me."

"I heard you," he murmured. "Thanks."

She had to chuckle. "I think that's my line."

"Nah, thank you for letting me have my wicked way with you. Fucking hot. I never thought phone sex was for me, but I could easily get used to this."

She stretched in bed like a content kitten. "I'm glad I was your first at something; it isn't every day one gets to soil a boy's sweet virginal Catholic soul with dirty talk. I feel so naughty; I'll probably end up in hell."

He laughed, the sound warming her, as if he were there, keeping her in his arms, cuddling her. "That wasn't dirty talk; that was amazing. And you won't end up in hell for it but in my bed instead, with me shoved deep inside you."

"Maybe. Odds are badly against us though. We may die from unfulfilled lust before we can have sex in this resort. This place is more closely guarded than boot camp."

He sighed. "True. The back of my pickup is starting to look like quite a desirable location."

"Really? You're taking me parking? Wow. I haven't gone parking since high school. I think I may be too old for that though. Isn't there an age limit for parking?"

She involuntarily yawned.

"I'm keeping you up. Go back to sleep, princess, and we'll talk tomorrow."

"Will you be able to sleep now?"

"Don't worry about me. Sleep, babe."

"Good night, James," she heard herself saying before closing the connection.

She wasn't fully awake anymore; she was floating, content. Pumped up on endorphins and on James. In a corner of her mind lurked the nasty impression this wasn't real, and the higher she flew, the harder she'd fall.

She didn't care.

It was barely noon, and the swimming pool area almost empty.

The second James spotted her, a wide smile broke across his face. She reciprocated shyly, blushing as red as a caramel apple.

So cute, she must have been remembering their session of phone sex. He knew he was, effusively.

He winked at her and strode to the edge of the pool. “Hi, princess. How come this place is deserted?”

“Palm climbing and coconut cracking exhibition.”

“Ah.” How that one was so popular eluded him, especially when the crowd was barely mobile. “And your mom?”

“There with Mrs. Nicholson,” she answered, the embarrassment on her face slowly receding. “Apparently the guys climbing the palms are um…exotically dressed. As in almost not dressed at all.”

“So that’s the reason it’s so popular. How’s the water?”

“Great,” she said and splashed some on him.

Tate crossed her arms on the side of the pool, her chin resting on her forearms, her luscious ass popping up as she let her body float. He couldn’t see what she was wearing clearly, but that was no one-piece swimsuit but one of those fashionable bikinis that barely covered the essentials. Damn he was screwed, no way to preserve his male dignity and leave the towel currently covering his bulging groin on the chair without flashing his hard-on at her.

Well, whatever, she was soon going to notice it. Praying she wouldn’t look down, he strode to the shower, turned the icy-cold water on full power with little result, and then jumped into the pool. He swam over to her and pulled her into his arms for a long, wet, steamy kiss. She stiffened at first but soon relaxed. Maybe she was ashamed to be seen making out in public, but he wasn’t going to let her put up that kind of mental wall. Not after last night. He liked expressing affection, no matter where he was or who was looking at him—or how short-lived the relationship was bound to be.

“Hi,” he whispered against her lips.

She circled his neck at the same time that she wrapped her legs around his waist. “Morning,” she answered.

Nope, no problems with public displays of affection. He groaned with lust, holding her tighter in his arms and grinding his shaft against her core. Jesus, this was getting harder and harder—in all respects.

"I see you're ready at all hours," she said jokingly against his lips. Framed by those long, spiky, wet eyelashes, her pale eyes sparkled with mischief, and he had to close his to block the sight of her away. His eager mind, though, conjured the image of her bent over the edge of the pool, wet and moaning, eagerly taking his dick, pushing herself back at him for more.

Shit, that was not helping. He forced his eyes open.

"It doesn't depend on me; it depends on you," he stated in resignation.

She snorted in disbelief.

"It's true, baby. You get near me, and in two seconds flat, I'm standing in full salute." Well, in reality, all he had to do was think of her and voilà! Hard as granite. Ready to hammer nails with his dick. A hard-on girl through and through, leave it to his old man to be right about things like that.

"The cold shower didn't help?"

"Nah." He shook his head. "At this stage, nothing will, except for the real thing."

"Maybe hot water will," she offered, pushing him toward the Jacuzzi. "Hot water leaves me all gooey. Maybe it'll have the same effect on you. You're too tense; you need to relax."

It might have worked, but as soon as they sat in the hot tub, he dragged her over his lap, her sweet ass nudging at his dick, and relaxation went out the window. No gooey effect for him this century. The water was fiercely bubbling, reaching up to his chest. She rested her head on him and sighed.

"Wouldn't it be great to stop time? Just for a while. Stay in here just like this. No worries. No responsibilities."

"Doesn't work that way, princess." And it was a pity because despite his blue balls, he liked having her in his arms. It felt…right. Go figure that one.

They were silent for a while. He had the nagging feeling Tate was musing about the restaurant. Something wasn't right with it, but she wasn't willingly forwarding any information, and he didn't want to ask too much. Every time he'd done so, she'd avoided the whole subject, or worse, shut down and distanced herself from him. He needed to distract her from those thoughts; the last thing he wanted now was for her to close down.

He kissed the side of her neck. “So, did you sleep well last night?”

“Mmmm, sure I did. Didn’t you?”

“You’re being a tease,” he reprimanded, tightening his grip on her.

She giggled and tried to free herself. That lap dance had him praying to the skies for control. “Stop massaging my dick with your ass, sweetheart, or I’ll fuck you right here.”

She stopped right away. “James, about us having sex...”

“Having second thoughts, princess?”

“No, but we should have the sex talk before, don’t you think? Just in case. Actually, we should have dealt with it before the attempt butchered by your father.”

“Sex talk? You mean the bee and the flower sex conversation? Your parents should have taken care of that a long time ago. Mine did.”

She elbowed him. “No, you bozo, I meant the safe-sex conversation where the bee explains in detail to the flower how he’s always worn a raincoat while buzzing around, and how he’d never gotten entangled with dubious pollen.”

He laughed. “Ah, that sex conversation. Okay, I’ve always been a very responsible bee, the only exception was with Elaine. Before and after my marriage, I’ve been tested several times. No dubious pollen, that is, all negative to HIV and STDs. Strictly hetero. Last checkup was around six months ago. I wrap religiously, so I’m safe. What about you, flower girl?”

“Me too. Me and Aidan both got checked. I haven’t been with anyone since him, so I’m clean too.”

“Good. You see, now we know we’re both safe for the environment.”

She vibrated in silent laughter, her fingers running along his forearm. How she touched his arm and he managed to feel it all over his body was a mystery to him.

“I fear I know, but tell me, what does your kind think about faithfulness?”

He shook his head in resignation. She really didn't get him; she was so stuck in thinking he was a "type," she couldn't see anything else.

"My kind? As in a bee or a black hole wrapped up in fancy paper? Be more specific, sweetheart, because it's kind of difficult to keep up with your imagery. I'm going to have to watch more National Geographical Channel from now on. I'm lacking facts here."

She turned to him and pouted. "You're making fun of me."

"No shit, sweetheart. You just make it too damn easy."

She went very serious. "I want to ask you something, and I want you to be totally up front with me."

"Shoot."

"We haven't talked about it, and I know we don't have the kind of relationship that would give me any say about it, but I need to be absolutely sure you don't have anyone back home waiting for you, because I don't have sex with cheaters. No matter how casual the involvement and no matter how gorgeously sexy the cheater."

She was so pretty. With her mane of hair slick against her back, her eyes looked huge. Damn expressive too. Now they were staring at him with uncertainty but resolution. He didn't doubt for a minute that she'd slap him and leave him to dry if he were indulging in a little side affair, which he wasn't. His type might; he didn't.

"You think I'm sexy?"

She crossed her arms over her chest and breathed out hard. "That's all you took from what I said?"

No, of course not, but he liked it when she berated him. It made him hot. Sick really. "No one back home. I'm not the cheating type. Despite my disreputable appearance," he added with a mocking smile and kissed the tip of her nose. "One flower at a time, that's my motto."

"Good to know." She turned around and rested her back to his chest.

They remained silent until he couldn't hold it anymore. "Don't you have anything to tell me? Or do you assume I'd be sleazy enough as not to care if I'm the only one in your bed?"

She snorted, her hand playing with the bubbles. "Of course."

His tone hardened. "Is someone waiting for you back home, princess?"

She didn't answer right away, continuing to play with the water. "I believe that's none of your business, Mr. Black Hole. All you need to know is that I'm willing." She was poking him on purpose, he could feel it in her demeanor, not that it made it less annoying.

"Humor me," he insisted, his tone unyielding. He wasn't sure where it came from, but he felt the unstoppable urge to fuck her into submission. Right there, never mind who was watching.

"Or what? Are you truly telling me you wouldn't fuck me if I had a boyfriend back home?"

He clenched his teeth. She got him there. He'd hate the boyfriend thing, sure, but it wouldn't matter; he'd do her in an instant if she'd allow it.

She looked over her shoulder. "Yeah, that was my thought too."

"Answer my question, Tate."

She sighed. "No, there's no one waiting for me back home. Not anymore. He dumped me. Happy now?"

"Yeah, extremely. Unless you're still hung up on the dude."

"Nope. It's been months."

"Good," he said, kissing the top of her head and relaxing again. "Why did the moron leave you?"

"Why do you care?"

"Just answer the question." Damn stubborn woman; there was no way to get a straight answer from her.

She rested her head on his shoulder, breathing out loud. "Jeez, where to start? Let me see. I was suffocating him being too needy and weepy. My dad and Jonah were dead, my mom was totally out of it, and my sis could barely cope with her own life, let alone the whole drama unfolding at home. I had to take care of the restaurant and my mom and all the bills—hers, mine, and the restaurant's. She was like a zombie, couldn't be trusted to pay her bills on time...hell, she could barely make it out of bed most days. I thought that entitled me to be a bit needy and weepy, but it turned out it didn't. He dumped me, told me I had my priorities all screwed up. He wasn't feeling appreciated. My so-called complete disregard of him was hurting his feelings. Aidan wanted my full undivided attention; you see, he was making partner, and I wasn't there for him."

"Fucking asshole."

"The restaurant and all the time I had to devote to it was unacceptable for him. I had to sell out and concentrate on his life and his career because those would ultimately be the basis for our life together."

James fought to tamp down his rising fury. "You were grieving. His life should have been put on hold for you. He was supposed to be there for you."

"Funny, that's what I thought, but I was wrong. He figured I should go back to my office job, very undemanding, a bit underpaid but with great hours. Weekends free, holidays too, not like in the restaurant, where I'm deep in shit 24-7. He was making the big bucks anyway, and Rosita's wasn't turning a profit."

"Why wasn't Rosita's turning a profit?"

A sigh escaped her throat. A sad, heavy sigh. "It's a long story," she said. "But I can't sell the place. I just can't. Every time I go in, I expect to see my father at the counter. Or my brother coming out from the kitchen. It hurts horribly, but I'm not ready to lose that connection."

"Of course you aren't, princess," he said. "And nobody should ask that of you. Who is this guy? Just tell me his name, and I'll beat the living crap out of him."

"No need. But thanks for the offer. I think the last time a guy offered to beat someone up for me was in second grade when Sean Wright slapped Timothy for stealing my shovel. At the end, it turned out Sean wanted the shovel for himself."

"I also want the shovel for myself," he whispered in her ear.

"Don't I know that." She laughed. "I don't care about Aidan, really, not anymore. In fact, it's been a very long time since I've thought about him. I've been too busy busting my ass at Rosita's."

"And it's a very fine ass," he whispered again, and she laughed. He wanted to insist and ask about the restaurant, but she was such a private person and she'd shared so much today he didn't want to push his luck. Besides, the last thing he wanted to do now was fight with her.

"Thank you very much. I also think so. A bit on the wide side, but fine nevertheless."

"Your ass is perfect, baby. Every part of you is perfect," he added, breathing her in, encircling her in his arms, ready to hold her for as long as she'd let him. Damn, he wanted so much to please her, sexually and otherwise, it was scary. She was so soft, her body fitting in his lap as if she'd been born to be there, born for him to hold. Oh man, what a sap! Look at him wishful thinking, panting and wiggling his tail. Pathetic. He had the weirdest, most unreasonable crush on this girl. The same girl who had reassured him time and again she wanted nothing serious with him because "his kind" were trash. Only sex, she'd said, and he'd eagerly agreed. Idiot. And the worst part was, he wasn't even getting any.

"Damn, you smell good." She had slathered on coconut sunscreen, which mixed perfectly with her fresh scent. She smelled exotic, like those cocktails one got served in the Caribbean on vacation. He nuzzled her throat, so delicate. In spite of her feisty inner fire, her body was all female, soft and pliant, molding to his. He scanned around. No one in sight.

He moved his hand down, stroking her stomach, drawing circles around her belly button while he flicked his tongue across her neck, kissing the sensitive spot where shoulder and neck met.

As he ventured further down, his fingertips brushing her bikini, she grabbed him by the wrist and squirmed, laughing. "Are you nuts?"

Yes, he was nuts. And desperate. The water almost completely covered them, and the foam from the bubbles left the view quite murky. She was sitting on him, her back resting against his chest. As far as he could see, this was quite feasible. "No one can see. Just lie on me and relax. Let me touch you."

Her laugh rumbled on his chest. "You're kinky. And dangerous. And horny."

Well, she got him on that, no denying it.

"Your fault. Before your lovely ass showed up around here, I was a very respectable man. Now I'm just a pathetic, scheming bastard dying to fuck you."

It took a while for her to settle down, but she finally let go of his hand. Good, because he was about to break her hold and delve into her bikini. He started with butterfly strokes over the cloth. Soon her hips were lifting to his touch.

He whispered in her ear, nuzzling her, trailing kisses and nips on her ear and throat. He pressed his fingers against her clit, rubbing it gently through the cloth. She jerked, but he held her down.

"Relax. I'm just playing with this pretty clit. You like it? I think you do. It's getting harder, and your nipples are poking out, sweetheart. I can see them even through the foam. You want me."

She let out a very unladylike snort, and he smiled, feeling like smooching her to death. "No shit, Sherlock."

"If you promise to be a good girl and not scream, I'll make it better," he said, sliding his hands beneath the waistband.

Another unladylike snort. "I'm curious, how much better are you going to make it if I promise to be a bad girl?"

His dick jerked in response, growing even harder. Fuck, that was painful. He groaned and pinned her to him, pressing his cock against her ass. He breathed in slowly, trying to regain control, weighing up the odds he'd end up embarrassing himself and coming against her buttocks. It had never happened before, but hey, there was a first time for everything. "Don't be naughty. And don't go making any promises you won't be able to keep. At any moment, a bunch of senior citizens could come strolling around the corner, and we don't want to offend their sensibilities. I wouldn't mind, though. I'll fuck you anywhere if I could be sure we'd finish in peace and repeat it a couple of times before getting arrested."

It was true. He'd been resisting, but by now he was ready to go at her on the table in the common area. During morning breakfast rush, even. "Now be a good girl and let me take care of you. Open your legs for me."

She spread her legs wider and arched slightly, offering

herself to his touch. He slipped his fingers beneath the tiny triangle of cloth and slowly began working her clit, playing with the ring, gently tugging at it.

She moaned, her nails digging into his arm, her eyes closed, her teeth nipping at her lower lip.

Jesus, she was sexy. Unable to resist, he delved one finger inside of her. Scalding hot and wet and tight.

"You like it, babe? Me inside you?" As she nodded, he continued, "Do you want more of me filling this tight, sweet pussy?"

He heard the hitch in her breath, and she tensed, trapping his finger inside her, sucking him in deeper. Shit, he was going out of his mind. This was a very bad idea. He was as tense as a bowstring already; her pussy clamping on his fingers would make him come. But he liked giving her pleasure; it gave him an amazing rush like nothing he'd ever felt before. Pleasing her pleased him.

She had other plans, though.

"Yes, I want more of you inside me, but I want to play too," she said, reaching behind her to his cock and palming him. He groaned harshly, closed his eyes, and pressed himself against her hand. It felt so damn good, his body so damn ready he could already feel his cum poised at the tip of his dick, pulsing. He'd just have to move aside the tiny strap of bikini and slip his cock inside her, skyrocketing them both into heaven.

With enormous effort, he opened his eyes and kept himself in lockdown, trying to block the images of him riding her from behind. "You better not. I'm liable to lose it, and we'd get arrested for indecent exposure," he said, kissing her shoulder. "Besides, Mrs. Samuels is heading this way."

Tate took her hand off him as if he'd burned her and closed her legs so fast she trapped his hand between them. She tried to scramble away from him, but he grabbed her. No way was she moving from on top of him; he wasn't sure his dick wasn't going to come poking out from the water if she did.

"Good morning, Mrs. Samuels," he said, turning to the old lady, his arms encircling Tate.

She looked at them, intrigued, one brow cocked. "Why don't

you make yourself useful and come by my place to pick up the pies? I've baked them especially for you to take home."

Oh God, now? "Hmm, can I pass by later?" He didn't want to get out of the hot tub and flash the boner of the century at Mrs. Samuels. It'd give her a stroke. And him. And anybody out there watching. Not to mention that after having Tate's buttocks pressed tight against his dick and her sweet hand squeezing it, he was pretty sure at the moment he was unable to walk without injuring himself.

"I have to leave in about fifteen minutes, dear. I have this thing with my sister I have to attend, and I won't be back for a few days."

Tate stifled a laugh. "I'll go, Mrs. Samuels. I've heard a lot about your pie. I want to see it before I leave."

James sighed in relief. He must have looked in serious need of rescuing.

"Besides, James just got in the water. I've been here for an hour already. I'm as wrinkled as an old prune. Give me five minutes, and I'll be there."

As she watched Violet walk away, she turned around and kissed his cheek. "Told you, sweetie, this place is more guarded than a boot camp."

Then she stood up, and he almost had a stroke. No prune at all. She was breathtaking, her whole body glistening under the sun, water skating down her curves, foam from the bubbles caressing her thighs. Like a damn goddess, with that little triangle of cloth barely covering her bare pussy. And the piercing. And that tight juicy place he was dying to lose himself in. At that image, his dick jerked, and he had to hold his breath not to come.

Fuck. That was it. He was getting them a room.

He'd suffered this unyielding boner for four days straight—day and night. Cold showers weren't doing shit. Hell, jacking off wasn't doing shit. The phone sex had been a mind-blowing revelation, but his damn psychic dick had known it was being fooled, because five minutes after coming, he'd been in as bad shape as at the beginning. Worse probably, his mind and body in overdrive. He had to have her. Today. Besides, the pain of going through the nine-hole golf course with that fucking king-size hard-on from hell tenting his pants was still fresh in his mind.

Despite the deplorable state his cock was in, he couldn't deny he was having a great time with her—it was almost worth the physical torture...almost. She was very funny. Smart and witty too, once you got under her defenses. And she was a shark when it came to playing—hated to lose. He was pretty sure he'd caught her cheating at bingo. So sweet, especially if one considered half her opponents had limited sight and hearing capabilities. She loved to laugh and to tease, and the only time she turned somber was when talking about the restaurant or her family. Yes, he was having a great time hanging out with her, if one could overlook the fact that his dick was falling to pieces from frustration.

No matter how much he liked her company—and he did—there was something else he wanted. Needed, by now. He'd kind of reached an understanding with his libido: he wasn't taking her in his car; he needed a bed. And privacy—something, as it turned out, very difficult to find in Eternal Sun. The moment his fly went down for any reason, he wasn't going to be able to stop.

Trying to be as inconspicuous as a huge guy with a raging hard-on could, he moved to the swimming pool, to the side closest to where his belongings were, jumped out, and reached for his towel, patting the chair until he found what he was searching for. He flipped the cell phone open, made a couple of calls, and then sent her a text message. Enough was enough. He was no teenager, for fuck's sake; he was thirty-four. Last time he checked, he was entitled to spend the night with a woman without owing anyone explanations.

"They smell delicious, Mrs. Samuels." Tate complimented the elder woman while she was busy packing the pies.

"Call me Violet please. I keep telling James to stop calling me Mrs. Samuels, but he keeps forgetting. I've known him for almost five years already. Great boy. His brothers too."

Beep. Beep. A message. Tate flipped her phone open.

U r mine tonite. Hotel Gold Crown, room 537. All arranged, u just bring ur pretty luscious self, I'll bring the condoms.

She couldn't suppress the nervous giggles. Violet looked at her, seeming intrigued.

"It's a message from James," she said while typing her response. "He's just being silly."

"You've grown quite close in these last days, haven't you?"

"Nah," she said without lifting her eyes from the cell, quickly pressing the buttons. "Just vacation fun."

At the end of your rope, huh?

She checked the sentence she'd typed once more and sent it. In her mind's eye, she could already see James chuckling.

She lifted her gaze to Violet and smiled brightly. The pies were all packed except for a small piece.

"That's for you, dear. Go on, try it."

"Oh, thanks," she said, bringing the piece up to her mouth. It was delicious, sweet and warm. "Tastes fantastic."

Beep. Beep. Another message.

Damn right I am. Been there 4 quite a while now. Will u have pity on a dying man here? I need 2 fuck u.

She read it, slowly shaking her head and smirking. "James again, fooling around."

Violet was quiet, and when Tate looked at her, she realized she was frowning slightly, her lips pursed into a tight, disapproving line.

"James is a great boy. I've never seen him fool around, as you call it, with anyone else here. And God knows I've tried to throw Tessa at him. He's always kept his distance from every girl. I don't want him hurt."

Hurt? Tate didn't know what to say. It was hard to think of James in those terms, as if he were a tenderhearted fifteen-year-old boy in danger of getting his sensibilities crushed.

She smiled at the old lady. "Don't worry, Violet, your boy is safe. I won't hurt him." She was in no position to do so; she was leaving tomorrow night. All they had time for was a quick tumble in the hay. Hopefully not so quick.

"All I'm saying is you be careful with him."

So this was how it felt to be grilled, to get the father talk when you went to pick up a girl from her home for the first time.

She nodded, resisting the urge to laugh. Oh man, did anyone around here ever take a good look at James? He was an imposing man. Huge, intimidating, even with his wicked smiles. He was definitely able to handle himself. She was no match for him.

The bitch had been gone for several days now. She'd taken off to Florida for a week, which meant his last two e-mails were still waiting to be read; she wasn't big on computers on the best of days, so there was no way she'd carry one on vacation.

He glanced around the restaurant; it was almost empty. Good, maybe he wouldn't have to finish off this place by himself; maybe it would die by its own lonely self instead. Two months more of this and it'd be over. She'd give in. He could hardly wait, because really, this place had cost him, and still did, so much on so many levels, it could never burn down enough for his satisfaction. Or maybe it could, he thought with a smile.

CHAPTER FIVE

She sucked at gin, no two ways about it, but poker was her kind of game. Not because she could lie worth a damn, but because her sweet smile made her look so fucking nonthreatening no one would believe she was bluffing. And bluff she did, constantly and shamelessly.

"I win again," she said with a smirk, splaying her cards on the table. "Pity we're betting pennies here; otherwise I'd have made a fortune off you by now." She offered James a big, smug smile and then addressed the others. "Do we raise the stakes, gentlemen, or are you scared?"

James hugged her tighter. "Careful, princess, this crowd is fearless. I've seen them betting their medication. You don't want to challenge them."

She turned to him, stupefied, then looked at an assenting Mr. Honbacker and burst out laughing.

She was breathtaking. Those roguish silver-blue eyes full of mystery lighting her whole face, that pretty bowed mouth, pink and soft and tempting, assuring him he was a swipe of her tongue away from heaven. Her long, wavy hair floating around her. She was a knockout, and every time she smiled at him, his dick twitched so badly he had to grit his teeth not to spill on the spot. By now he wasn't even trying to keep his hands to himself; it was a physical impossibility. Tate's mom was frowning at him as much as she did at his dad, but whatever. James couldn't help himself; he was a goner.

"Let's get out of here," he whispered into her ear. Playing cards was now the last thing in the world he wanted to do.

She laughed that earthy laugh that had tortured him for so many days now, encircled his neck with her slender arms, and kissed him on the cheek. She was having fun at his expense. And why on earth did those tiny pecks on his cheek feel even more intimate than a blowjob?

"Wait a sec, let me win enough to pay for supper. You're putting up for the room, after all," she said morosely.

"Forget supper, baby; we'll raid the minibar." Tomorrow she was going back home; they were running out of time.

"It feels like prom night all over again," she stated as they walked toward his car.

"You ended up in a hotel room? Boy, your prom date must have been happy."

"Hardly. He actually never got me into the hotel room."

"Poor bastard. I know how he felt."

She clicked her tongue in clear disapproval. "His fault. Tony Masero shouldn't have been groping high school homecoming queen Big Boobs Cynthia the day before at the mall. In front of my friends, I might add. Dirty sneak. Besides, he'd been nuts to think I'd lose my virginity to him to begin with. On prom night, in a sleazy hotel room, with a half-drunk teenage imbecile going prematurely senile from testosterone poisoning. This is a step up—you aren't drunk, and you haven't been groping Big Boobs Cynthia Smith, have you?"

He barked out a laugh. Jesus, she was hilarious. "I swear on my grandmother's grave, I haven't laid a finger on Big Boobs Cynthia. That I know of." He'd always been a die-hard fan of big boobs, but he couldn't honestly recall any Cynthia Smith. And now it was a moot point anyway; his preferences had recently shifted, and he was finding out perky, smaller tits did it for him big-time.

She wrinkled her nose, assessing him. "Well, okay then. I think I'll let you take me to that hotel room. Better not be a sleazy one, mister." He shook his head, and her lips turned up. "Good. Although I can't offer you my virginity, buddy; that's long gone."

"Perfect. What I have in mind would scare a virgin." Besides, virgins were not for him—too draining.

She averted her gaze, color creeping up her cheeks. Such

contradictions; one moment she was being raunchy, the next blushing like a shy teenager.

He'd planned to take his time with her, savor the moment, build up the heat, make her wait and beg for it, but the second they entered the room, he pinned her to the door, bracketed her with his arms, and lost it. He fell upon her like a starving man, kissing her savagely, his tongue ruthlessly taking over and exploring every inch of that sweet, hot mouth.

A choked moan escaped from her throat, and he greedily swallowed it while he gripped her hips with urgency and ground himself into her. He felt feverish, out of control, famished, like he'd been waiting for this for ages. There weren't going to be any fancy moves from him. Just stark-naked hunger. He'd endured four days of maddening foreplay, and by now he had her scent so deep inside him it was all he could smell day and night. It had finally driven him insane. Total mental leave of absence. That was the only way to describe his current behavior. Talk about testosterone poisoning. Hah, Tony Masero had nothing on him; he hadn't drunk a damn thing, but he was as good as fully loaded.

He yanked her skirt up, using his thigh to part her legs wider and press against her pussy, forcing her to ride it. He greedily licked her throat, then went down to her collarbone. He closed his lips around one of her hard nipples and tugged, getting her to ride him harder, her juices seeping through her panties.

"I'm too far gone to last this time, or to go slow, but I promise I'll make it up to you," he managed to say between kisses. Hopefully she was okay with it, because he was unable to even stop to check for her reaction. Lifting her leg to his hip, he ground his denim-clad erection against her folds, and she gasped, clutching his shoulders with her short nails, holding him tight. Man, this was madness; no matter how desperate he was to be inside her, he had to slow down. But apparently there had been a coup d'état in his brain, and there was no one up there enforcing his commands. He was drunk on her scent, and his dick was calling the shots.

He urgently gripped her ass, lifting her, keeping her locked between him and the wall. She was hot and wet. And panting loudly against his mouth. He needed to fuck her right now, hard and fast, or he was going to die. He reached for her panties, and with a swift movement, he ripped them off her.

He had about a couple of seconds before losing it completely, if not less. He unzipped his fly, took himself in hand, and barely remembered to sheath himself with a rubber before plunging inside her. She cried out, her pussy clamping on him, her legs trembling as he seated himself root-deep, and without giving her time to adjust, he began pounding into her. Thank God she was wet, because he'd been hijacked by his dick and couldn't stop. No sense of dignity and decorum or timing. Or technique. He just needed to get deep inside her—deeper than anybody had ever been before. Stake a claim on her he didn't even understand himself.

She reached for him, sinking her fingers into his scalp. Panting even louder. Trembling and shaking.

"Oh God..." She breathed into his mouth while he hammered her into the door.

He had the fleeting thought he was being too rough; she was small and tight and delicate, and he needed to get her off now, before he came completely undone, which was a handful of thrusts anyway. Making her climax might later be the only redeeming point of this whole wham-bam fiasco. The only thing keeping her from kicking him to the curb.

Changing the angle a bit, he dragged himself over her clit, slamming his pelvis into her with every plunge, nudging at her swollen clit and rubbing at the ring. He gripped her ass, opening her cheeks wide and forcing her to take all of him while she kept panting, her breath choppy and loud. He couldn't take the pressure anymore; the mounting vortex of need inside him was fast swallowing him. He was about to move his fingers to her clit to throw her over the edge when suddenly Tate's body tensed, and she screamed against his lips, immersed in a powerful orgasm that instantly milked the rest of his sanity out of him. Her pussy convulsed around him, demanding his seed. Holding her tight in his arms, he pounded inside her and came like a wild man.

When he regained his senses, his throat felt raw, his mind foggy, and he wasn't sure if his legs would work again—ever. What the fuck had happened? Had she killed him? Whatever it'd been, it was so out of his sexual experience he wasn't sure whether he'd come or had a massive stroke. They were both breathing fast, no one saying a damn word. Man, he'd fucked it up nice this time. Talk about sexual technique. He should be ashamed of himself. Shot on sight. Fuck.

He struggled to find his voice. "Are you...okay?" He didn't know what to say. "Did I...um...hurt you?" What a moronic question; of course he had. Going at her like a madman, without any foreplay. She'd been wet, and she'd come, but still. That had been rough. She would be within her rights to chew his head off.

She shook her head. "It just surprised me," she whispered, her sexy eyes turned up to him. "Your Conan the Barbarian act caught me off guard. I came, of course. I always do when you touch me, no matter how rough. You just do it for me."

"I ah... Sorry, princess," he mumbled, feeling like a fucking jerk. "I lost it. All that pent-up lust fogged my mind. Let me get rid of the condom, and I promise I'll make it right for you. No more three-minute fiascos." He stared at her, her face all soft and rosy from her release. She smiled at him. Thank God she wasn't kicking him out on his ass. Yet.

While he disentangled himself from her and got rid of the rubber, she stood still, leaning against the door, the spiked heels making her body sway dangerously. She looked dazzled and fucking beautiful. Like a manga character, huge hair and huge eyes wrapped up in a sexy, petite body that was all his. For the time being, at least.

He'd been so beside himself he hadn't even watched her orgasm. Damn pity, for he loved seeing her fly apart in his arms. If he'd learned anything during the past days, it was that Tate climaxing was a treat. This time though, it'd been a little difficult to see anything with his eyes rolled all the way to the back of his head. He'd been immersed in a maelstrom of fire and desire so strong it'd blocked out everything, even what he wanted to see the most.

He lifted her into his arms and placed her on the bed.

"Lose the top."

"Don't you prefer to rip it off me with your teeth?" she said jokingly.

Yeah, no sense trying to play it cool and civilized now. Too late for that; she'd already seen the caveman.

He lunged for her. “Now that you mention it...” Besides, that knuckle-dragging, Neanderthal part of him didn’t seem satisfied yet. Maybe after he’d fucked her three or four times more, he’d be able to calm down and take it easy. In fact, his dick was already hardening at the prospect of nailing her again.

“Oh no no. Stop right there.” She giggled while scrambling away. “I can ruin my own clothes without any help whatsoever, thank you very much.” She pulled her top up and over her shoulders, leaving her naked to his eyes, except for the bra and the stockings and the skirt rolled at her waist, entangled in the garter belt. His eyes surveyed her body, memorizing every curve and hollow. He was going to taste all of them. Lick her clean and then make her sweaty and dirty again.

“Take the skirt off too,” he ordered and watched her shimmy out of it, her tits jiggling with the movement. Shit, she wore a demibra. The devilish little thing barely covered squat and offered her tits on a platter—nipples peeking out, in plain view. They were tight and red, begging to be licked. “Lose the bra.”

She went to her knees on the bed, got rid of the garment, and moved to unclasp the garter belt. “No, leave that on. The shoes and the stockings too. For now.” Dying to touch her, he strode toward her, his hand held out, but she surprised him by grabbing his cock. Her hands were cool and soft, and they began working their magic while she kissed and nuzzled his chest.

He let out a ragged groan at the sight of his gorgeous, wicked princess nibbling at his nipples. A jolt of pure lust jerked his body. Her mouth was dangerously trailing down, until it landed on his dick, and James felt his mind exploding.

She pleasured him with her hands and mouth. Several times he moved his hands to her head to make her stop, but it was as if his hands were free agents and he had no control over them. Panting and sweating, he found himself on the brink. Abruptly he pushed her away. “Not yet, princess. I want to come inside you, with your pussy clenched around me.”

“But—”

“No buts.” He flipped her on her back and settled between her legs and prodded her gently with his fingers. She was ready, but he didn’t want to risk it again. She needed to come a couple of times more to be soft and wet and needy enough for what he had in mind. Besides, he had to redeem himself. Then he got sidetracked by her breasts, so cute and small and nicely shaped, rising and falling fast, the red nipples beckoning him. Yes, his time of being a hardcore fan of big boobs was gone. He raked his teeth over one nipple and then sucked—hard.

Tate's back bowed, and her pussy convulsed around his finger. He sucked again, and she convulsed again.

"God, James, I don't know how you do that, but every time you get close to my nipples, I feel it between my legs."

"Funny," he whispered, lavishing her other nipple, making it wet and hard, getting her inner muscles to jerk around his finger and greedily clasp it. "Every time I kiss your nipples, I feel it all the way down to my groin too."

He kissed his way down from her tits to her stomach until he pressed his mouth to her bare pussy, needing to taste her again. With a moan on her lips, she opened her legs wider. He ate at her folds, kissing and petting them, making them flush a deeper red, and then suckled her clit gently, humming against it while Tate arched her back and lifted her hips to him, begging for more. He loved her taste. Like hot honey melting around his taste buds. It was sweetly addictive. He could lap at her all day long and never tire. Keeping her wide open, with his hands under her ass, he fucked her with his tongue and was rewarded by a deep, ragged moan. She was madly bucking beneath him, willing his tongue to fuck her deeper. Desperate. So damn responsive—like she was made for him.

He moved to lick her clit, rubbing at it with the flat part of his tongue while two fingers filled her. A little more pressure on her clit and there she went, screaming into orgasm. He rode it out, petting her until all that was left were tremors. Then he went at it again. And again. Until she was whipped-cream soft and limp in his arms. Now she was ready. She whimpered, but he flipped her on her stomach, lifted her ass up, and forced her onto her hands and knees.

"I told you this is one of my favorite positions."

She turned her face to him, insecurity written all over her.

"I'll make it work for you. I promise. I can get very deep

inside you like this; you'll come so hard you'll pass out."

He rolled a condom on, and in one stroke, he drove into her to the hilt. She gasped but took all of him. She was scalding hot and fucking tight, her muscles fluttering around him, grabbing him. He backed out slowly and pushed in again, feeling her flesh yielding to him, her heat bathing all of him.

"Man, look at you," he whispered into her ear while he kept still. James reached over, brushed her clit, and slid his fingers down. He touched her folds, feeling how wide open she was for him, for his penetration. "You're so fucking sexy." He licked and petted the back of her neck, her throat, her ear, until she was moaning and pushing against him, urging him to get on with it. Harder. Faster. He loomed over her, gripping her hip with one hand while his other continued to gently rub her clit. And then he snapped again.

Soon the slamming thrusts were rocking her whole body.

"Do you like it, Tate? Do you?" he said insistently while she released a ragged "yes."

He didn't recognize himself. So needy, so out of control. No detachment, no distance. He was letting this girl get to him...get inside him.

James felt his orgasm rising in his head and in his balls at the same time, his sac drawing tighter to the base of his dick, but when it hit him, he was totally unprepared. It was like free falling. The world exploded around him as he tensed, and his semen furiously spurted out of him. In between his haze, he noticed her falling apart with another of her earth-shattering screams. Good. He'd made her come. Again. The number of orgasms he brought to a woman was always a matter of pride, but now it was also a matter of survival; the more limp and satiated he kept her, the less she would try to ditch him. Plus he had that episode against the door to make up for, the intensity of which had startled him. Startled him? No, scratch that, it'd scared him to death. He didn't do intense. Sexually intense, yes, but that was pretty much the extent of his involvement. He'd always prided himself on remaining a bit detached, even during the hottest of fucks. Not anymore. He was thinking with his dick, he knew it, but he couldn't help it. She was blowing his mind away, nothing else left but his glands to dictate the rules. What a poor state of affairs for a guy who always ran the show with a cool head.

He rolled off her and gathered her in his arms, hiding his face in her hair.

His throat was swollen shut.

"Jesus, you're fantastic. You fried my brain. Again," he murmured after reassuring himself his voice wasn't shaky anymore. She was dismantling him, true, but at least he was going to go a happy man.

One extremely well-used condom later and Tate was totally limp. She opened her eyes and licked her dry lips. James had one arm over her waist, holding her tight. Slowly she rolled onto her back. Feeling boneless, glowing, and adrift, like she'd float up to the ceiling if James moved his arm.

She lowered her eyes to his still half-erect cock and groaned. "I don't know what it'd take to lay that beast down. Probably nothing I should be contemplating right now seeing as how I can barely move."

"Two or three rounds more with my pirate princess and it'll calm down."

Tate laughed. "Then I better raid the minibar. Get myself some sustenance." Although she doubted nuts and chips would be enough to get her through this bout of sex. Maybe she'd get lucky and hit pay dirt, find some high-power energy drink there—or some go-all-night amphetamines, for that matter. Then again, raiding the minibar would imply her walking to it, so she decided to pass. At the moment, her legs were too wobbly for such a colossal effort. The spiked heels she still had on would ensure she broke her neck.

As James reached for her, the chime of her cell startled them both. She looked around, trying to remember where she'd left her bag. Ah, yes, near the door, with the rest of her clothes. And her brain.

Scurrying from James's embrace, she decided to brave neck injury and went to fetch the cell. She flipped it open and read the message.

"What's it?"

Her airline putting a crush on the best sex of her life, that's what it was.

"My flight has been rescheduled. It leaves at one p.m., not in the evening."

"Ask them to book you a seat for a later flight."

She shook her head. "No, I better confirm my seat for the one o'clock flight," she said, quickly composing a message.

He propped his back against the headboard, the sheet bunching around his hips. "You know, I'll be leaving in two days. You could travel back with me. We could stop along the way for some sightseeing. Check in to a different motel every night and hump like crazed rabbits all the way to Boston."

"Tempting, but I can't wait that long before arriving home."

"Pretty please?"

She avoided his gaze. "Sorry, no. I'm really in a hurry. I can't afford to cruise around the country." *Without a care in the world, while her personal world was falling to pieces.*

"What is it that you're in such hurry to go back to? Or should I say who?"

She gave him a "duh" look. "There's no one back home, I told you already. Not that it's any of your business."

"Don't be mistaken. You're in my bed. It is my business."

"For now."

He looked at her as if she was kidding herself but didn't press the matter. "It's the restaurant then, right? The reason you're so twitchy to go back? Why, Tate? And why is Rosita's not turning a profit?"

She stiffened. She remembered telling him that and not elaborating further. "It does turn a profit, it's just that…"

"What? Spit it out, will ya?"

She sighed and sat on the corner of the bed. What the heck; in several hours, she'd be gone anyway. "Well, a couple of months after the car accident, we had a fire in the restaurant. It started in the kitchen; apparently, someone left a stove on. There was a rag nearby, and, well, the place went up like a torch in the middle of the night. By the time the firemen got it under control, the damage was considerable. The insurance policy my parents had was old and full of loopholes, as it turned out. Dad was planning to update it before passing the restaurant to my brother, but he never got around to it. So as the fire was our fault, the money for repairing the damage had to come basically from our own pocket."

"Are you sure it was an accident? Maybe someone broke in. A prank from kids, maybe."

"The police ruled that out. According to the arson expert, the fire was an accident caused by negligence. The firemen pinpointed the origin. The stove had been on. And there were no signs of breaking and entering." She was dead sure it hadn't been an accident, though. She had her e-mail in-box full of threatening messages, for Christ's sake. How clearer could that get? Those had begun a week after the fire, threatening her, among other unpleasant things, with torching the place up for real this time if she didn't sell out. But the police said there was no evidence of foul play, that for all they knew she could be the one sending those e-mails in the hopes of getting the insurance money. She wasn't telling James any of that, though. She wanted to; it would feel nice to unload onto someone, but she didn't even want to utter the words. Besides, no one wanted to hear them. Her mom would freak out about the e-mails, Elle too. The police weren't taking her seriously. Aidan had bailed out. She barely had time for her friends, who would actually also flip about the threats. James wouldn't freak, she was sure, but it wasn't his problem.

"So cutting a long story short, I got stuck with the bill." She smiled, trying to play it down, but it came out as a grimace. Her mouth didn't seem to be able to stop now that she'd opened Pandora's box. "Rosita's lost not only my dad and Jonah, but my mom too. They were the heart of the place, irreplaceable. I'm a lousy cook, can't help in the kitchen but for the basics, and I suck as a hostess. It's difficult to smile and make people feel welcome and have a good time when you're broken inside."

He reached for her. "Jesus, Tate. You don't have any close family that could help you?"

She shook her head. "There's only the three of us: me, Mom, and Elle. If I give up, Rosita's is as good as gone. Elle and Mom won't set foot in it, won't fight for it. I'm sure after they've had some time to heal, they'll relish the place and all the memories that it holds, but now they can't see it. Hell, most times I can't either. But if I give up now and sell out, then Rosita's will be truly lost to us. We won't be able to revisit those memories in the future when Mom and Elle are ready for them."

His face tightened. "You're putting too much responsibility on your head."

She shrugged. "It's the only head around."

"You need a vacation, a real one. Take the road trip back with me."

She snorted. Was he kidding? "Please don't make me laugh. My gut cramps every time my cell rings. I need to be there. I'm already scared shitless the place has gone to hell during this week I've been away." Or up in flames.

He waved at her dismissively. "Don't dramatize. In my experience, most employees work better when the pressure is off somehow, when they're given some space. Give them another week to show they can come through."

Yeah right. "I can't afford it."

"You need to disconnect. We could leave tomorrow if you don't want to wait two days. I don't think my dad will mind, and I'm flexible that way."

"I bet you are," she said ironically.

His tone hardened. "What does that mean?"

"Tell me one thing; how can you run a business if you're absent whenever you feel like hitting the road and coming to Florida, or feel like inviting a girl to a sex marathon while crossing a bunch of states?"

"I'm there when I need to be, which is more than most people can say. Besides, I have time to spare."

"Sure you have."

"I don't like what you're implying, princess."

She dismissed him. "I'm just saying I can't go with you. I'm a grown-up, have grown-up things to do." Ouch, that had come out too snotty, even for her ears.

"And I'm just a brainless, irresponsible stud that turns

wherever the wind blows, is that it?"

"No, it isn't like that. You talk too much."

He stood up. "True, this was just sex, after all. Better use our time efficiently," he said, grabbing her by the wrist and pulling her out of the bed. "Get the stockings off."

"Don't bully me," she snapped at him, straightening her back.

He gave her that devilishly sexy grin and palmed himself. At the sight of his fully erect cock, throbbing and pulsing, her own body began melting. Maybe she could use a bit of bullying after all.

She strode to the chair, lifted her leg up, and, offering him a back view he'd surely appreciate, rolled one stocking down slowly, taking her sweet time fussing with it and unbuckling the high heels. She'd never stripped in front of anyone, was probably sadly lacking in form and technique, but if his deep groan was anything to go by, or the way he stared at her, she was doing just fine.

"Now the other," she heard him say and kept going. Lifting the other leg, dragging down the stocking, and fussing a little with the shoe. When she lifted her eyes to him, he had his gaze fixed on her, a condom dangling from his free hand.

"Roll it on me."

"Let me touch you first," she said, moving toward him. She wanted to explore his body, kiss him all over in the same way he'd done to her.

He caught her hand before it could reach his chest. "Forget it, princess, not part of the deal."

"What deal? I had no idea we had a deal," she complained.

"You've decided to shove me in the same box you shoved all your sister's bad-news boyfriends. Losers only good for fucking. I'm just playing the part, sweetheart."

"I've never said such a thing."

"No talking, remember? Let's fuck. That's what we're here for."

He looked mad. She shouldn't let him touch her while mad, much less push her on her knees, as he was doing, but her treacherous body went along. She thought he'd force his way into her mouth, but he didn't. James stood there, waiting for her to rip the foil packet and roll the condom on him.

As soon as she was done, he pulled her up and tossed her onto the bed. Before she could complain, he grabbed her by the ankles and dragged her to the edge, her ass almost dangling in midair. Lifting her legs up and wide, he unceremoniously seated himself in one long continuous thrust inside her quivering core. His cock was much too big for her, but he'd made her come repeatedly, and her slick flesh accepted him.

"Touch your clit," he instructed her, his splayed hands gripping the back of her thighs, keeping her wide open and totally exposed to his gaze. "I want to see how you make yourself come. How you jacked off the other day on the phone with me."

She licked her lips, a bit uncomfortable with the situation. This level of exposure was new for her. If he'd just press against her, she could easily work herself toward release without having to masturbate in front of him. But he was clever; he didn't let her lift her hips to him. In fact, the bastard had stopped moving altogether.

"Make yourself come."

"Please, move."

He shook his head. "Nuh. You start petting that beautiful clit; I'll start moving again."

She pursed her lips in annoyance but slid her hands down her stomach and closed her eyes.

"Open your eyes. Look at me. Watch me watch you."

Damn obnoxious control freak! She was about to yell at him to fuck off and stop ordering her around when he suddenly moved, his cock surging deep inside her, brushing that inner hot spot that made her flesh flutter in anticipation, and finishing with a devilish grind that set her insides on fire. Gasping, she arched her back, ready for more, but the asshole pulled back and stopped moving again.

Fine, let him have it his way! Tate opened her eyes and, staring at him, cupped her breasts and caressed her nipples. Then she slid one hand down until she brushed her clit with her fingers. Yeah, it looked like she could play at this teasing game too. James growled at the sight and watched, mesmerized, his cock pulsating inside her, twitching and growing even bigger.

"That's it, Tate; touch yourself for me, baby," he said in a ragged breath, slowly driving into her. "Let me see how you do it."

She delved her fingers down around her slick folds to dampen them, and then went back to pet her clit, drawing circles with the pad of her finger and grinding the piercing on it. This felt so good she was fast losing herself to it, to the pleasure. And James's hungry stare worked as a powerful aphrodisiac. Her breasts were aching and throbbing, and her pussy was clamping. She added a bit more pressure on her bud, and her pussy walls jolted. James's dick twitched inside her in response.

"Fuck, babe." He gritted his teeth as he fought to regain control. Yep, pretty interactive toy, she'd say. She jumped; he jumped.

Although the show was visibly eroding his amazing control, he kept his strokes slow and soft and his eyes glued to her as she continued touching herself. She pinched her nipples, pressed her fingers over her clit, and played with the ring some more, tugging at it while he tried to stay true to his words and look as detached as possible. But she could see he was having a hard time with that. Especially every time she reached to the base of his cock and caressed him, raking her nails slightly over his thick shaft until she'd reach the spot where they were joined, and then continuing up to pleasure herself. This drove him mad. And her too. It felt very intimate.

His dick had swollen to huge proportions, the veins throbbing and distended. He was sweating and looking very tense. Keeping their hips separated and the rhythm excruciatingly slow was obviously taking a heavy toll on him. He was, as usual, power tripping and calling all the shots, but she felt empowered too, and extremely aroused.

Soon she found herself passing through the point of no return. She couldn't torment him anymore—she was going to come.

"James, I need you to fuck me harder. Now," she pleaded between breathless pants, rubbing herself harder. Her orgasm was already pounding at her clit, growing at the base of her spine. Her pussy was fluttering, and she badly needed him shoved deep inside her. He understood her urgency and buried himself balls-deep in her, catapulting her right away into full-blown orgasm. She watched him, fighting to keep her eyes open as her climax roared through her. His jaw was locked, his lips drawn in a thin line, his body trembling. His eyes were awestruck. Then everything went black for her.

"That was awesome," she heard him mumble when her spasms had passed. He lifted her from her ass and moved them over so he could lie on top of her. "It was like having an iron fist squeezing me, sucking me in. I could see your pussy strangling the hell out of my dick."

She focused her eyes on him. "Glad you liked it. I did. I'd have preferred you taking a more active part in it, though."

"What do you mean? I was there watching you like a hawk, my dick shoved up inside you. Hard as steel. What more did you want?"

She laughed. "You slamming against me like crazy," she said, arching her back, moving against him.

"But then I wouldn't have been able to watch you milking my cock."

She locked her legs around him, reaching over to his ass. "Stop watching. Start banging."

"Yes, ma'am." He grinned.

By the time he was done with her, she was exhausted and sweaty. And euphoric too. He'd made her dirty and licked her clean all over at least twice. She was going to miss sex like this. This wasn't hormonal relief; this was something more. This was going to set a damn hard precedent to beat.

CHAPTER SIX

"Do you want to tell us why you're so sulky, man?" Cole asked. "Anything to do with you coming home ahead of time from Dad's? You made the trip in record time..."

James was quiet for a second while he sipped his beer and considered the benefits of lying to his older brother. He decided against it. "I met a woman there."

Cole grimaced. "Oh, Lord, please tell me she isn't someone's grandma. I don't think I'm ready for that."

His younger brother, Max, barked out a laugh, and James almost choked on the beer.

"No, you asshole. It's the daughter of Dad's new neighbor. Her name is Tate."

"So after all your constant preaching against it, you finally dipped the wand into the granddaughters' ink, uh?" Max said to him. "I hope now you'll stop whining at me for being nice to them."

"Nice to them? You fuck everything that moves, Max."

He laughed. "Sooo not true. I have my standards, only cuties. And absolutely no men, no virgins, and no moms."

Cole frowned at Max but soon gave up and turned to James. "I don't understand; you met a woman and that's why you ran away? Let me guess; you nailed her and then bailed as soon as she began introducing you to her elder nosy relatives."

Ha, as if! Nothing could be further from the truth. She'd been the one running out on him. After leaving that hotel room, his smoky-hot pirate princess had turned into the Ice Queen of Evilland, barely looking at him. When it came time to say good-bye, she'd all but offered him her hand. Offered him her hand! Imagine that one.

James had found himself hurrying back to Boston a whole day ahead of schedule, and not only as a means to avoid his dad's cracks. Instead of enjoying the trip back, as he always had before, he'd been off balance, ticked off. No stopping for sightseeing or chitchatting with locals, nothing other than fueling, eating, peeing, and sleeping. He couldn't get back fast enough. To what, he wasn't sure. Well, he was, he just wasn't ready to admit it to himself.

The night with Tate had been spectacular. All the heavy-duty, hard-core imagining he'd indulged in hadn't even come close to the reality of fucking her; Tate had blown his mind, not to mention his dick, which might never recover. It'd seemed to him so much more than sex, but as soon as he'd hinted about seeing each other back home, she'd panicked and given him the cold shoulder—the "Oh, better not, we'll both be pretty busy" speech. Best-case scenario; hot sex away from home, no complications, and no follow-up. So why on earth was he so pissed off? After all, sex without strings was something out of his personal mantra. He should be happy at the way things had gone down. But he wasn't. The truth of the matter was he hated she was walking away from him that easily, especially as he was having trouble doing the same.

"You're way off." James sighed. "She's actually here now. Flew back to Boston before me. Do you guys know a place called Rosita's?"

Both his brothers shook their heads.

"It's an Italian restaurant on the outskirts of Boston. It belongs to her family. She runs it."

"So let me get this straight; you aren't running away from her but after her?" Max asked. "Nice turn of events. First time, I'd say."

"I thought you said no sex in Eternal Sun," Cole reprimanded him. "Too complicated, you said. Not worth it."

James huffed. Lucky him, today he'd come home from his first workday in time to be dragged off for burgers and beers with his nosy brothers. The beers and the burgers were fine; the third degree sucked big-time.

He decided to play it down and, faking indifference, shrugged. "What do you want me to say, man? My dick got the better of me." Although to him, it seemed Tate's grip was somewhere more northern than his family jewels. Not that he was ready to admit anything to anybody yet. Hey, just the fact that he wanted to go to her, among other things to make her smile, gave him a stomachache. "The road to hell is paved with good intentions, right?"

"So you're saying you made the trip back in record time dragged by your cock." Cole sounded suspicious, and with good reason. It had been ages since James had let his dick drag him anywhere. "What's so special about her?"

"Tate is… I don't know. Different."

"What do you mean 'different'? Different how?"

Fuck. He really didn't want to get into this; he had no straight answers.

Max beat him to it. "I'll tell you how; James here has spent his vacation acting like a lovesick puppy. Drooling and smooching this Tate every chance he got. I hear she's cute and sweet. Too young though." At James's glare, he just shrugged unapologetically. "Dad called."

Max had his own place, but as he had yet to discover how the dishwasher and the washing machine worked, he pretty much still lived at home with their Aunt Maggie—in Gossiplandia.

"She's twenty-six; that's hardly cradle robbing."

"How come you're here with us and not with her?"

Good question. His silence was just making his brothers more curious, so he gave it up. "She blew me off before leaving. Apparently she doesn't want to get involved with me."

"She said so?" Max asked.

"Not in so many words no, but she doesn't see me as dating material. Can you believe it? She claims she knows my type; it turns out I'm a black hole wrapped in fancy frilly paper." Talk about being reduced to a fucking social stereotype.

"What?" Max all but yelled, eyes wide in surprise and amusement.

"Exactly my thoughts. Her sister had some bad-news, tattooed, low-life boyfriends. It seems I fit the picture. She wanted to keep it light."

"I told you those tattoos would come back to bite you in the ass someday," Cole said with a grunt. "So what's the plan? Are you going to go see her at this Rosita's?"

James looked intently at his bottle, hoping they'd miss the words *sucker* and *sap* written all over his face. No such luck.

Max chuckled. "Man, you're worm meat. You've already been there."

"I just passed by, didn't go in. She seemed too busy, and I didn't want to get in the way. Besides, she made it clear she doesn't want me."

"She fucked you and dumped you," Max stated. "And now Mr. Detached Dick has had his sensibilities offended." Max was being ironic and crude, but yeah, he'd gotten offended. Mr. Detached Dick wanted more. More sex for sure. Maybe something else too, which made him officially insane. This juvenile infatuation had definitely gotten worse after getting laid. He was beyond pathetic now.

"What is it that *you* want?" Cole asked, ignoring Max. "Because let's face it, dude, what should amaze us isn't that she doesn't want to get involved with you, but that you want to with her."

Yeah, he had trouble swallowing that one too. No wonder his brother was skeptical. "I'm not sure what I want. Her father and brother died a year ago, and she's taking care of the family restaurant, which seems to be in difficulties." To their questioning gazes, he added, "Don't know many of the specifics; she was too skittish about that. I presume there's much more than she led me to believe, though. She's going through a rough patch, and I understand her reluctance to give me the time of the day. I don't want to mess with her, but I want to be more than a vacation fling."

"Are you sure? It sounds as if she has her plate full. If you just want to get laid, she may not be the most appropriate choice...too much baggage."

"I don't just want to get laid." It slipped out before he could stop himself. And damn if it wasn't true, never mind the frigging sweats his body was breaking into at the realization.

Cole and Max looked at each other and grinned. "This is going to be fun to watch."

"You need to go to that restaurant and woo this girl."

He rubbed his face and grimaced. Wooing wasn't really his speed. Sporadic fuck-and-run was more like it. "She may not want to talk to me. Hell, for all I know, she may throw me out." And why that prospect knotted his stomach, he didn't know.

Cole frowned at him. "Well? So you pick yourself up and try again. Make her listen."

"Or you pick yourself up and go throw yourself onto the feet of another more receptive chick," Max suggested.

"Max." Cole growled at him in warning.

"What?" he said, lifting his hands. "Just offering a plan B, man. Everyone should have one, just in case."

Tate dragged herself upstairs to her tiny apartment. She was dead on her feet. Stress and adrenaline had kept her going all night, but now the restaurant was closed, her employees had gone home, and she didn't have to pretend she wasn't beaten up.

She was supposed to check invoices and scout for new suppliers, but she was too tired. Without turning on the light, she undressed and threw herself on the bed. She should check her computer and see if there were any new reservations for tomorrow. On second thought, no thank you. She'd put up with too much shit already today. After being given the silent treatment by her maître d', Clint, and after hearing her chef complain all night long, she was too strung out to face any e-mails from Prince Charming. The sicko had been writing every day, as if he knew she'd been on vacation and wanted to catch up on any lost time. Asshole. They were never long, the e-mails, just a couple of sentences each time threatening her with torching the place if she didn't close it up or sell, pointing out how unsuited she was for running it, calling her a whore and stupid and incompetent. Well, the incompetent part he had down right. She sighed.

Low on battery, her cell blinked in the dark, and suddenly she felt the irresistible urge to call James. God, how she'd love to hear his voice. Check on him, see how he was doing. Laugh a bit. Or a lot. He always made her smile, and she so badly needed to smile. Five days in Boston and her facial muscles were again atrophied. No more laughter for her. Although it was little by little freezing to match her reality, her body still remembered him, shivered in excitement at the thought of him. If she concentrated hard enough and closed her eyes very tight, maybe she could block everything out and imagine she was still with him. Still feel his hands on her, and the tingling and the fuzzy feeling would be back, or so she hoped.

The surroundings were less than encouraging; she'd never been able to override the sadness impregnating this place long enough to give herself any decent amount of pleasure. Not that she truly tried. It felt...wrong. Like laughing at a funeral. But maybe now... Her mind discarded that thought right away; she couldn't fuck herself the way James did it anyway, so why bother? Besides, her Bob, in whichever moving box it may be, totally paled into comparison with the guy, whose mere voice made her instantly wet. And she hated those tight orgasms she got by herself, so brief they were almost finished before they started. Those short, almost painful releases had absolutely nothing to do with the long and mind-blowing ones James got out of her. Maybe if she really, really concentrated on their time in Florida... No, she scolded herself. She couldn't pretend she was on vacation anymore, so no, no masturbating to his fantasy. And absolutely no calling. After all, she was the one that gave him the cold-shoulder routine before she left.

She was a big girl; she ought to behave like one.

He'd thought about the correct approach hard and long, for as many days as he'd managed to stay away from her, which in honor of the truth hadn't been that many to begin with, but as he finally stood at the counter waiting for Tate, he still hadn't decided which angle to play. He probably should smile innocently, get her defenses down long enough to cajole her into talking to him, maybe convince her to go out for a beer with him if he got extremely lucky. He wasn't sure how to behave. He'd go with the flow, look into her face, evaluate her mood, and then go from there. Nothing pushy, though; starting light would be the best option at this point. She was a tough cookie, he knew, and pushing her would get him nowhere.

From his post at the counter, he watched Rosita's maître d' walk to the kitchen door and heard him say there was someone there to see her. He didn't seem prone to long sentences, grunted more than talked. His disdainful expression perfectly matched his manners as he walked away from the kitchen door muttering, "Don't know who he is, too busy to run your errands." Tate had said Clint was moody. No hell, Clint was moody. An asshole would be a better description for the guy.

Soon after, a harrumphing Tate came into the restaurant area, her gaze fixed on the rag with which she was wiping her hands, her forehead creased in annoyance. She was as beautiful as ever if not more so. Man, he'd missed her.

James's chest clenched, the unfamiliar feeling making him damn uneasy. Suddenly he realized what the deal was with him acting out, being twitchy and irascible all those days without her. It was withdrawal. He'd been suffering some kind of withdrawal...from her. He needed a lobotomy. He grimaced inwardly.

The second her gaze met with his, she stopped abruptly. The excited glint in her eyes gave her away; she was happy to see him, although, by the quick and savage way she suffused and replaced it with one of suspicion, it was clear he wasn't that welcome.

"Hmm...hello," she greeted curtly while taking a step back, crossing her arms over her chest and tilting her chin up. Setting boundaries again, like she'd done the second she stepped fully dressed out of that hotel bathroom. Putting him in his place.

All his good intentions of taking it easy flew out the window. Fuck slowly. James narrowed his gaze on her and shook his head. Enough. He reached for her, grabbed her by the neck, and before she could react, his mouth fell upon hers. He'd missed kissing her. She tasted so good. It was a short but possessive kiss, one she didn't fully return yet didn't fight.

"Hi." He breathed on her lips as she stared big-eyed at him. "I thought I'd take you out to dinner. Any chance of you escaping for a while?"

She shook her head. "No." She tried again to step back, but he had her secured with a hand on the small of her back. She was going nowhere.

The place was busy, but that wasn't the reason she was rejecting him. He could see it in the frenetic way her pulse beat in her neck, in the way she avoided looking at him. It was too scary. This wasn't a silly fling in Eternal Sun miles and miles away from home; this was too real. Too close home. That's why she was keeping him at arm's length. She was scared of this thing between them. Good, that made two of them.

"I'll wait then," he said, keeping her in his arms.

She seemed too startled by his behavior to fight his closeness, but she wasn't ready to give in just yet. "I don't think um…it's a good idea. You should go."

His mouth quirked up. Yeah right. "I don't think so."

Her lips puckered. It looked like him being his arrogant self was throwing her off. She looked ready to snap at him, but he knew she wouldn't; the place was quite full. The last thing Rosita's needed was a soap opera scene, and Tate would feel guilty kicking up a fuss. Guilt. He'd make guilt work. If need be, he could get all sorts of mileage from guilt.

"As you wish," she said between clenched teeth. "Clint here will serve you a beer. It may take a while though. Feel free to bail at any moment. I won't hold it against you."

He grinned, totally ignoring her flippant remarks. "No problem, I'm not in a hurry. I'll wait."

After brushing her lower lip with his thumb, he released her. Tate stepped back and retreated to the kitchen, looking dazzled, outmaneuvered, and a bit pissed.

James glanced around and prepared for a long wait. Calling beforehand and getting her to agree to go out for supper would have solved this problem, but that wouldn't have worked. He didn't want her to have an excuse to cut him loose. Face-to-face, his chances grew exponentially, and although he liked to believe he was a gentleman, it wasn't in him to pass up such a clear advantage.

It took the better part of two hours to get things quieted down enough that they'd be able to make do without her. James hadn't complained or checked his watch in impatience. She knew because she'd sneaked as many peeks at him as she could get away with. Her hand had three new knife cuts to prove it; it looked like tonight she'd been a bigger hazard to herself than usual. He'd just sat there, sexy as hell, following her every move with an intensity that had her edgy and nervous. She wasn't sure why he was there, but she couldn't deny feeling giddy about it. Happy to see him. Expectant. Damn and double damn, she was a moron.

When she'd found herself almost face-to-face with James, she'd got goose bumps even in her damn hair. He'd said he'd stop by, but she hadn't believed him. Not really. After all, he'd already got to nail her. Repeatedly. The I'll-call-you line didn't carry too much weight in her book, especially after the actual deed was done. But here he was, sitting at the counter waiting for her, after she'd been less than civilized before her departure.

Despite how many times she'd wiped her mouth with her hand, she could still feel the warm, commanding weight of his lips on hers. His kiss had pretty much mashed her brain, the easiness and security oozing from him overwhelming. And the way he smelled and tasted...dear Lord, it made her legs wobbly. He was even better than she remembered. And damn, he made her needy. Today hadn't been a good day, and it was a busy night. The kitchen was a mess, her chef was as usual in full-blown hysterics, and Tim had called in sick. Some weird disease again. Sneaky bastard.

At the sight of James, her first instinct had been to throw herself into his arms, tell him all about her shitty day, kiss him silly, and drag him somewhere where he could fuck her worries away. She'd suppressed that need pretty fast though, self-preservation kicking in. After all, she'd been the one to draw the boundaries in the first place. Just sex. No follow-up of any kind once back home. Not because she didn't want to, but because it would be too dangerous for her. He was too dangerous for her. She could so easily get used to him. She'd realized that during their time together, especially during their last night, not that she'd said a word to him. She'd played it *Sex in the City* cool until the very end—so not her.

At closing time, she approached him. "So, you're still here."

His smile was still dazzling. "Yep. Hungry as a wolf. Let's go to dinner?"

She threw a dirty look toward her maître d'. About an hour ago, she'd asked him to serve James something to eat; it was the least she could do seeing as how he'd stoically put up with hours of waiting. Apparently she was also being ignored by her staff on the inconsequential things. What a surprise. What the hell was wrong with Clint anyway? He'd been so supportive after Aidan dumped her, urging her to confide in him and talk about her problems, but lately he looked pissed at her all the time. As if she wasn't doing anything right.

"Let me make it up to you. Dinner's on me," she heard herself say. "Right here. I have contacts with the kitchen, and I can guarantee they'll serve us. Even at this ungodly hour. And believe me, despite my best efforts, the food here is good."

His expression was so wickedly pleased, she felt flustered and uncertain, as if she'd walked head-on into a trap. After a quick visit to the kitchen, she directed him to one of the booths at the far end of the dining area. It was an intimate setting, and she should have chosen another table in more neutral territory, but what the hell, there was no neutral territory in Rosita's, all the tables were intimate even to a fault, and the kitchen personnel were already bringing out the food. "I hope you like Italian. We're kind of specialized."

"Perfect." He grinned, and she felt it down deep in her bones. Damn, this was a bad idea.

They ate pretty much in silence. She was tired and tense and too aware of him, replying to his questions with monosyllables. Any more would get her saying only God knew what.

Soon the last patrons left, and right after that, Rosita's staff began leaving. In another lifetime, they would have had supper all together, but those times were long gone. Clint looked downright livid. Tina the waitress had to hurry to her kid. The other waitress, Kelly, also left in a hurry, the chef had been spitting fire all night, and the kitchen personnel was too tired of dodging bullets. Talk about team spirit. They couldn't get out of there fast enough.

"This is a very nice place you've got here." James complimented her when she came back from turning the lights down and locking the entrance door. Although the restaurant was in shadows, she looked around, inspecting her surroundings. Yes, the place looked cozy. Thousands of pictures around of her almost nonexistent family. It might look homey for most people, but to her it felt like the cruelest cosmic irony. So much of the warmth it used to radiate was now missing. Nowadays it was like an empty carcass. Pretty, sure, but soulless.

She shrugged. "You should have seen it before, with my father at the counter, greeting the clientele. Serving them drinks while they waited for their tables. Making them laugh. He was good at that, the same way you are actually. My mom would be floating around the tables, a bit more reserved than my dad, but everyone would feel relaxed and welcome because of her. The food was always good, but even if it wasn't, it didn't matter; people would have flooded in anyway. My parents were that good."

"I'm sure they were, but you shouldn't underestimate yourself; you're doing a hell of a job too."

She gave him a yeah-right look. Tate had spent all morning dealing with her suppliers, which hadn't done anything to improve her general mood. She really didn't know how long she could put up with their shit without snapping. She missed her father. And Jonah. They would know what to do and how to keep those assholes in line. And sure as hell, they would know how to keep Rosita's afloat, which she didn't. And she was the one doing a hell of a job? *Please, don't make me laugh.*

Trying to regain her composure, she changed the subject. "Anyway, how come you're already in Boston? I figured you'd still be on the road."

"I left right after you."

"Why?" she asked suspiciously. "And why are you here?"

He frowned. "Why are you in cold-bitch mode? So tense and defensive?"

None of your business, she was going to snap back, but she was too tired to gather the necessary energy to work herself into a tantrum. "Has no one ever told you it's rude to answer a question with another question?" She waited for an answer, but James just looked intently at her. Her expression softened, her eyes lowering. "Sorry. Bad day."

"Tell me."

Oh hell. Just two words. Two tiny words and she was laid bare, completely undone. Shaking like a fresh-baked soufflé left forgotten next to an open window. It had been so long since anybody had asked her that or cared enough to want to hear; she almost broke down into sobs. She shook her head, blinking back tears. *Pull yourself together; don't act like a crybaby.*

"What's the matter, princess?"

"Never mind me. It's this place," she said, waving around. Elaborating further would just make matters worse.

"The diners seemed happy enough. There's a weird vibe going on with your staff, but it's hardly noticeable if you aren't paying attention."

"And you are?"

"Yes, I am. Come on, Tate, don't be such a tight ass. Let me in, baby."

Holy shit, the man really knew how to say the right things at the right time. And she was so desperate for the comfort he was offering, even if it was only a temporary thing.

She swallowed and looked at her lap, trying to keep her tears locked inside. "I feel like I'm drowning here, James. All these memories surrounding me. Choking me." As the last of her staff had left and she'd closed up the place, Tate had turned off all the lights except for the flickering candles on the table. She needed to save on her electricity bill, but more importantly, the less she saw of her surroundings, the less likely she was to lose it. The idea was sound and had merit; pity it wasn't working worth a shit. Every inch of this place, photos included, was engraved in her long-term memory, eating at her like a fucking bleeding ulcer she couldn't eradicate no matter how hard she tried. She blinked some more, desperate for the tears and the lump in her throat to recede. "It's not only the financial pressure, it's this pressure valve in my chest that's about to explode. I miss them so much. The dead and the ones left behind. I miss seeing Elle and Mom here, laughing and pitching in. Even fighting with them. It's like everyone died in that accident. Even me."

"I'm so sorry, babe," he said, reaching for her.

She jerked away. She didn't want pity. "I should've sold the place like my mom wanted. Signed the damn papers just after the funeral and never looked back." Her voice was shaking badly, and she tried to cover it by clearing her throat. "But stubborn me couldn't. Still can't. I'm a fool. Just the thought makes me feel like I'm selling them out; can you believe that?"

"You're not a fool. And you'll get this place on its feet again."

"I won't." Now that she'd gotten started, she may as well go for broke. Let it all out. Well, almost all. She wasn't going to talk to James about the stalker. No way. She couldn't. Talking about it made it seem much more real, and she couldn't afford that. Tate was hanging by her last thread as it was; taking the stalker threat seriously would obliterate her. She'd crumble into tiny pieces. Besides, she didn't want to rely on James of all people. That would be a huge mistake, one she wasn't risking. She'd go down that road, and in no time she'd grow attached to him, start depending on him, and when he walked out on her, which he invariably would, she'd be crushed. No thank you. She had to remember he wasn't there to stay. His kind never were.

"You see, when I refused to sell out, the owner of Old Vito began boycotting me and convinced my suppliers to refuse delivering to me. When they do, more often than not, they serve me products of lower quality. My chef is in hysterics most the time, threatening to quit because of it. His assistant calls in sick every other day, and Clint is—"

"An asshole," James finished.

She couldn't find it in herself to deny it, so she just shrugged. "They're grieving, we're all grieving, plus there's the economic strain from the fire, which, believe me, is no joke. The kitchen personnel are defensive as hell, convinced I believe they had something to do with it. For a time, they blamed each other." Yeah, until she had the bright idea to show them one of those e-mails to get them to stop the blaming game. Great move; they stopped blaming each other and started quitting. "I want to keep this place, I really do. I owe it to my father and brother, but I don't know how. I'm losing it. I'm losing it all."

Her eyes welled. Damn, damn! This was so undignified. She didn't want to fall apart. Not now, not in front of James. She was a modern woman, a grown-up, capable of handling anything life threw at her. She certainly didn't need to go crying to anyone. But her tears didn't care about being politically correct and burst furiously out of her. She covered her face, ashamed and appalled at her tear ducts' clear lack of decency.

James pried her hands off her face and tugged her to him, circling her with his strong arms and hugging her. She went along reluctantly, but he was so warm and felt so safe, soon she was gripping his shirt and letting it all loose. All her pent-up feelings, all her anger, all her frustration were being wrenched from her in hard, angry sobs.

He held her tight while she cried. It took a while before all the grief worked itself through her, leaving her limp and exhausted. Tate could feel his thudding heart against the palm of her hand, against her cheek, so soothing.

James was the first to break the long silence. "Tell me something, sweetheart. The curiosity is killing me."

"Mmm?" she mumbled, her face still buried in his chest.

"Who the hell is Rosita?"

Her shoulders shook in silent laughter. "Rosita is...was...my grandmother from my father's side. She was from a small town called Lucera, in the south of Italy. My granddad fell madly in love with her when he was stationed there during World War II. He snatched her up and brought her to the United States. She was a great cook, so they opened an Italian restaurant and named it after her. I never got to meet her, but she was a true Italian beauty."

"So that's where you got your devastating looks from," he murmured to her hair, kissing the top of her head. "No wonder I never stood a chance against your magic."

Yeah right. "Not really. Elle is more like her, with her olive skin and her big black eyes. I got my granddad's eyes and my mom's fair skin. The mane of thick hair may come from Rosita though, the wide ass too," she added and chuckled, very much aware he was trying to divert her attention and grateful for it.

"Sorry for this," she said, mopping her tear-drenched eyes with the palm of her hand. "I didn't mean to bum you out."

She moved to disentangle herself from him, but he wouldn't let go. "You didn't bum me out," he said, assuring her while tucking some strands of hair behind her ear.

She must look like a hag from hell. Her cheeks and nose red from crying, her eyes black from the smudged mascara, her breath still in hiccups, and her loose braid half uncoiled. She unwound it totally, self-consciously running her hand over her hair while his hand kept stroking her back.

"I must look hideous," she said, still wiping her eyes with her hands. "Sorry for this crying jag."

"You're beautiful, Tate, and you know it, babe." He smiled at her, something worryingly close to tenderness in his eyes, while his thumbs wiped the last of her tears from her face.

Tate lifted her hand to his. So rough yet so gentle. "You came." She was so glad he was there but didn't dare to say it. She wasn't sure where they stood; they weren't in Eternal Sun anymore. And she was a mess.

"Of course I came. I said I would, didn't I?"

"Yes, you did. And I laughed at you. Sorry for being a bitch." And she'd been quite a bitch. Not on purpose of course, but that hardly changed anything. After coming back from the hotel, she'd pretty much dismissed him. He'd offered her a ride to the airport, but she declined and left almost without saying good-bye. "After what I said and how I behaved, I thought I wouldn't see you again."

He grinned and lifted her chin so her gaze met his. "I'm stubborn that way. I don't hear what I don't want to hear."

She laughed. "Well, I'm glad for your selective deafness."

He coaxed her closer. She didn't need any coaxing, though;

she needed him to kiss her again, desperately wanted to lose herself in him. James was such a great kisser, the right amount of pressure, of aggression and possessiveness. She placed her arms around his neck, bringing him down to her, and as she opened up for him, his lips took charge immediately, making sweet love to her mouth while his body pressed tightly against hers.

There was nothing like kissing James. His taste was intoxicating, not to mention his touch. As he kept eating at her mouth, his hand glided to her breast, stealing a shudder from her. With effort, she broke the kiss and pushed him away.

Startled, he looked at her.

She just smiled.

This was such a bad idea, but hell if she could stop herself.

"Lie back," she whispered to him, going to her knees between his thighs.

"Tate? What on earth…?"

She wickedly looked at him. "Boy's Happy Hour is finally here. Enjoy."

CHAPTER SEVEN

Oh man, he was in trouble.

She'd looked so damn beautiful bathed in candlelight, her eyes the color of quicksilver, her dark eyelashes still wet from her tears, the mere sight of her took his breath away. On her knees, though, while unbuttoning his jeans, those sexy eyes of hers wickedly turned up to him, and her breath coming rapidly from her soft lips, she looked more than beautiful. She looked fucking astonishing, so much so that his heart all but stopped and his throat swelled shut.

He stopped her hands. "Tate, are you sure you want to...?"

"Give you head? Yes, I'm pretty sure I want to suck your dick," she whispered as her sweet, small hands moved from under his and undid his pants. "Do you have anything against that?"

Fuck, he was so going to hell for this. Her words alone were going to do him in, not to mention that curious, wandering hand approaching his cock. The second she palmed him, a jolt of energy hit him so hard he hissed, his hips instinctively lifting to her. It took all his mental control to talk.

"You were upset. I don't want you feeling forced into anything," he pressed on, horrified at his own words. Mental. Since when did he let chivalry get in the way of a blowjob? Talk about boycotting oneself, jeez.

Tate ignored him. "Does it look as if I'm being coerced into anything?" she asked while nuzzling his shaft, her soft smooth skin burning him alive, his dick twitching like a motherfucker. "Now shut up and enjoy the ride, big man, before I decide I don't want to do it anymore."

He threw his head back in a harsh groan as her wicked tongue made an appearance and flickered over him. This was going to kill him, those luminescent eyes intense on him, her sweet mouth stretched over his dick, ready to suck him into heaven. He wasn't going to survive it.

"This is one of my favorite sex fantasies."

She looked at him in surprise. "Do I dare to ask which one, Catholic boy?"

He concentrated on talking, trying to regain a bit of control. "The Corleone fantasy of course. An Italian restaurant, a classic one, like in the movies, with the white and red tablecloths, the homemade curtains on the windows, the old pictures on the walls, the smell of good old Italian food all over. Me in a private booth with a sexy, voluptuous Italian beauty on her knees in between my legs, her long, dark curls all over my thighs, jacking me off with her luscious, talented Mediterranean mouth."

Tate snorted, her lips sweetly brushing his throbbing cock. "The only voluptuous part of me is my ass, thank you very much."

"Your ass and Sofia Loren's, baby, tight as sisters. And you know I'm a sucker for the classics."

She laughed, the sweet vibration slamming at his cock, forcing him to grit his teeth to hold it all together. And she hadn't taken him into that sweet piece of heaven yet. When that happened, his head was going to explode.

"You're incorrigible. I shouldn't encourage you. Pity I can't help myself," she added and then continued lavishing him with sweet attention. "Go on, tell me more; let's see what I can do to accommodate you."

He tried to concentrate on talking. "Where was I? Oh yes, the Corleone fantasy. She's the daughter of a very powerful mob guy, the most beautiful woman I've ever seen, and the most dangerous too. Her godfather is a scary dude from the old country who loves her and dotes on her to a fault. He's made many guys disappear for just talking to her. At any moment, her family bodyguards may discover us, and I'll end up in the river with cement shoes at the very least. And I don't care. Best blowjob ever," he said, tucking her hair behind her ears and then sinking his fingers into that dark mass, pulling at it.

She smiled at him and held his gaze, leisurely licking him from his balls to the tip of his shaft, giving special attention to the underside of the crown, under the ridge, until he was ready to beg for her to take him into her mouth. Damn, he wasn't going to survive unscathed from this. There were no walls with Tate, no defense he could pull up to distance himself from all the things that petite woman made him feel.

She shook her head in amusement. "A very detailed fantasy. You should give up security alarms and go into porn script writing," she murmured, her hot breath bathing the head of his shaft, torturing it while her sweet fingers lightly caressed the throbbing club. She was teasing him, denying him access to her mouth, driving him ballistic with need.

He grabbed his cock at the base and held her from the back of the head, his dick nudging at her mouth, his hips lifting to her. "Don't be a tease, baby, please. Open up."

Poised on the top of his dick, her mouth hot and wet, she looked at him and then parted her lips, his dick slowly pushing in. James hissed, and his body tensed like a bowstring.

"Tate, baby, you feel so good," he breathed out while she hummed something he didn't catch, mainly because his ears were so madly roaring he could only hear his blood rushing. He was losing it...again...like always where Tate was concerned.

And she knew it, for she kept pushing him, taking him deep in her tight throat while one hand gripped the base of his cock and the other caressed his balls—a killer combination. She was so sweet, so giving. And so wicked, loving. And killing his cock at the same time.

James tried to stay still, but his hips kept lifting up of their own volition while his hands held Tate's head to him, forcing her to take more and more of him every time.

In a moment of clarity, he pinned her with his stare. "I want to come in your mouth, princess. Deep inside your throat. If you don't want it, you better stop right now because in two seconds flat, I won't be able to stop myself." His tone was deep with warning as he caressed her hollow cheeks with his thumbs. He stared mesmerized at her, at those beautiful lips stretched over his dick. She held his stare, slowly releasing his cock.

James right away felt her absence and was trying to control his disappointment when she sweetly kissed the tip of his crown, her small fingers opened the small slit and her tongue took a hot swipe over it—in it. His cock jerked so fucking bad it was a miracle he didn't come there and then.

"I wouldn't have it any other way," she said and sucked him in again, making him groan and curse.

He wanted to make it last, but that was a physical impossibility. Tate was taking him deep into her throat and then releasing him slowly, licking and sucking him until he thought he was going to lose his mind along with his cum. He was unable to control it all; the sex, his attraction to this girl, his response to her, it was all out of his control, his mind, his body, his feelings.

"Tate, baby, I'm going to come," he said, halfheartedly trying to tug her head away. He didn't want to scare her, and pushing himself all the way in her throat and filling her up with his cum would probably constitute scaring her.

She ignored him.

"Fuck, baby, I can't hold it," he said with a harsh growl as she mimicked swallowing and closed her throat on him. "Aw shit." The pressure was unbearable, his whole body in overdrive, spikes of pleasure erupting all over him while she kept swirling her tongue around him, suckling him into oblivion.

He felt raw, his need to get deep inside her terrifying even himself. His hips went up, his back arched, and he shouted his release as Tate took all he had to give. He felt his orgasm all over his body, raging through him like a wildfire, from his toes to the top of his head, robbing him of his breath and his sanity while she sucked the last drop of cum out of him.

When he came back down to earth, she was tucking his dick in and taking a sip of water. An overwhelming need to have her in his arms overtook him, so he lifted her from the floor and brought her to him. She was so small yet so full of strength, able to bring him to his knees with just a wink of her eye.

He needed to kiss her. Weird, he'd always avoided kissing someone who had just consumed his release. Not now. He took her mouth gently, reveling in her taste and his. "Take me home,

Tate," he said urgently into her lips. "I promise you won't regret it."

James was as stubborn as the next man, arrogant and proud too, but he recognized a lost cause when he saw it. He was done in. He couldn't walk away from her. And damn if he was going to allow her to do walk away from him.

She looked at him and softly laughed. "Well, it's good that I live upstairs, uh?"

He didn't wait for her to say anything else and lifted her in his arms. "Lead the way, princess."

Laughing, she circled his neck with her arms and placed a soft kiss on his cheek.

As he took the stairs two at a time and then put her down so that she could open the door, his head was already simmering with ideas, already plotting how to solve her current problems. She was living on top of her restaurant, in an apartment that as far as he could tell had seen much, much better days. She was overworked and overstressed with financial burden and employees' grievances. Overwhelmed and sad, wary and grieving. Although he was dying to help, he knew she'd hardly accept any of it, so he decided to keep quiet for the time being. That didn't mean he was going to sit in silence and let her deal with all those assholes on her own. No way. She wasn't alone anymore, never mind what she thought. She was so strong, trying to do battle all by herself, not asking for assistance from anyone, but he wanted to help and take all those burdens away from her. He wanted to pound those suppliers into the ground, get her staff in line, make her smile the same way she'd done in Florida.

"Get naked," he heard himself say once he was in.

She lifted her eyebrows, clearly ready to give him some attitude, but he backed her to the table and took her mouth, licking at her tongue, while he let his hands go over her body, caressing her curves. She responded right away, her body undulating against his.

"I said clothes off, princess. If you don't want me to rip them off you, that is. You know how I enjoy playing Conan the Barbarian..."

She smiled wickedly at him, her little teeth punishing her

lower lip, and shimmied out of her black skirt. She had on thigh-high stockings and a lace piece of almost nothing covering her pussy that would make any grown man stutter. It left him speechless, then confused.

"Sexy underwear… Who were you expecting to meet tonight?" he asked, frowning.

She laughed throatily. "I always wear sexy underwear, never mind how uncomfortable it is. Didn't you notice in Florida? It's my only vice."

"This is uncomfortable?" he asked, signaling at her crotch.

She slowly turned around. "A string up your ass? What do you think?"

"I think it's the best invention ever."

"I bet you do," she whispered and smiled knowingly.

He dropped to his knees and kissed her lace-clad mound, a hot, devouring, openmouthed kiss that got her crying out. She was wet, her folds puffing, her clit quivering, the piercing in it shiny with her juices.

"I'm dying to see that precious clit ring of yours again," he said while taking her panties off. She watched him, already out of breath. So fucking sexy.

"So you missed it."

"I missed *you*. The ring is just a nice extra bonus."

With those words and one swipe of his tongue over her bare pussy, her bragging attitude was gone. She leaned on the table, a sexy moan escaping her lips. She was slick and hot, halfway there already. He smiled against her tender folds, raked his teeth over them, played with the ring. He loved a responsive woman, one that got as excited taking pleasure as giving it. Without further instructions from him, she lifted her leg to his shoulder, her heel digging into his back, and ran her hand through his hair, keeping him at her pussy—not that she could have kept him away.

He'd missed her taste, her sweet smell, her clit ring, the way she arched, offering herself to him. The way she spilled hot girl juices on his mouth when she came. He'd even dreamed of it. He reached for her breasts and played with her nipples as his mouth sucked her clit. Just like that, Tate began panting. She had very sensitive breasts, amazingly responsive nipples that had her jerking madly in no time, her pussy throbbing in need.

"I've missed this," he said with a groan. "The way you fuck yourself against my face."

James would have loved to lick her forever, but Tate was getting very loud, pressing his face against her, lifting her hips to him, the muscles of her legs tensing, her pussy fluttering against his tongue. She was very close, and so was he. From his position, he could clearly observe her, the sexy curve of her throat, the soft swell of her breasts against that tiny blouse that at some point had been closed but was now half-open, missing a couple of buttons actually.

He was holding her wide open, spearing her with his tongue and rubbing her clit with his thumb when she came in his mouth. So beautiful, her inner flesh convulsing around his tongue. He could die happy if he could have that in his bed for the next forty years. The second he acknowledged that thought, it scared the hell out of him. His dick, though, was fearless and got even harder. Man, he really needed a lobotomy.

He stood up, shucked off his jeans and underwear, and rolled on a condom, his eyes never leaving her.

"You're so fucking beautiful when you come," he said, cupping her face, nuzzling her mouth. "Now turn around and bend over. I need to ride you."

Tate opened her eyes and let out a shaky laugh. "Bend over the table? After being on my feet the whole night? I don't think so, buddy. I want on my back, pronto."

"And I want in you. Now," he said as he lifted her left leg, hooked his elbow under her knee, and entered her. Her laughter turned into a gasp. Her pussy was swollen from her release and so damn hot he could hardly breathe. Foreheads touching, they both looked where they were joined, how his dick parted her puffed-up folds, impaling her.

"That's it, sweetheart, watch my cock going inside you," he instructed while sliding in and then pulled almost totally out, his shaft glistening with her juices. He surged all the way in and then nudged at the ring with his pelvis. Her pussy clenched, and her nails dug into his shoulders.

"You just came in my mouth, and now you'll come on my dick."

Her voice was just a whisper. "I don't think I can come again right now."

"I'll get you there, princess," he said reassuringly as he carried her to the bed without leaving her tight embrace. "You can be sure of it."

"We'll have to do something with this bed. One whole night sleeping here and I'll be injured for life," she heard James murmur into her shoulder.

"Why? Planning to make yourself at home in my bed?" she asked, still half-sleep.

"Yes."

Those words entered her sleep-fogged mind slowly, but when they did, all sluggishness disappeared. Her eyes opened to find James wrapped tight against her back. Oh dear Lord, she'd had sex with him and fallen sleep with him in her bed. *Very smart, Tate, way to go*! She tensed her muscles and got ready to jump out of the bed when she realized she was sore all over. Yeah, gymnastics with James at two o'clock in the morning was not the best of ideas. Hell, gymnastics with James wasn't the best of the ideas at all—for her heart, mainly. She furtively glanced to the window. Still dark. Well, that was good; they hadn't spent the night together, so not all was lost yet.

This guy would break her heart. It was unwise to have a sex-based relationship with someone that could do that to her, much less invite him to get comfy in her bed. That was a sure recipe for disaster and heartbreak. She should screw only those who couldn't emotionally touch her or get inside her head. As things stood, James had gotten there, among other places.

She swung her legs over to the side of the bed and tried to get up. "James, I don't think this is a good id—"

Before she could finish her sentence, James had grabbed her and tossed her back onto the bed, his strong arm encircling her waist.

"I won't let you walk away from me, princess. Not out of fear. You don't have to fear me," he whispered in her ear.

"You know how we agreed this was just sex..." she began.

"You agreed this was about sex. You were the one putting on all the conditions. I wasn't given a say. But if you just want sex, then sex it is."

"Yeah, well, I've changed my mind. This isn't what I want." She couldn't afford to have sex with him again. She couldn't afford to have anything with him, period. Too risky.

"Great, because this isn't what I want either."

That threw her off. "If you don't want sex, what is it that you want?"

"More. I want you, Tate. All of you, not just the sex. Although I'm not going to lie to you, that I want badly."

Oh boy, worse worst-case scenario. "I can't give you what you want."

"What is it that you're so frightened of? You want me. Just look at you; your body beams, and you're rosy and satisfied, humming with residual pleasure. You obviously find me attractive; I can make you come like crazy and make you laugh. Why can't you give me a chance? Come on, Tate, don't be scared."

"I'm not scared, I just think—"

"Don't think."

"Don't you tell me what to do, much less what to think, you big lout!" she said, squirming. "I'm very capable of doing that by myself."

Although no one would have guessed it with the way she was letting him get away with everything. He didn't answer, just chuckled and kissed her head. The condescending bastard.

She frowned at him over her shoulder. "Are you hearing me?"

"Nope."

"You don't really know me. That happy-go-lucky Tate down in Florida was not me. The raving lunatic crying her eyes out down there, that's me. The crazy person hiding in this shoebox, that's me."

She began ranting about how she couldn't deal with a sex relationship, and how he couldn't offer her more, how he was the frilly black hole that would suck her in and yada yada. How her life was all screwed, how she didn't have time for him, how this was not smart. To drive the point home, she should have said she didn't want him, but that was such an outright lie she knew she couldn't get away with it. She continued rambling, working herself into a frenzy, while he kept silent and held her tight, sometimes snorting, sometimes chuckling. He held on to her until she ran out of steam.

His whisper caressed her ear. "Listen to me, baby. We'll go as slow as you want; you don't need to freak out on me. Let me get to know you. I promise I won't place any unreasonable demands on you. We'll take this one tiny step at a time. We'll go out, get to know each other, have wild sex every other second—just the usual, baby." She snorted, but he didn't relent. "I haven't dated for a very long time, and I'm a bit rusty, but I really want to try."

"James, don't do this to me. I can't take a chance on you." James was out of her league, and by the time he'd finished with her, she'd be mincemeat. "We better stop right now..."

"Turn around, princess. Look at me."

Yeah right, like she could keep half her mind working if she turned around and watched those warm hazel eyes. She shook her head vigorously. "I don't want to talk about this anymore, James; I can't." She wasn't strong enough to kick him out of her bed, yet she wasn't strong enough to withstand the devastation that having a relationship with him was going to cause.

He sighed. "Okay, princess, we'll do it your way. For now, let's agree to disagree. I'll be waiting here when you decide to turn around and face me. Literally and figuratively. For the time being, I'll humor you and we'll talk about something else. Something neutral."

"Ha, we don't have neutral subjects, James." True, everything revolved around some land mine: the restaurant, her family, his lifestyle... "You'd better go."

He ignored her. What a surprise. "Tell me, sweetheart, what are you doing living here in this crowded apartment on top of the restaurant?"

That took the fight out of her. The way he didn't give up but steamrolled over her and still made her feel cherished.

She glanced around, knowing what he was seeing. A cluttered, tiny matchbox full of old, mismatched stuff.

"I can't afford to live anywhere else," she said, hoping her mouth would have the good sense to stop talking. It seemed good sense, though, was gone, along with the rest of her working brain. "This was my brother's monument to bachelorhood. He could have afforded a house, but he liked this place, said it had character." Or at least it had when Jonah lived there.

"Kind of smallish, don't you think?"

"Small? Now it's huge. You should've seen it before, with Jonah's humongous king-size bed occupying half the living room." He'd been a true ladies' man, and this had been his private retreat. He'd torn down a couple of walls and turned the place into a loft, bought the biggest, comfiest bed he could find, and with his slick moves managed to acquaint it with half the female population of Boston.

James chuckled silently. "Tell me about your brother."

She let out a groan of disbelief. "That's what you call a neutral subject?"

"No, princess, that's what I call life. He was a very important part of your life, and I want to know about it."

A sigh escaped her throat. "Jonah was the best, a bit overbearing with him being the older brother and all that, but he was great. He and my dad used to fight a lot, mainly because they were very similar, but they still managed to work together for many years. You know, Jonah was the only one of us who spoke Italian. He used to say an Italian chef that didn't speak Italian was like trying to eat pizza without any tomato sauce. He learned from Grandma and then from Granddad." She wished she had a photo of Jonah to show him, but she didn't. All the photos had gotten shipped out along with all his other belongings—by her. Her way to rid herself of unwanted memories, as if it'd be that easy. "Jonah didn't die right away in that damned accident; the doctors managed to keep him alive for twenty-four hours in the hospital, hooked up to several machines, tubes coming in and out of him, until he died from a brain hemorrhage. If that hadn't killed him, complete organ failure would have. His body was beyond help." Until now, she hadn't been able to talk about the accident without breaking down. But at the moment, she was all cried out. And it felt good to talk about it.

"I am so sorry, princess."

"Fucking drunk driver had the balls to die too, so there's really no one left to hate. The asshole was speeding and ran a stop sign while driving home, loaded, from some business meeting."

She remembered that fateful night. There had been bad weather that day, poor visibility and icy roads. Not that it was an excuse. "Dad died before they had time to get him out of the rubble. He'd sustained such severe injuries from the crash that we couldn't have an open casket at the funeral."

James caressed her gently for a while, silently offering her his comfort.

"If this was Jonah's place, why did you move here?"

There, she admonished to herself. Even he understood how crazy that move had been.

Tate shrugged. "When I left my job to take care of Rosita's, I had to let go of my downtown apartment. Too expensive. And too far away from here. For a while, I was at Aidan's, but well…soon I had to leave. At first it was…difficult to be here." Ha, that was the understatement of the year. The first time she entered the apartment after the accident, the pain had brought her to her knees. Jonah's memory was everywhere, embedded on the walls, on the furniture. She'd closed the door, called the movers, and got all her brother's stuff packed and sent to the family house. She'd also hired a cleaning company, mainly to rid the apartment of her brother's scent, but that had been unsuccessful. She could still smell him everywhere. Sometimes she thought she could see him too. "But I'm sure it'll get better, eventually. It's better than my parents' house, anyway…"

"What do you mean?"

"What do I mean? I'm the biggest cheat you've ever seen, James. You know how I told you Mom and Elle can't stand setting a foot in Rosita's? Well, I can't get myself to cross the threshold in my childhood home. How about that, huh? I haven't been there since the funeral. I can't go there, so I hide here. I sent all my brother's belongings there so I wouldn't have to face that either. I'm a mess, James; you don't want to get involved with me." And she didn't need him making a bigger mess of her.

"Hey, selective deafness here, remember?" he said jokingly over her shoulder and tightened his embrace. Then he kissed her ear. "You are not a cheat, princess; you just need time to recoup. You're doing the best you can, and that's more than anyone has the right to demand from you."

Jesus, how did he always know the right thing to say to her? His warmth seeped into her, little by little, making her feel at peace, and for the first time since moving into that apartment, she couldn't smell Jonah.

"Turn around, baby. Trust me. I only want to make you feel better."

It took a while, but finally she turned to face him. He was so handsome, warm and rumpled from sleep. She placed her palm on his cheek, caressed his lips with her thumb.

"This is a bad idea, James." The sex was already a bad idea, let alone this kind of intimacy. She was going to get attached to him—not a good place to be.

He stroked her back, his fingers finding all the curves and hollows, from the small of her back up to the back of her neck. His eyes were so intense that they held her captive.

"Let me kiss you, Tate," he said as he drew her closer, her nipples gracing his chest. "Let me show you how good an idea this is."

By the time he released her mouth, her breath was choppy and she had all but forgotten her own name. His huge hard-on was resting on her lower stomach, pulsing and flexing, but in spite of it, James didn't put any moves on her. He seemed content just to caress her.

After a while of him kissing and fondling her, he wasn't the only one visibly throbbing with need; she was so turned on she could hardly think straight.

"Do you plan to do something with that?" she said, signaling to his cock. "Anytime soon, I mean."

"I'd love to, princess, but I don't have any more rubbers with me."

Her eyebrows lifted up. "You came here to seduce me armed with just one condom? What were you thinking?"

He breathed out hard. "Oh come on, Tate, don't be nasty. I wasn't sure whether you'd talk to me. I didn't want to jinx it by being cocky and coming here with a string of latex. You know you would have had my arrogant, self-centered ass for it," he muttered. Well, maybe he was right. "I gather you don't have condoms around, right?"

She shook her head. They were doomed. Before the housekeepers swept over Jonah's place, she'd have found condoms everywhere. And not only condoms, but other more colorful stuff too. Not now.

James nuzzled her face, dropped kisses over her eyes and mouth. "I can make you come with my hands and mouth all night long, no problem, but I'd love to be inside you bareback if you let me. We had the sex conversation, baby; we're both safe."

Tate froze at his words. "It's not only about being safe, James. There're other matters to consider. I'm not babyproof."

"I won't come inside you, princess, I promise. As a matter of fact, I'll lay here and let you have your wicked way with me," he said, falling to his back. "Whatever you want to do with me, I'm game. I'm here to serve you. I won't even move. Unless I am ordered to."

She laughed and dismissively rolled her eyes at him, but he was staring at her with those killer eyes and *wham*, she lost her mind. Or maybe she'd lost it in Florida and this was just the last straw. With her gaze intent on him, she lowered her lips to his chest. The man was so tasty she couldn't help but trace his nipples with her mouth and revel in his shudders.

She straddled him, lowering herself onto him. Tate knew this was the worst of the ideas so far, but for the life of her, she couldn't stop herself; she wanted him inside her too. She was wet and slick from all his kissing and cuddling, sensitive from their lovemaking. Tender and swollen. And needy.

"Slowly, baby," he said, holding her by her waist, ensuring she didn't rush it. "You can't take me all at once, and honestly, neither can I. You feel too good, princess. Tight and hot."

She rode him, slowly and a bit awkwardly at first, then faster and harder, her hands splayed on his pecs, while James looked at her in awe, his fingers gripping her thighs, clearly fighting the urge to thrust up. He reached for her and brought her down on himself, kissing her possessively as she cried out at the change in position and fucked herself against him, hard and deep, grinding her clit against him while he murmured encouraging words to her in between kisses.

"Give it to me, princess," he ordered. "Let me have it. I want it."

She came long and hard and sweet, but even then, true to his words, James didn't move.

She fell onto his chest and rested there for a long moment. She could feel his dick twitching and pulsing inside of her, hard as steel, yet James just lay there, hugging her and nuzzling her head. Her moves to unsaddle him were fast halted as he pressed her to him.

"Where are you going?"

"You didn't..."

"No, I didn't, but I'm in heaven deep in you. I want to stay like this. Let's talk."

She burst into laughter. "Talk? Are you nuts? I can't talk while lying on top of you with your cock shoved deep inside me."

He grabbed her by her waist and, without pulling out, he rose to lean on the wall, rearranging her to straddle him. "There you have it, no more lying."

She laughed some more. "It wasn't so much the lying as the hard club inside me distracting me, thank you very much."

His fingers traced her lips. "You're breathtaking when you laugh, do you know that? You should smile more. In the restaurant, you're so serious; your mouth is tightly stretched in a grim line most the time. You break my heart."

She lowered her gaze. "There hasn't been too much lately to smile about, much less laugh. Mom's always been somehow more serious, but Elle is hilarious—when she feels like it, that is, which she hasn't lately." She lifted her fingertips to his face and stroked his beautiful features, his strong chin, and his warm lips. She could feel him inside her, flexing and throbbing. Every one of her caresses got a response from that unyielding shaft inside her, rushing liquid heat down to her core. "I used to laugh a lot. My dad and Jonah were quite overbearing but always got me laughing. In a way, you remind me of them."

"I'm not overbearing," he said.

She rolled her eyes. "Yeah, sure you aren't."

As his hands brushed her collarbone, her skin prickled in goose bumps. Then he reached for her breasts, caressed her nipples, and as her pussy contracted, he also jerked inside her. Their bodies were talking to each other, answering each other's pleas. He continued exploring, and soon she was on fire.

"James, I'm sorry but I have to move. I need to."

"Go on, princess. Ravish me all over again; I can hardly wait. This time I may move though."

She smiled at his comment, pressed her fingers over his mouth, and began rolling her hips. "Shh, James, let me feel you."

With his hands gripping her, holding her in place so he could push into her, he brought her to another powerful orgasm and helped her ride it. When she opened her eyes, his expression was hard with strain, the cords in his neck standing out.

He was sweating, his white-knuckled fists grabbing the sheets. "Make me come, Tate. Now."

She reached for him, his hips thrusting up, seeking her, and after a couple of deep-throated strokes, he bent over her and growling found his release in her mouth.

CHAPTER EIGHT

After a couple of days of having to battle with Tate for almost everything that had anything remotely to do with gaining her trust, James knew her well enough to foresee that this wasn't going to go down easy. She wasn't fighting their attraction or his presence around her or in her bed, but she was fighting his need to help her, which, truth be told, was damn hard on James. Helping the people he cared about was ingrained in him; he was a protector, a provider, but she was stubborn and independent, and although he was getting under her defenses, she kept huge chunks of herself locked away, inaccessible, as if her problems were her own and he had no right to even ask about them.

He knew Tate had been expecting her suppliers, and when she saw James entering Rosita's, surprise bloomed over her face. Then suspicion. Her eyes widened even farther as she realized he wasn't alone, that behind him followed two men, and behind those, three men carrying boxes with fruits, vegetables, and other food items. They were her new suppliers, not that she knew it yet.

"What the hell?" he heard her grunting as she narrowed her eyes on him. It wasn't a friendlier greeting than the one he'd expected. He offered her his killer smile and reached over the counter and brought his mouth to hers, trying to dazzle her with a kiss. Damn she was gorgeous, even while looking suspiciously at him.

"Hi, princess. These are my associates, Zack and Sean," he said, pointing behind him. "Don't mind us; we're just going to pass by your kitchen," he added while releasing her and signaling the others to follow him.

She looked totally dumbfounded as the line of parading men greeted her with a nod of their heads. "James? What on earth are you doing? And who are these men with the boxes?"

He'd expected to go with the silent cryptic act for as long as it would carry him, but it seemed it wasn't meant to carry him too far. "Guys, the kitchen is this way," James said, signaling to the end of the corridor, where the chef's head was already poking out. "The owner and I will be there in a sec."

"Start explaining this minute, mister!" Tate almost shrieked at him once the others weren't close by. "What the hell do you think you're doing?"

"My friend Jack runs a biker bar. It isn't a fancy restaurant, but he also serves some food. He got me in touch with his suppliers."

She crossed her arms over her chest. "James..."

"Don't fight me, princess. You go in there and see if those goods meet Rosita's standards. I haven't promised them anything. They brought along samples so that you can decide whether or not you want to work with them. I'm not running over you, sweetheart, but I'll be damned if I'm going to sit with my arms folded while some assholes make your life impossible." For two days now he'd done just that, sat quietly and observed her breaking her back in that restaurant; damn if he was going to endure another day of that without even trying to make a difference.

"I can find my own suppliers, thank you very much."

"I'm sure you can, never doubted it for a second," he said, crossing his arms over his chest too. If she thought he was going to budge, she better think again. "Now go to the kitchen and do your boss thing."

She glared at him, but he won the staring match.

Her finger tapped at his chest. "You and I will have a talk about doing things behind my back," she said and turned toward the kitchen.

"Tate, honey, you know I love doing nasty things behind you. And you like them too," he whispered to her and chuckled. She turned to glare at him, but he offered her his most charming smile, and she just shook her head.

Her chef was ecstatic, and with good reason. The goods were first class, James knew, just as he knew that after going through them and the price lists, Tate would be stupid to let this opportunity pass. And his woman was not stupid. Stubborn to a fault, yes; stupid, no.

"We aren't taking on any more clients, but Mr. Copeland called and..."

"Jack," James explained as she turned a questioning glance to him. "He got them out of a tight spot once, and they were more than happy to repay the favor."

"I don't need charity," she all but snarled at him.

"This isn't charity. Jack owes me a couple of favors, so he made some phone calls for me, that's all."

"We've checked up on this place, Miss Cooper, and your reputation speaks for itself. This isn't charity, I assure you; we'd be more than happy to work with you."

Tate doubted for a second, but then nodded. "Okay, you got yourself a new customer," she said, shaking his hand.

No sooner had they unloaded the goods than some voices came from the restaurant side. The other suppliers. Perfect, just in time.

"Tate, princess, send them into the kitchen; we're going to have a chat with them."

"What are you going to do?" she asked, eyeing him suspiciously.

"Nothing, love, just some talking," he said as Zack and Sean smiled innocently at her.

"I can also fire those suppliers on my own."

"And I wouldn't deprive you from that pleasure. You fire them, just make sure they leave through the back door in the kitchen," he said.

She was going to complain, but she must have seen something on his face, because after a long second, she threw her arms up.

"Okay, what the hell, let the assholes be intimidated for once."

Half an hour later, James left Rosita's with a huge smile. Well, that had gone smoother than he'd expected. Tate had been a bit pissed at the beginning, but she'd soon gotten on board. Plus he'd gotten to deal with her old providers. Huge bonus. One by one, they'd passed by the kitchen, where James, Zack, and Sean had made their point clear—no one was to mess with Rosita's. His fingers had been twitching the whole time. After all, beating the shit out of them would have been a fitting payment for all the times they'd made Tate cry, but those boys were just employees following orders. So they'd gone verbal and just threatened the hell out of them.

"Lovely woman you got here," Zack said while they walked to the car. "She's feisty."

"Not my woman yet, but I'm working on it," James answered. He didn't like that Tate kept her heart guarded from him, but she'd come around.

They went to eat, and then to the office. By six o'clock, there was only one more client to deal with.

"Do you guys mind if you start the Browns' job without me? I have another errand to run."

"Sure," Zack replied. "Anything to do with the sweet piece of ass you introduced us to today?"

"Her name is Tate, and you better keep your eyes away from her ass. From any part of her, actually."

Sean laughed. "What happened with the 'women come and go, no need to sweat about it' attitude?"

James didn't answer; he just grunted. "Got it, chick's off limits. Fucking assholes, those suppliers, by the way. Good you got that all straightened out."

"Yeah well, there are other matters there that need addressing too." Like the kitchen assistant's constant Houdini stunts, for example.

"Take your time, man; we have everything under control. Go to your woman."

Not yet, but soon, he thought. First he had some things to do. He'd dealt with the providers, now it was time for Tim. For a couple of days now, he'd observed the chef's assistant at Rosita's.

He was barely twenty and, as far as James could see, not a bad boy if one could overlook the fact that he was showing up to work whenever it suited him, which was causing a huge strain on the other kitchen staff, especially the chef. And the place needed Tate outside, greeting people and making them feel at home, instead of having her grounded in the kitchen, stressed-out and grouchy.

After a short ride, he parked in a mall and headed for Technogeeks, where Tim not only worked in the mornings, repairing computers, but—as far as James could tell—also spent all those evenings that he'd been dead sick with European swine flu or whatever. Today was no different. It was already six o'clock; he should have been in the restaurant doing prep with the others, yet he was in the back, hands deep in the desecrated bowels of some computer.

The second he saw James, the kid flushed a bright red. To his benefit, he didn't try to lie.

"I need this job, man. I can't not stay and do overtime when I'm asked."

"Yet you can lie to Tate," James stated coldly.

"Come on, man, I already feel like shit about it, but there's nothing I can do. Rosita's only opens in the afternoons, and I need this job too; I can't afford to lose it. I actually can't afford to lose either of the jobs."

Yeah, James knew that; Tim came from a dysfunctional family and was taking care of his two siblings. That was probably why Tate put up with all that crap about weird illnesses and never-heard-of allergies.

"I know you can't, but this isn't working, kiddo. Tate needs you there."

"In a month or two, this place will quiet down. I may not have to come in the evenings to deal with the difficult computer meltdowns."

Maybe, but James wasn't ready to wait for that.

"Tell me, do you like working with these gadgets?"

The kid shrugged. "I'm good with them, and it pays well."

"What do you know about security systems?"

"Plenty. Arming or disarming?" he asked casually.

"I'm going to pretend I didn't hear that," James warned him. The last thing he wanted on his hands was a lawbreaking punk. Although he knew Tim was clean, just a good kid in a shitty family situation.

"Just kidding," he said, holding his hands up. "I can't risk getting caught. I have...people depending on me, so I stay out of trouble."

"What if I were to make you an offer? Would you be available?"

Tim threw him a casual glance. "Sorry, old man, you're cute, but I don't swing that way."

James snorted. Just what he needed, a mouthy smart-ass. "Very funny. You better start taking me seriously, or this old man is going to kick your lily ass to kingdom come. Now let's talk business. We're swamped, and we need help installing security alarms. I was thinking about hiring someone. Are you interested?"

Tim's eyes lit; then he tried to play it cool and damp down his growing enthusiasm. "Don't know. You pay well?"

James looked around. "I'm sure much better than what you're getting here. There's one condition, though: you'll work from ten to three p.m.—hard work, I'm warning you—but you'll never stay overtime, so you don't have any reason not to go to the restaurant. If you miss even one day at Rosita's without being really sick, and I mean really, really sick, puke your guts out sick, your ass is fired. Are we clear?"

Tim assented right away. "I really didn't mean any harm to Tate..."

James nodded curtly. "And that's the only reason you're getting this chance. Now call your employer and get him to find a replacement for you right away because you're heading to the restaurant."

Tim worked fast, and in fifteen minutes, everything was arranged. His employer wasn't too happy about his hasty departure, but well, he didn't have the boy contracted, so there was really nothing he could do about it. And James's attitude didn't leave room for compromise, much less bickering.

He'd dealt with the providers and Tim. Old Vito was on his standby list of unresolved matters should he ever try to fuck with

Tate's business again. Although he seriously doubted it, judging by the way the providers trembled when they'd left Rosita's; the message had gotten through loud and clear. Should Old Vito dare to come up with new tricks, he'd reassess the situation, but until then he'd consider that matter settled. There was one more thing disrupting the atmosphere at Rosita's, and that was Clint, who occupied the first position in that list of shit to come, not that James planned to do anything about him just yet.

It was evident to anyone with eyes in their head that Clint had the hots for Tate and, by the way he behaved, that his ego was too bruised to keep waiting for her to fall at his feet. He was in punishment mode. Although he was an asshole with as much interest in the girl as in being the boss and calling all the shots, putting him in line was something Tate should do by herself. Besides, James didn't want her thinking he couldn't handle a little competition. James had made clear without words that Tate was his, and he could get awfully territorial about her. As long as Clint kept his hands to himself and his shitty behavior inside the minimum bitching decibels range, James would do his damn best to tolerate him, even if that meant gritting his teeth at the sight of the guy. If Clint didn't get the hint about how precarious his situation was and got disrespectful or more contemptuous and confrontational with Tate, then all bets were off and James was going to start talking with his fists first. He wanted Tate to stand up for herself, but he wasn't going to let anyone manhandle her, not even verbally.

After dropping Tim at Rosita's, he headed back to work. There was still some paperwork to do for the Browns, but he could hardly wait for the evening to be over and get to Tate. He knew he would have to appease his little woman, and he was looking forward to it.

Tate couldn't bring herself to be pissed at James; she was too happy for that. Nils, her temperamental chef prone to drama queen outbursts, was whistling. Whistling, of all things, and joking. Unheard of! He was more than pleased with the goods they'd got, and the promise they'd keep coming. On top of that, Tim had appeared for work, apparently fully recovered. She didn't know if that last thing had anything to do with James; Tim wasn't talking, but she had her suspicions.

For several days now, James had gently but unstoppably steamrolled over her every time she'd tried to tell him their...whatever...was going nowhere. He'd just smile at her and melt her with one of his sweet comments or one of his I-am-in-charge stunts. He came to her every evening after work, waited for her to finish, intently watching everything and everyone around him, listening in silence, never interfering. She knew he was assessing the restaurant, but he hadn't said a word about it. If the suppliers' trick was anything to go by, then he was done sitting on the sidelines. She should be raving mad for his interfering, bitch about boundaries and how he was supposed to not overstep them, how she could take care of herself and the restaurant, how she didn't need help. But damn if it didn't feel nice to be taken care of for once.

With the kitchen personnel happy and in no need of immediate help, she was free to be outside, where she was supposed to have been all along. The downside was that she had to deal with Clint's moodiness firsthand. Or assholeness, as James had eloquently put it more than once. He was right, of course, but Tate wasn't ready yet to part with people her own father had hired. This continuity gave her a small measure of comfort, and that was why she kept putting up with his shit. Although she had to admit, her father had never meant for him to be the maître d'; Clint had been just a waiter, a fairly new one at that when her father and Jonah had died, and it was just the mess resulting from the accident that had put him in the position of running the dining area, especially as she was swamped with problems or stuck in the kitchen almost all the time.

Seeing how he behaved with Tina and Kelly, the way he was fast to snap at them, she doubted her father would have kept him around very long; he was just too mean, more so now that he was pissed at her. Clint seemed to have a thing for her, not that she'd ever thought about reciprocating. For a while after Aidan left her, he'd been very nice, but she'd kept her distance and his true nature had popped up. James's appearance had worsened the situation. Clint had gone from not talking to her to sneering at her. In front of James, he somehow refrained, but not so much when he wasn't around. In spite of all that, and when he wasn't being a moody, spiteful asshole, he was an excellent waiter, fast and clean, and he probably deserved the benefit of the doubt—for a while longer at least.

She spent all evening greeting patrons, and between that, dodging Clint's attitude and snide comments, and helping the waitresses, by eleven thirty she was physically and mentally wrung out. Even if she'd go to hell and back before admitting it, she was dying to see James coming through the front door. The good part of being in the kitchen was not having to face the looks full of pity from all those regular customers who'd known her and her family for decades. Almost a year had passed since the accident, and she still had to deal with their covert condolences on a regular basis. It was all so draining: the meaningful stares, the silences, the way they discreetly asked how she or her mom or Elle were doing. The way they tried to look cheery while talking to her yet not quite pulling it off. Out of respect and uneasiness, everyone avoided referring to Jonah or her dad. The way all of them tiptoed around that big pink elephant in the room, not wanting to acknowledge its presence, would have been funny if it weren't so sad.

With James it was different. No big pink elephant to politely ignore. He asked up front, and Tate realized she liked talking about them; it helped her process all the grief inside her.

When she heard the door, she turned hopefully. It was too late for customers to show up; this had to be James.

But it was Aidan.

He looked impeccable in his expensive suit, with his black hair perfectly cut and his million-dollar lawyer smile. It was the first time she'd seen him after the breakup, and funnily enough, it didn't hurt; her mind was too preoccupied with James.

"Hello, Tate."

She smiled at him, moved to embrace him, then stopped herself. She didn't harbor any bad feelings really, not anymore, but that didn't make them friends. Real friends didn't dump you while you were in a difficult situation, not to mention lovers.

"Hello, Aidan."

"I see you're still trying to keep this place afloat," he said, throwing a look around. She followed his glance, glad tonight had been a busy night. Even at this late hour there were still a couple of tables occupied. She might still be deep in shit, bills, threatening e-mails, and worries, but that didn't mean she wanted him to know. If she had anything left, it was pride.

"Yeah, well, I'm hanging in there. How are you?"

"I'm fine, very busy all the time. They offered a partnership. I accepted, of course, and now I'm in charge of several corporate accounts, very demanding clients—lots of responsibilities. Plus I was also asked to handle a couple of pro bono cases."

She knew all about his success stories; after two years of being together, they had a bunch of common friends over whom they now had shared custody, and although she hadn't seen much of them lately, for some annoying reason they insisted on telling her about Aidan and his marvelous accomplishments, like she'd been the one dumping him and should be sorry for it. Especially irritating were her former coworkers at her old office, where Aidan had been considered something of a superb catch. Lose her comfortable job and then him over a stinky little family restaurant? Slave over the place all evenings, weekends, and holidays? Please! She was out of her mind, they repeatedly said. But they seemed to forget she hadn't lost her job, she'd quit, and Aidan had quit her.

"I'm glad for you," she said, feeling awkward. He'd meant the world to her, once upon a time; now there was nothing left but an uneasy feeling. "Did you come for dinner?"

"No. I was in the neighborhood, just wanted to see how you were doing. I hoped you'd have the time to go for a drink with me."

"I…um…I'm a little busy," she said.

He disdainfully scanned his surroundings. "You're the boss of this place. Surely they can manage without you for a while."

His response annoyed her. How typical of him. "Actually no, they can't." Despite the decrease in customers, without her dad, Jonah, her mom, and Elle pitching in, they were badly understaffed. Not that Aidan could ever understand that.

At her hard tone, he softened and reached out for her. "For old time's sake? I just want to talk a little. Check up on you, see how you're doing. Some of our friends are worried about you."

His hand on her arm felt so uncomfortable she moved back to break the contact. "I really don't think this is the time..."

At that very moment, James strode into the restaurant and headed for her, a takeout bag dangling from his left hand. A smile broke across her face immediately. It was amazing how despite her attempts to the contrary, James's mere presence made her feel safe and comforted.

"Hi, princess," he greeted, cupped her face, and kissed her. Thoroughly. Then he turned to the man standing near her, his intense gaze inspecting him. "Are you going to introduce us?"

It took a while for his words to seep in. "Ah, sure, yeah. James, this is Aidan. Aidan, James."

Aidan looked uncomfortable and surprised. "Nice to meet you," he mumbled, offering a well-mannered smile that didn't reach his eyes.

That was just as well, because James was not smiling. He just answered with a nod, one of his hands curled around Tate's waist.

That gesture didn't escape Aidan, who actually looked...pissed? "I see. Well, hmm, I'd better be going. I can see you're busy. Take care."

"Yeah, you too, Aidan."

James didn't say a word, just followed Aidan's retreat with his gaze. When he disappeared from view, he turned to Tate.

"Are you ready, baby?" His casual tone was much at odds with the intensity radiating from his hazel eyes—he wasn't pleased about Aidan, but he was fighting not to let it show. "I brought Thai food, figured by now you'd be a bit tired of Italian."

She loved Thai food. She'd mentioned it in passing while they were in Florida, and he'd remembered. So sweet—for a pushy domineering guy trying to run her over, that is. Still, food won the battle. "Give me half an hour."

After forty minutes, they were climbing the stairs to her apartment.

"You know, we'd be more comfortable at my place. We could lay down naked in the bed and eat there."

She shrugged unapologetically. "I like my bed."

A snort, harsh in disbelief, escaped his lips. "Please, honey, your bed is not a bed; it is an instrument of torture."

Once in the apartment, they left the food on the counter, and as she began opening the boxes, he leaned on her from behind and bracketed her body with his arms, palms splayed on the counter.

"So that was Aidan," he said, nuzzling her hair.

She was silent for a second. "Yeah, that was Aidan."

"I see. Is there anything you want to tell me?"

She snorted, turned around, and poked at his chest with her finger. He didn't budge an inch. "Do not think for a second I don't know you're diverting the matter at hand. Aidan is not important."

"I sure hope he isn't," he said.

She rolled her eyes, more than exasperated with his hard tone. "Of course not, what kind of slut do you think I am, uh? You're the one I'm sleeping with. Although I may reconsider that if you don't stop bullying me."

A proud male smile spread on his lips, and he fell upon her mouth. It was a hard, possessive kiss that all but took her breath away. If she didn't regain her bearings soon, she'd be outmaneuvered—by the dick poking at her belly and by the fragrant smell of spicy coconut chicken coming from the bag.

"I'm glad you don't consider him important," he said into her lips. "Nevertheless, next time I see his hands on you, I'll chop them off."

"You won't do any such thing. It was nothing, and I can take care of myself." She hadn't liked the feel of his touch either, no matter how light, but she wouldn't let him distract her. "Forget Aidan; he means nothing to me. Let's go back to the matter at hand."

He smiled. "Which is?"

"You, Zack, and Sean intimidating the hell out of my suppliers in my kitchen."

"Ex-suppliers," he corrected her with a cocky smirk. "And intimidation? Nuh, that's called public relations, princess."

"It's called meddling, mister," she reprimanded him. "Did

you know Tim showed up tonight for work, no sign of being sick? Did you have anything to do with that too?"

"Me? No. What makes you think I did?"

She so didn't believe him. She crossed her arms in anger, her chin stubbornly tilted up. "I won't be handled, James. And believe it or not, I don't need rescuing."

"I'm sure a badass chick like you doesn't need rescuing, but I do enjoy being the heroic type. Let me indulge, babe." He caressed her cheek, her swollen lips, the side of her neck. How could anyone stay mad at him?

"You, mister, are really lucky this badass chick loves Thai food. Otherwise she'd have to hurt you."

James smirked. "Come sit. Let me feed you. Afterward I'll take you to bed and make love to you until you fall sleep from exhaustion. How does that sound?"

It sounded perfect.

CHAPTER NINE

James had been in charge of supervising the security for one of their clients' events until two o'clock in the morning, and now, despite being dead on his feet and badly in need of sleep, he was on his way to Tate's. Alden was literally around the corner, but he wasn't considering it.

It had been almost three weeks since that first time Tate had let him in her apartment, and despite the harshness of the damn bed, he hadn't slept in his own since then. Except for yesterday, when he'd also worked until the wee hours and, against his better judgment, had decided to stay at his place. It'd been a restless night, his huge, comfy bed never seeming so empty before, so today he wasn't repeating the experience, never mind his bone-deep tiredness and that Lilliputian bed of hers that was prematurely destroying his back. Her place was small and crowded, full of boxes and mismatched furniture, but weirdly enough it had started to feel like home to him. Although probably by now a cardboard box with Tate in it would feel like home to him.

She was getting to him in a way no woman ever had before. And the way she fought him every step of the way was adorable. Like the fight about the keys. She'd given him the keys today, grudgingly, repeated insistently they were not *his* keys, that they were on loan just because he was going to come in late and she wasn't going to be awake. She assured him she was going to take them back the next day and that was it—no getting cozy with them. He'd laughed, taken the keys, and kissed her silly. Tate could say whatever she wanted; those spare keys had his name on them. He'd get her to give them freely to him, if not today, then someday soon, and not on a short loan.

He entered her apartment and quietly closed the door, getting rid of his shoes and his jacket and heading toward her. The place was a mess, like always, and the fact that it didn't bother him in the least spoke volumes of how deep he was in.

She was sleeping, curled in what looked like a big, brand-new bed. Wow, that was a surprise; she hadn't mentioned it to him. His chest swelled; she'd taken the trouble to buy a new bed so that he'd be more comfortable, even if she'd insisted repeatedly that a big bed was a waste of space in that tiny apartment. The underlying assumption being, of course, that he wasn't going to be around long enough for the buying of the bed to be worthwhile.

After undressing, he slid in and reached for her, pulling her on top of him. He'd gotten used to having her blanketing him, to which she'd agreed mainly because the bed hadn't allowed for them to sleep side by side, but James was now spoiled rotten and needed full-body contact, from the tip of his foot to his head. He needed to feel her breath on his chest, the light heartbeats against him, her light weight on him. He absolutely loved feeling her hot core against his thigh, loved the way she wrapped her legs over him.

She looked so tired; she didn't even wake up when he scooped her up and positioned her on top of him. She mumbled something he didn't understand, but he kissed the top of her head and wrapped himself around her, effectively cutting short all her rumblings. In spite of his body's tiredness, he went instantly hard, like always when he touched her. He kept waiting for this insane attraction to wear off, at least to manageable proportions, but it just got stronger and stronger; the more he had her, the more he wanted her and the more out of control he felt. Sighing, he tried to ignore his body's reaction; she was tired, needed her sleep, especially now that the restaurant was picking up.

Tate was looking much more relaxed and in charge, and damn if it wasn't showing. He liked to believe he was partly responsible for that change, but he wasn't sure, she wasn't forthcoming about that. Be that as it may, the restaurant's atmosphere had undoubtedly improved a lot. The chef was happy, and Tim was around every day, but that wasn't the main reason for the general improvement in Rosita's—Tate was. She'd gained confidence in herself and her abilities, making diners feel at ease and welcome. A superb hostess, she was able to handle just about anything and anyone. He knew firsthand because he'd observed her transformation from a beautiful yet insecure young woman, overworked and overstressed, into this take-charge knockout that oozed charm and security. She was even standing up to Clint, who nowadays was more than pissed that she was taking over the dining area. And everyone was noticing the change. With that loose, thick braid swinging around her sexy self, that wicked smile and those smoky eyes, she was his private wet dream. Much to his distaste, other men seemed to do their share of fantasizing too, so these days, possessiveness was riding his ass hard.

He had a vivid recollection of one night in particular, just some days ago, when he'd been about to beat a couple of pricks for being too friendly with Tate. They hadn't been overtly rude or anything like that, but he saw their eyes, the lust in them. Those assholes talked to her while she was taking their order and bringing their wine, joked and flirted with her, admired her ass every time she turned around, even whistling in admiration.

Tate had handled herself perfectly. She really knew how to deal with customers, how to draw the line without them getting offended. Apparently James wasn't that capable or mature—or evolved, for that matter. As their flirting intensified and one guy had moved to grab her wrist, he had jumped from his chair and darted toward them.

If not for Tate's ability to defuse situations, he'd have rearranged their faces. She admonished the guys at the table with a smile and then dragged James away to the counter, sternly looking at him as he'd sat and fumed and mumbled under his breath about how those guys were going to meet an untimely death if they didn't remove their gazes from her. He was sure she was going to chew his ass, but she hadn't; the vixen gave him a wicked smile, came closer, and had whispered into his ear.

"Behave now. Those guys are just a bit rowdy. They won't lay a hand on me because I won't let them. If it were your hand, then it would be another story. I'd let it wander anywhere it wanted. And not only your hand, but other parts of your body too. You just behave now, and I'll prove it to you after we close."

Then she'd kissed him and walked away, leaving him out of breath and with the biggest hard-on in recorded human history.

Closing time didn't come for ages, or so it felt, but when finally they got all the patrons out and the last of the personnel left, James was already walking a tightrope.

"I want you now," he said as he'd walked toward her. "Here. Bent over that table."

It was the same table where those assholes had been sitting. He hadn't got to beat them up, but in a wounded maleness sort of way, he'd needed retribution.

She looked at him as he approached and smiled one of her sultry, sexy smiles. "Oh hail James the Barbarian. Macho power tripping again?"

He reached her, brought her to his chest, and kissed her, hard and deep, ravaging her mouth like he'd been dying to do all night, while she'd encircled his neck and held on tight. When he'd broken the kiss, she was short of breath too, her eyes glistening, her lips swollen.

She'd looked mischievously at him and taken a step back toward the table. She rolled her black skirt up enough for him to realize she wasn't wearing any panties.

"Fuck, you're killing me here!" he'd cursed as he began unbuckling himself. "You've been twitching your gorgeous ass all night long without wearing any underwear?" Thank God he hadn't known at the time, or it would have given him an aneurysm.

"No, silly. I recognized the way you were staring at me from the counter after those guys flirted with me. I could feel the lust coming in waves from you, so a while back, I took them off, I wanted to be ready. I'm starting to know my man."

She might have said something more, but his ears were so badly roaring he hadn't caught it. All that he heard again and again was her calling him "her man." Hers. His chest swelled, and his cock throbbed in urgency.

Then she'd turned around, bent slightly over the table, and offered him a view that almost stopped his heart. "You like it?" she'd asked, parting her legs a bit.

Did he like it? His eyes were fixed on her luscious behind

and her bare folds, puffing out from arousal, glistening, waiting for him. Without bothering to ask, he'd checked his pockets for condoms, got one, and rolled it on. Nowadays he was worse than a teenager, carrying condoms all over himself—his wallet, his pockets, his car—hoping to get lucky anywhere and everywhere.

He should have probed her with his fingers, checked out if she was slick enough for his penetration, but he couldn't wait. He'd needed to claim her, to mark her as his own, so he pushed his way in. Her pussy was hot and wet and so damn tight it almost blew his head off. She whimpered, and he stilled, afraid he'd hurt her. Reaching back, her hand grabbed his ass and pushed him all the way in.

"Don't go easy on my account. I've been thinking about this too for the last hour."

That did him in. He couldn't have gone easy even if his life depended on it. She'd broken the last of his restraints by forcing him in to the hilt. He fucked her deep and hard, watching the spectacle in the mirror in front of them while she'd taken all of him, moaning and urging him to give her more. She had her eyes closed, her mouth slightly parted, her cheeks flushed, the pleasure he was giving her written all over her face. She was so damn beautiful he could hardly breathe.

Without slowing the rhythm down, he'd glided his hand up and under her blouse. He opened his hand on her stomach, reveled in her smoothness; then he'd reached up to her breasts. Her nipples were puckered and hard, begging to be touched. As one hand gripped her waist, he rolled and pinched the pearled beads with the other, getting Tate to jerk and moan louder. She arched her back, urging him on, her pussy clamping around him.

"Yes, James, like this. Please. Harder. Please."

He'd smiled. Her nipples were very sensitive and very demanding, requiring constant attention. He knew how much she enjoyed him being a bit rough with them, so he pinched them harder, and a ragged moan rushed out of her.

He pumped her hard, the tip of his cock slamming at her womb with each plunge, her pussy pulsing in need. "I love fucking you. I can't get enough. Your pussy is so sweet, clenching so nicely around my dick."

She'd reacted to his talk, like she always did, and her body had tensed, her tender flesh fluttering around him. She was close, and so was he. He'd bent down, kissed her neck, and whispered into her ear, "Touch yourself, princess. I'm short of hands. Take your hand to your pussy and touch your clit. I'll take care of the rest."

She'd whimpered but obeyed, and the view of her in the mirror reaching for her pleasure almost undid him.

She came right away after barely grazing her clit, her pussy had convulsed so strongly it instantly milked all the cum out of him.

James was still panting hard when she'd chuckled between breaths. "Yeah, I do really love your Barbarian side."

That had been the closest he'd gotten to telling her about his feelings. He'd had to grit his teeth to stop himself from spilling his guts. He knew by now that he wanted more than a casual involvement. He wanted her, all of it, quirks and bad moods included. Forever. The trick was getting her to accept that. She'd already accepted they were sexually involved, even reconciled to the idea that no matter what she said or did, or how difficult she was about it all, he was stubbornly sticking around, before and after the fucking. She liked to pretend she didn't like it, but he knew better, could see through her, and she wasn't fooling him; he was getting to her. He could still sense, though, how sometimes she kept herself at a distance as if a huge secret was eating at her, could almost see the distress in her eyes when she caught herself relying on him and hating it. In spite of how much closer he'd gotten to her, Tate still didn't trust him fully, and her determination not to give him an inch was driving him crazy. He wanted to give her time, but the whole situation didn't sit well with him; he ached to protect her, dammit, didn't appreciate being left outside like he didn't matter or worse, like he was the enemy.

He fell asleep hugging and nuzzling her head. He would get Tate to trust him and open up, to give their relationship a chance. Hell, the bed, no matter how shallow a gesture, was a huge step forward already.

She was floating, aroused, having the nicest dream. Her nipples were aching, her pussy felt on fire, and her clit was throbbing. Surprisingly enough, the feeling didn't go away as she drifted into awareness. When she finally opened her eyes and found James on top of her with his mouth working her nipples, her breath caught in her throat. And that was not all he was doing; his cock was halfway in her and his fingers were rubbing her clit. No wonder she was sopping wet.

"Good morning, princess."

"James?"

"What do you mean 'James'? Is there anyone else that wakes you up in this manner?" he asked, trying to sound outraged. "Because if so, then we need to have a chat, baby."

She laughed. "No, James, you're the only one that wakes me up by molesting me."

"The only one that wakes you up, princess. In any way," he corrected her, slipping another inch deeper.

"The only one," she repeated, unable to think as he slowly worked another inch of his cock inside her. He was almost fully seated in her, stretching her tender flesh to the limit.

"I see you bought a bed for me."

She shrugged casually, but he wouldn't let her play it down—he caressed her clit a bit harder, getting a throaty gasp out of her, and rained kisses over her: her eyes, her nose, and finally her lips. He ate at those, licking and kissing until she was breathing hard. "Thank you, babe. Nobody has bought me a bed before. I'm so taken by your gesture."

"Don't get cocky. I'm quite partial to your body, and I don't want it to crumple into arthritis before its time. That's the only reason for this concession."

James pushed that last inch inside her, now fully invading her. "Yeah, that and that you love me," he said so naturally that it stopped Tate's heart. It amazed her how giving James was. He didn't seem afraid of anything; he was so sure of her it scared the living shit out of her. "But don't worry, you're stealing my heart away too, princess."

"I didn't know your kind had a heart."

"Yes, I do, even if you're set on stomping all over it."

"James..." She looked at his eyes and didn't know what to say. She did have feelings for him, of course she did. It was impossible not to have feelings for the guy, but she wasn't ready to admit it to him yet, or herself, let alone say it out loud. James probably knew she wasn't ready yet because he didn't press the issue, he just smiled at her and kept working her clit, tugging at her piercing as his mouth trailed over her throat, taking small bites, his tongue flickering here and there. Soon she found herself bucking at him, desperate for him to move.

"James?"

"Mmm?"

"Don't make me hurt you. Move," she said demandingly, wrapping her legs around his waist and squeezing him tight. "Fuck me already."

"You're so romantic." He laughed. "But you'll tell me those words, princess. Sooner or later you will."

"Whatever," she muttered, but she was glad when he began moving and occupied his mouth with hers. She wasn't ready for this conversation. Besides, she still doubted a guy like James was relationship material. Who was to say he wasn't going to leave the second this got old for him? She had to protect her heart.

James propped himself on both his elbows and didn't break eye contact during their lovemaking. He kissed her all the time, all over her face, her throat, murmuring to her how beautiful she was, how much he wanted her. Damn him. With his tender words, he'd long ago transformed their sex into lovemaking, and despite knowing better, she was getting addicted to it.

Her clit was so sensitive, every time he nudged at it after the plunge, she felt like exploding. James was also in bad shape, tense and sweaty, trembling from the need to stay under control. Every time he pushed in, she lifted her hips to him, welcoming him, while her nails dug into his shoulders, urging him on. Soon they found their release together, breathing into each other's mouths.

They stayed in that position long after their hearts had stopped racing. She couldn't breathe but didn't care.

"What do you think if we stay in all day, testing the bed?"

She laughed. "Don't you have to go to work? It's Monday, you know..." Rosita's was closed on Mondays. She was free, but James wasn't.

"I've arranged it with Zack and Sean. I'm free for you to command all day long," he said, rolling onto his back and taking her with him.

"I was thinking about going to the mall to get some clothes, but if you don't want to spend your free day shopping, we could..."

"Are you kidding? Running after you all day, bringing you tiny clothes into the dressing room, checking how they fit you? That's another of my fantasies."

"You're mental."

"Fucking you up against the wall, surrounded by mirrors, an almost transparent curtain separating us from the world, damn quiet so that the people in the other dressing cubicles won't hear us. I'm ready. Bring it on."

"Oh no, you can forget about me enacting any more of your raunchy fantasies."

He didn't listen. Hell, he never did. "Are you thinking about shopping for lingerie? Because those should be tried in the store..."

She laughed, and as she tried to jump out of bed, her cell rang. She reached out to her nightstand, where the phone was, and James, taking advantage of it, tackled her down, wrapping her in his arms.

Squirming and giggling, Tate checked out the caller. Elle.

"Shh, it's my sister. Behave and be quiet."

He barked out a laugh and nuzzled her throat. "Who am I, your dirty secret?"

She rolled her eyes at him. Yeah right, dirty secret her ass. Like the way he'd behaved in Florida left any room for their relationship to be a secret. Or the way he'd behaved in the restaurant from day one. Hell, half her regular clientele were already treating him like he was family—there to stay.

Ignoring him, she answered the phone. "Hi, Elle, aren't you supposed to be in class?"

"Hi, Sis, good morning to you too," Elle said mockingly.

"And yes, I'm going to class, just running a bit late. Mondays aren't my forte; you know that."

She hadn't talked to Elle since the day after her arrival back in Boston. When Elle had visited their mom, she'd heard about the whole James affair from her and several in-house informants, so she'd of course called Tate right away wanting all the details. By then, there hadn't been much to tell, just that she'd had a one-nighter of earth-shattering sex with the tattooed bad boy next door, and that there wasn't going to be any follow-up. Now, however, the story had gotten a bit more complicated; that tattooed bad boy was still in her bed, presently driving her crazy with his touch.

She threw him a glare, even slapped his hand, but it didn't do any good. She steeled herself, trying to concentrate on the conversation. "How are things going?" That was code language for *has Mom snapped yet*? James must have sensed her distress, for he tensed too.

"Actually, things are quite good. Mom seems…less sad. Less mental. And the kittens have improved dramatically. We have people asking to adopt them."

Tate laughed. That was good. Last time she spoke with her mom, several weeks ago, she'd effusively accused Mr. Bowen of Amy's new condition. Apparently the cat had begun overeating and throwing up afterward. According to her mom, emotional distress had thrown Amy into the clutches of bulimia. Tate hadn't known whether to laugh or cry.

"Listen, I'm a bit in a hurry now, but I wanted to give you a heads-up. I'm thinking about coming to Boston for a visit next week."

"That would be great. Just let me know when, and I'll pick you up from Logan." They used to be very close, but since the accident, Elle had been on the run. Maybe now she was done running and Tate could have her sister back. One could always wish.

"Great. By the way, sorry to call so early on a Monday."

His mouth on her ear and his hands on her breasts were a bit distracting, and she lost track of what Elle was saying. She giggled.

"Tate, are you there? Are you listening?"

"Yeah...no, what? Sorry, I didn't hear you, what were you saying?"

"I said I was sorry I called so early on a Monday."

"It's okay, I was about to get up anyway," she said as another giggle escaped her. She slapped at James, but that didn't deter him as he continued kissing and nipping her ear. *Stop*, she mouthed at him.

Elle was silent for a long second.

"Tate, are you with someone?" She waited too long to say "no," and Elle, who was no dummy, was all over her. "Oh my God, you have someone in your bed," she said with a squeak. "While we've been talking. Groosssss! What's he doing there? No, no, erase that; don't tell me! Aw shit, it's not that asshole Aidan, is it?"

"No, it's not him."

As James narrowed his eyes on her, very much daring her, she braced herself and said it out loud. "It's James, Mr. Bowen's son. Remember I told you about him?"

"The tattooed guy with whom there wasn't going to be anything more than a vacation fuck?" Elle sounded stupefied.

"Yeah, that one. We've been...seeing each other."

She felt herself blush at her own admission, and James laughed.

"We've been doing more than that, princess," he mumbled to her.

"Seeing each other?" Elle's tone was shocked. "But I thought you only liked soft-handed, expensively perfumed, self-centered metrosexuals with an acutely developed sense of fashion and themselves, not 'tattooed Neanderthals'! How did you slip to the dark side? Oh wait, he's that good, uh?" she said morosely, her words tinted with laughter. Then she stopped abruptly. "You've been keeping up a conversation with me while going at it with tattooed Wonder Boy? Oh Jesus, I need a shower! Yikes. I'm hanging up now. Have fun. I expect a full report when you aren't...horizontal. Talk to you later."

Tate glared at James as Elle hang up. "That went well. Now

she thinks we're a couple of horny rabbits that can't keep their hands off each other."

"Well, as long as she's already thinking that..." he said, delving his hand between her thighs.

"I don't think so, you sex maniac," she said, giggling and squirming away from him. "I'll take a shower; you start with the breakfast. And no, you can't come with me to the shower. I've told you a million times we don't both fit in there."

His heated gaze followed her; she could feel it. "Yes, we would. It's just a matter of you squeezing tight against me."

"Yeah, right!"

"Spoilsport," she heard him complaining.

On her way to the bathroom, she turned on her laptop and opened her e-mail. She was waiting for the price list one of the new suppliers was supposed to send her, along with an old invoice.

As she turned the water on, she heard the chime of the e-mail.

"You got an e-mail," James said.

"Check it out; it's probably from the suppliers. I'm expecting a new price list for the cheeses."

Then she remembered. Oh shit! Prince Charming's e-mails were there too. Fuck, fuck! She flung a towel over her and all but ran out of the bathroom. Maybe there was still a chance James hadn't noticed those.

The second she saw him, she realized it was too late. He was sitting in front of the computer, knuckles white. She looked at the screen. Damn, it had been that asshole e-mailing her again, not the suppliers. It'd landed in the folder named Prince Charming, where all the other filthy messages were, and James was now scrolling through them.

His body was tense, and his eyes looked at her in fury and disbelief. "What the fuck is this?" His harshness drew her back.

"No one gave you permission to look at those," she said, trying to keep up the bravado.

His hands fisted even more. His tone hardened. "Cut the shit out, Tate! What the fuck is this? There must be over a hundred e-mails here!"

Yep. One hundred fifty-seven to be exact, Tate thought. She winced as James began zapping through them. There were all so filled with filth, she winced at the thought of James reading them. "I have a bit of an assholeish admirer, that's all."

He shot up to his feet so fast the chair flew backward. "So I'm good enough to fuck you, but not to know there's a wacko stalking you? Is that how little you think of me?" He darted toward her and grabbed her upper arms. "When the hell were you going to tell me, Tate?"

"I didn't think it was that important."

"Not that important? Not that important? You've got to be fucking kidding me!" he said with a snarl, looming over her.

"I had no clue I was supposed to tell you every damned thing!"

He ignored her. "I knew you were hiding something from me, but never in a million years would I have guessed you'd keep something like this from me." He was so pissed and hurt, rage marred his voice and darkened his eyes. "Did you at least go to the police? Or did you think it wasn't necessary?"

She shrugged him off. "The police? Hah! Don't make me laugh. They were the first to suggest I was making those up to get the insurance to cover for the fire. They were useless!"

"The hell they will be once I have a little talk with them. This asshole almost burned your place down once already, Tate!"

"You don't know that for sure, and you don't have the right to meddle in my things."

"Right. Pack your things up; you're moving in with me."

"What?"

"You heard me!"

She giggled nervously. "I can't move in with you. Be reasonable. Besides, you live a thirty-minute drive from here. I need to be close to the restaurant. My car's old and unreliable."

"You'll take my car."

She made a face at him. "Your monster truck? Don't be ridiculous. I can barely reach the pedals."

"Then we'll buy you a new car."

She frowned and crossed her arms, thinking about the benefits of storming out in a huff. "No!"

"Fine, then I'll move in here."

His words effectively stunned her. "What? Why? No!"

"What do you mean why? You have a wacko stalking you," he yelled, more furious now that she wasn't complying. "I'm not letting you out of my sight. And don't test me on this."

She tried to calm him down. "You're exaggerating, James. I don't have a stalker problem. I really don't. Listen to me. You know how annoying yet harmless it is when you open your e-mail box and a hoard of spam plops down? Well, this—my problem—is like spam, annoying yes, but basically harmless."

His pacing came to a halt, his body trembling from anger. "Have you lost your ever-loving mind? Haven't you been paying attention? It's escalating; this last e-mail is more aggressive than the one before that. He isn't only threatening the restaurant, he's threatening you. Dammit, Tate, you're in danger. You're dealing with a sick fucker; he won't be content with messages. Sooner or later, he's going to want to meet you face-to-face. I won't allow that; I want you safe."

She jutted her chin up. "Even if you're right, that's not a good enough reason to move in together."

"Do you need another reason? Well, here's one: if we lived together, I could fuck you all the time. Having you 24-7 in my bed is very attractive."

She laughed. "You can come over and stay in here as often as you want. I bought this bed for you, after all. But I'm not moving in with you. And that's final."

He looked ready to spit bullets. "I'm installing alarm systems here and in the restaurant. And you're getting a panic button."

"I can't afford—"

"Not another word!" he roared. "This is final too. I'm getting those for you, and that's that. And don't push me right now, Tate. I'm not in the best of moods. Take your shower, get dressed. The mall will have to wait. We're going to my place to pick up the alarms; then we'll come back here to install them. And that's only for starters. Then I'll call the police."

"But—"

"Not. A. Word!"

She wanted to drive her point home; she was no child and not to be muscled out by his bossiness every time he got his feathers ruffled, but today wasn't the day to take a stand. He'd reached his limit. Looked so tense, so pissed. She wasn't scared of him—he'd never lay a finger on her, of that she was dead certain—but she didn't want to add to his anger. Besides, he was right to be mad, and she knew it. She should have said something to him a long time ago, but her mouth had remained stubbornly closed. Out of fear, out of uneasiness because even if she hated to admit it, she'd come to depend on him a lot, on the strength his presence infused in her. The last thing she wanted was to lay more burdens on him, or heaven forbid, come across as a drag, too needy or clingy. She knew how that one had played out last time.

She finished her shower and dressed hastily, half afraid he'd left. But he hadn't; she found him already dressed and sitting on a chair, tapping on the table, on edge but still there. She felt so relieved a wave of tenderness and gratitude washed over her, leaving her breathless.

"You're still here," she mumbled.

His stormy eyes locked on hers. "For fuck's sake, Tate! Of course I'm here. What did you think, that I'd walk out on you?" His accusatory tone made her feel ashamed. Shit, she'd gotten him furious again. She should have known James wouldn't scare easily. Tate shook her head and averted her eyes.

She went to him, sat on his lap, and gently caressed his shoulders. It felt like petting a wild tiger. He looked so highly strung and hurt it broke her heart. For the longest time, no one said anything.

"Sorry, I didn't mean to leave you in the dark," she whispered. "Please don't make a big deal out of it. I didn't tell you because I thought it wasn't that important. Please don't be mad." Not sure of her reception but not really caring either, she moved to kiss him. At first he didn't reciprocate, but she continued brushing his lips with hers, taking small flicks with her tongue, and soon his own desire betrayed him. He roughly cupped the back of her head and forced her mouth open, kissing her deeply, his tongue ruthlessly thrusting in. He was making a point too; he was in charge. She wrapped her arms around him and pressed herself against his hard chest, letting his warmth and strength soak into her, dying to reassure herself of his presence. He hadn't walked out on her; he was pissed, true, but he was there.

"Who is this asshole, and why the fuck are you calling him Prince Charming?"

She lifted her shoulders. "Don't know who he is. As far as the name goes, well, it just seemed ironically fitting."

His face was tense; he didn't find it funny. "How long has this been going on? And don't even think of lying to me anymore. I want the truth, Tate. And I'll get it, even if I have to tie you to the chair."

She sighed and nodded. "It started a couple of months after the accident. First, I thought it was all a prank, but with the fire... The police never took it seriously, and I kind of did the same. I don't even like thinking about the whole thing. Maybe the police were right and the fire was an accident. This could all be just a nasty coincidence."

He let out a harsh groan. "You're deluding yourself."

"Yes, I know, but things haven't been easy on me. Taking those threats seriously is too much for me to deal with."

James ran a hand through his hair and spat a curse. "You didn't have to deal with that alone. I'd have been there for you, would have taken care of it, if only you'd have let me."

She bit her lower lip and told him the truth. "I didn't want to bother you with my problems. You aren't responsible for me."

He grabbed her by her shoulders, looking ready to strangle her. "You haven't gotten the dynamics of our relationship down yet, have you? Let me explain it to you: we're involved, very involved. You're mine, and your problems are also mine. No one messes with what belongs to me. Don't fight me on that, because you'll lose, baby. And be aware next time you hide something like that from me, I'll turn you over my knee and spank your ass red. Do we understand each other?"

She nodded, stunned into silence. Shivers raked her body. She did like hearing she belonged to him; she'd never belonged to anybody before.

"Good. Now, are you positive you don't know who this Prince Charming could be? The owner of Old Vito?"

She shook her head. "No, not his style. He's a much more direct person, preferring to intimidate straight up front. Old school, you know. E-mailing me to death strikes me as too modern for the likes of him."

He scowled her. "This is serious, princess. Have you tried to change e-mails?"

"It's Rosita's address. We do quite a lot of business through the Net, especially group bookings. I can't close it down." She'd tried to block his address, but the bastard kept changing it.

"You can't ignore this. The messages are full of rage, very personal—the fucker knows you. What about Clint?"

She rolled her eyes. "No way. Besides, what would he gain from hurting me or the restaurant?"

"Never underestimate the power of a wounded ego, princess. Aidan?"

"Aidan dumped me, not the other way around," she said, sinking her fingers into his hair, luxuriating in the way it felt around her fingers.

"The asshole dumped you while you had a stalker after you? Or didn't you tell him about it?"

James was such a protective man; of course he couldn't understand how a guy could leave any woman to fend for herself, even if she were more than capable of taking care of herself. It was in his DNA, part of what he was. "I told him, but Aidan was too busy with his own life, and those e-mails weren't on his priority list. He said I should just cut my losses and sell the place."

"You told him, yet you didn't tell me." The accusation was clear, and she took immediate affront of it.

"I told him, and I learned my lesson; I was needy and clingy and suffocating him with my problems. I wasn't about to repeat the same mistake with you." And James had come to mean so much more to her than Aidan, she hadn't wanted to jeopardize it.

"I am not like Aidan, and I resent being compared to him. I

don't run when things get tough, and I don't leave people I care about hanging."

She stared at him. "I've realized that on my own. You're nothing like him." Yep, Aidan and James were as different as they came.

"No more comparisons, okay?"

She nodded, and that seemed to appease him. "What about ex-employees? Did you fire anyone recently?"

Tate shook her head. "You've seen what I've put up with in order not to fire people my dad hired. No, I haven't fired anyone. Some people left, yes, but it was voluntarily." She lifted her gaze to him, almost pleading. "There's no need to overreact."

"I'll be the judge of that, princess. Let's go, and we'll get breakfast on the way."

He was still pissed, but it seemed that by agreeing to the alarms and the panic button, whatever the hell that was, the fight had partly gone out of him.

"Will we get to the mall in time after installing the alarm? I still want to buy clothes. I may even let you take a peek while I change in the dressing room."

He studied her for a second, his eyes serious. "Do not think for even a second I don't know that you're playing me like a fiddle."

"I am, and you like it," she whispered. "Although you'll like it better when I take you lingerie shopping. By the way, why are we going to Alden? Don't you have alarm systems at the office?"

"I have one brand-new prototype we just received there. I want you to have that one."

"You know what I think?" she asked, throwing him a casual glance, trailing her fingers over the back of his neck. "I think that's an excuse to get me to your place. You've been talking about it for weeks now, about your big bed and your nice hot tub, the lake views too. You should be ashamed of yourself, mister, trying to take advantage of a damsel in distress."

He narrowed his eyes on her, frowned at her jovial tone. "Don't you joke about this."

He wanted to look stern, but she could see his lips

beginning to turn up.

She pushed on, waving an admonishing finger at him. "You Catholic boys are sneaky. A girl can never be too careful around you—too many repressed dreams and fantasies."

He shook his head in mock desperation and stood up, offering her his hand, his gaze daring her not to take it. She'd never held his hand willingly; he'd always had to grab it. Now was her chance to show him how much he meant to her. She reached for his hand, entwined her fingers around his, pressing hard, and smiled at him. James looked so surprised it felt like a sucker punch to her gut. Had she really been so damn bitchy that a simple lovers' gesture had surprised him?

CHAPTER TEN

Tate left the recruiting office with a huge smile; she was so hiring Goth Girl. Paige might have come across as a bit on the weird side with all that metal and black paint on her face, but she was witty and perky, and they'd connected right away. She'd spice things up in the dining area and fit perfectly with Kelly and Tina. Not so much with Clint, but hell, with the way he was behaving and how sick and tired Tate was getting of it all, who knew how long he was going to be working for her?

Without letting that last thought mess with her current Zen mood, she started her car and began driving back to Rosita's, singing happily to the tunes on the radio. It was a nice morning, unseasonably sunny, and for some reason, her spirits were totally up. Maybe she'd pass by James's office and take him for some waffles, try a traditional breakfast that didn't include monkey sex and coffee being slurped from her belly button. At the mere thought of her lover, a warm, fuzzy feeling blossomed inside her, which didn't make sense; the way he'd been behaving lately, the only thing blossoming inside her should have been a helluva tantrum the size of Texas.

It'd been several days since James had installed the state-of-the-art security alarms up in her place and at the restaurant. She was no techie, but those were top-of-the-line babies, equipped with cameras, motion sensors, direct connection with the police—you name it. The whole shebang. Nowadays she felt safer than she would in Fort Knox. The panic button was installed in a cute wristwatch that she kept forgetting to wear, and for that she was taking too much shit from James.

He'd gone to the police and got some detective to come read the e-mails. He didn't make any promises but assured them he'd look into it, which, coming from the police in regard to a threat that may or may not become a reality, was damn impressive. James hadn't stopped there, though, and had Zack and Sean watching her when he couldn't. They hadn't come out and overtly acknowledged they were babysitting her, but really, what other reason would there be for them sticking around when James wasn't present? Even that scary dude, Jack Copeland, the owner of the biker bar, had been in Rosita's a couple of times. She'd confronted Zack and Sean, ordered them away, but they always came up with the most absurd excuses for being there. They were so easygoing and so sweet she couldn't stay mad with them; it felt like kicking puppies. Jack Copeland, on the other hand, intimidated the hell out of her. Not that he'd been disrespectful or said more than two words to her, for that matter, but the guy looked as intense and as focused as a damn Terminator fresh off the assembly line—he didn't need words to scare her. There was no way she was confronting him. Let him be in Rosita's as much as he wanted.

As far as she was concerned, James was blowing everything out of proportion, but he wouldn't listen to her complaints; he just smiled sweetly at her, fucked her senseless, and then continued to bulldoze her.

James was taking over, and Tate, too dazzled to oppose his advances, was letting him.

When he wasn't making love to her or purposely melting her into a goop of irrational happiness, he was driving her insane with his clever mix of male arrogance and sweet, grand gestures. She spent most of her time either rolling her eyes at him in exasperation or muttering curses, which, needless to say, had not the slightest effect on him. The guy had no shame when it came to getting his way.

In spite of everything—or maybe because of it—she was falling for him. Big-time. It really wasn't how attractive and how amazing a lover he was, which of course didn't hurt a bit, but also how cherished he made her feel, how damn happy she was with him around. How her life was better—richer—with him in it. She loved that he was always in Rosita's at closing time, helping her out. Absolutely loved the way Tim and the others had taken to him, and him to them.

He and his personality took up a lot of space, especially now that he'd taken out the big guns and gone all protective on her, but she liked "handling" him. And not only that, she was getting used to him and, horrors of all horrors, missed him horribly when he wasn't around, or when he couldn't sleep with her, which, in honor to the truth, was very rarely. He would drag his tired body from wherever he'd been working and come to her. And damn, she loved him for that too. Actually, she loved everything about the guy, bossiness and tattoos included. Yes, tattoos included. She'd often found herself mesmerized by the beautiful dragon on his arm and shoulder, tracing it with her fingers, with her mouth. She was pretty sure she'd shamelessly licked and nibbled each one of its shiny, sexy, gorgeously mouthwatering green scales. And the same went for the Oriental symbols on the left side of his abs. Frigging scary, really.

Her overall situation hadn't changed, it was as precarious as before, but since coming clean with James, she'd been feeling damn light-headed—happy and high. The same way religious grannies felt coming out of the confessionary: squeaky clean and light and liberated. Now she wasn't carrying the weight of Prince Charming's existence all on her own shoulders. The threat was still there, and the debts too, but they didn't feel so heavy anymore. Although she'd convinced herself those e-mails weren't his business and therefore not worth mentioning, the ugly truth was she'd dreaded telling him about it, afraid he'd bail on her. But that hadn't happened; if anything, opening up to him had the opposite effect. He was around even more than before.

While stopped at a red light, Tate looked through the window and suddenly realized where she was. Her breath caught in her throat, and adrenaline came rushing in. She hadn't realized her trip to the recruiting office would bring her through this neighborhood. Her first instinct was to floor it and run away, but she forced herself to stay calm and just clutched the steering wheel. She was stuck in traffic, that little sensible voice coming out of somewhere deep inside her head said to her, nowhere to run, at least not at this very second.

Time seemed to slow down, leaving her alone with her

thudding heart almost coming out her mouth and that voice of reason nagging at her, telling her that this was her chance. The lights must have changed because the car behind her honked loudly and angrily. She released the brake and cautiously pushed on the gas, not trusting herself. Maybe that voice was right; maybe this was a sign. For better or for worse, she was there. Could she deal with this now? Probably not, but what the heck, when had she been that close to this place anyway? What was the worst that could happen? Things were looking up; the restaurant was doing better, and she was feeling better, stronger—emboldened. Maybe now she could step into her childhood bedroom, roam through her childhood house.

Or maybe not.

Without allowing herself a second thought, she took the next turn and navigated through the labyrinth of suburban streets she knew so well. Her hands felt sweaty and shaky, clammy against the wheel. Her mind and body were so damn wired up all she could feel and hear was her heart thumping loudly inside her head. *Thump, thump, thump.*

Tate stopped in front of a two-story Victorian house. Her house.

The street was quiet. Everything seemed normal, life as usual. Yeah, right. Tate clenched her teeth and fought the anxiety tearing through her. Oh man, what the hell was she doing here? She'd avoided this place like the damn plague since her mom moved to Florida; hell, even before that. If her memory wasn't failing her, the last time she'd been home was for Dad and Jonah's funeral reception. With her mom's relocation to Eternal Sun, Tate had arranged a cleaning service to come once a month to keep the house spotless, but she'd gone to painfully great lengths to ensure she was never around when that happened. She'd always find something extremely important to do, like watching her chef, Nils, prepare tomato sauce. Luckily for her, Mrs. Copernicus took her neighborly duties very seriously, so it had been a piece of cake to talk her into watching those guys for her. Tate claimed she was too busy to come all the way from Rosita's to open the door for them. In reality, she was too terrified.

So for her to now be at 34 Bridge Lane, voluntarily, all by herself, and not running in the other direction like a possessed woman...pure madness, there was no other way to describe the situation. She'd finally jumped off the deep end. She knew she should split; yet there she was, having trouble breathing and thinking, but not leaving. Although that may have more to do with her muscles being frozen in place than with any cognitive decision on her part.

Shit, this was all James's fault; his presence in her life and that exhilarating feeling he brought along had got her believing she could handle anything, and look at her now, tricked by her endorphin-cooked mind into coming here to shoot herself in her foot.

She breathed out, anxiety and dread and a tiny bit of hope warring inside her. "What am I doing here?" she mumbled to herself, her voice barely making it through the knot in her throat. She reached up, repeatedly pulling at the neckline of her pullover. It was too tight, dammit! She wasn't getting enough air.

She couldn't do this, no way. Going in there was the same as committing emotional suicide. Okay, so what if she was there? She didn't need to do a damn thing or get out of her car, for that matter; she'd sit there for a while, get her shit together, and then go back to Rosita's. Yes, that was the smart thing to do: collect herself, turn the ignition on, and be on her merry way. Then she looked at the front lawn, the lawn that Jonah used to take care of, the same one that Mr. Copernicus now kept trimmed and neat, and *kaboom*, she lost it. Her hands moved on their own, and suddenly the door of the car was open and she was stepping out. Although her brain wasn't ready for this, her body refused to respond to the red flags and kept lunging forward, as if anxious for this standoff to be over. She looked at her actions in panic; she felt torn, as if there were two of her, the one lunging forward with complete disregard for her mental stability, and the one running after that wacko, trying unsuccessfully to grab her by the shirt and bring her to a halt. Her body had been hijacked.

This was crazy. She didn't want to be there, couldn't deal with it really. The closer she got to the house, the louder her breathing got, until she couldn't hear a thing besides her panting, adrenaline pumping so hard through her that her vision narrowed. This was going to do her in. Unable to put a stop to it, she saw her legs bringing her to the front door, her hands grabbing the key and opening the door.

The second she saw the familiar hallway and, from the corner of her eye, the living room, an avalanche of memories slammed at her, one triggering the other and another in a never-ending free fall of flesh-cutting memories, and she almost lost her stomach. Luckily she hadn't had breakfast yet. The pictures on the vanity in front of her didn't help a bit either. Mayday, Mayday! her mind screamed. Back off, get out of here. But her traitorous legs weren't obeying as they took a step forward.

This was a floodgate she shouldn't have opened. She was so going down.

James stepped out of the car, his gaze narrowing on Tate, who didn't see him, not even when he came to a halt in front of her.

She'd done the right thing calling him.

He'd been at the office with Zack when his cell rang. The caller ID hadn't recognized the number.

The person on the other end of the line was anxious as hell. "James?"

"Yes. Who is this?"

"Elle, Tate's sister. I got your number from your dad. Sorry to bother you, but I think something's very wrong with Tate."

James went on alert right away. "What do you mean?" He'd left her this morning still tucked in bed. There had been nothing wrong with Tate then.

"Mrs. Copernicus, our neighbor from Boston, called. Tate came by our parents' house today. She's been sitting on the stairs on the front porch for over an hour already. According to her, Tate didn't even sound articulate when she went to ask her what she was doing there. Sorry for bothering you, but I'm worried about her. She isn't answering her cell... If she's there alone, she's in deep trouble and...ah...I have no one else to call that could check on her. Your dad wasn't sure about giving me your number, but I threatened to unleash my mom on him, so he caved in. He said I could call you only in an emergency. I think this constitutes one."

"What's the address?" he asked, already shrugging on his

jacket. He wrote it down. Good, that wasn't too far away from his office.

"Thank you, I appreciate it. I wouldn't bother you, but—"

Bother? Was she joking? "I'm on my way."

And Elle had been right; this was a damn emergency. Tate was weirdly still and seemed disoriented, her swollen eyes glazed and nonresponsive, empty, set on something far away, as if she couldn't see anything around her. Why on earth had she come here alone? What for? And more important, why hadn't she called him?

This must have been a huge shock for her. James knew Tate hadn't processed the deaths of her dad and brother yet; she just walked around life, sidestepping over the huge void their deaths had left, careful not to get close to it so she wouldn't fall into that pit. She was a master at soldiering on. The family was in trouble, the situation demanded strength and restraint, and she'd stepped up to the plate. She could keep it up, not letting herself remember or feel, but the downside to this was, of course, that all the grief was kept locked inside without an outlet, itching to get out. At all costs, she had to avoid emotional land mines or risk falling victim to one. Her childhood home was the biggest land mine of all, and this time she hadn't kept clear of it.

It took a while, but finally Tate looked at him and actually saw him, as if waking up from a drunken slumber. She attempted to smile, but her lips started trembling and tears began rolling down her cheeks. She covered her face, hiding her mascara-smudged eyes from him. She'd been crying. A lot. Without a word, James lowered himself and sat beside her on the stairs, enveloping her in his arms.

"Hi," he whispered.

She just shook her head, her hands still hiding her face, her shoulders shaking, clearly unable to talk.

They sat there in silence for a good ten minutes. Her body was cold to the touch, so he scooped her up in his arms and surrounded her with his heat.

"What happened?" he finally asked.

She took a while to react. As he repeated the question, she turned to him and, looking resigned, lifted her shoulders.

"Talk to me, babe. Did you go in alone?"

She nodded, wiping the tears with the back of her hand. "I wanted to take you out to breakfast. Waffles. On my way to you, I realized how close I was to this place. I was stupid…thought I could come here." She shook her head, tears flooding her eyes again, her voice broken. "I must've been out of my mind. I didn't make it to the second floor. Couldn't breathe in there."

Yeah, well, by the looks of her, she couldn't breathe out here either. "Do you want to talk about it?"

She shook her head vigorously.

Okay, fine. They'd discuss this later. "What are you doing sitting here?"

She shrugged again. "Don't know. I…didn't think… I wasn't sure how to get to Rosita's. I'm a bit…upset."

No shit.

"Are you ready to leave now, princess?"

She nodded and clung tight to him, encircling his neck with her arms while he stood up.

"Yes, please, take me home," she whispered.

He carried her to the car, tears still running down her cheeks. She wasn't ready yet to take the trip down memory lane, and, he wasn't going to be the one forcing her to. But he hated seeing her like this, so broken, her spirits so down. She looked…lost—grief-stricken.

"Come on, Tate, didn't you say you were taking me to breakfast? What about my waffles? I know of a quiet place, won't be too many people at this time of day. Let's go there; we'll talk."

"I said home," she snapped back at him, the words full of fury. "You go eat your damn waffles by yourself if you want to."

She'd come out of her stupor, and anger and conflicting emotions were raging inside her. He wouldn't put it past her to ditch him and get a cab, she was that independent, and that upset, so he just kept his mouth shut and got her into his car.

She didn't say a word on the whole way back, those damn silent tears running down her cheeks nonstop, knotting his gut and making him feel useless.

As soon as they got back to the apartment, she went straight to bed and mumbled something about him being free to go. Yeah right, like that was going to happen anytime soon. He called Zack and Sean, arranged for them to pick up her car from Bridge Lane, contacted Elle to let her known everything was okay and then laid down and spooned her. She was still crying, curled there on one side of that big bed.

"Everything's going to be fine, Tate. I'm here," he whispered to her, but she didn't answer and moved to disentangle herself from him. No way was she keeping him at arm's length. He just tightened his hold on her, and she gave up. She might think she didn't need or want his comfort, but she was damn well getting it.

He rocked her. At some point, she dozed off, but not even then did she stop crying. Now that she wasn't consciously repressing it, the sobs tore free from her chest. It was breaking his heart; those broken sobs were killing him as surely as the silent tears before them had. He whispered to her, trying to soothe her in her sleep. Thank God she seemed to respond to him, and little by little, she settled down.

They spent all day there, him hugging her, Tate dozing off and on. At one point, he felt self-conscious at being so pushy. Maybe he was intruding in her grief.

He loosened his grip on her. "I better go..." he said, releasing her waist.

She turned around, the force of that sudden movement sending him onto his back, and grabbed him by his chest, plastered herself on him. "Please, don't go," she whispered, squeezing him hard. "Please don't leave me."

She then blushed, as if ashamed of her admission, but he wouldn't let her take it back. He squeezed her back and nuzzled the top of her head. "I won't."

It took a while for her to relax again, but she did.

Poor little thing, she was so precious to him, so frail and so strong at the same time. There was no way in hell he was going to let anybody terrorize her. There was nothing he could do about her dad and her brother's deaths, apart from being there for her, but hell if he was going to let this fucking Prince Charming mess with her. James had spent quite a lot of time on those e-mails, which despite Tate's claims to the contrary were much more than a spam problem. The first ones mainly concentrated on threatening the restaurant. The creep wanted the place sold out, but the latest ones were more directed toward her. He guessed Prince Charming was getting impatient, and that was usually bad news; it meant the one being stalked was running out of time.

He'd get this straightened out. That fucker's days were numbered. Jack was on board, and the man had more contacts than anyone had a right to have. One of Jack's friends, a damn good computer expert, had agreed to check out the e-mails, and if anyone could find the sender, it was him.

As 95 percent of stalkers were somebody known by the victim, they were concentrating on Tate's closest circle of friends and employees. Ex-boyfriends were always a good place to start, so they had put a tail on Aidan, but so far they hadn't uncovered anything suspicious—the guy did nothing but work and attend business brunches. Pity, he'd have loved to smack the shit out of the arrogant fuckface, but even James had to recognize the asshole ex-boyfriend scenario worked much better when he hadn't been the one doing the dumping.

They had gone to see Old Vito's owner to feel the waters a little, and Tate had been right. He wasn't the kind to stalk anyone with e-mails; the suppliers' trick was more his style. What Tate didn't know was that Vito's son Andrew was stepping in, and he and his goons were computer savvy and therefore more than capable of trying new tricks. Although in the sense that they could break all your bones or set your place on fire, they really were old school. Besides, according to Jack, Andrew Vito ran several shady gambling operations, and surprise, surprise, Clint owed one of his bookies several grand. It must really suck to be an unlucky gambler on top of being an asshole. James had run a background check on Clint some time ago and wasn't surprised to find he'd been arrested several times for drunk and disorderly conduct and for getting too intense on people and situations. He, with his list of mandatory anger-management courses ordered by the judge and his debts, would be a perfect candidate for Vito to use to run Tate out. After all, with no signs of breaking and entering, the fire had to be an inside job.

James spent hours in bed with Tate. They spoke little. By

the afternoon, Tate was not asleep anymore but idly caressed his chest.

"I heard you before on the phone."

"I sent Zack to pick up your car."

Her face blushed a sexy shade of pink. "Yeah, well, about that... Sorry. Again. I seem to have a nasty habit of breaking down around you," she said, shifting a bit uncomfortably. She was so proud, meltdowns in front of anyone were a damn hard pill to swallow. "I'm not really a crier."

James hugged her tightly, tucking her head under his chin. He was as freaked out by women's tears as the next man, but if she were to heal anytime soon, she had to unload all that grief choking her.

"How long is this going to hurt, James?"

"I don't know, princess. For a while. For a long while, but it will get better with time, I promise. The day will come when you'll be able to think about them without being sad."

He knew it was going to take time; she'd been left all alone, no safety net to catch her and help her. He'd had Max and Cole and his dad and Aunt Maggie when his mother had bailed; he'd been protected and cherished, surrounded by people who loved and cared for him, but even then he'd dealt with some abandonment issues those first years. Tate had been abandoned in a more dramatic way, left all of a sudden to fend for herself without any support. Not only were her dad and brother gone, but the rest of her family as well. This wasn't going to blow away overnight, or anytime soon for that matter.

"I avoid thinking about Jonah and Dad so systematically I'm afraid I'll forget them," she whispered.

"That won't happen, baby. You may not see it that way now, but it's good that you were there today. Next time it'll be easier, you'll see. And I could go with you if you want."

"I'd like that." She was quiet for a while, her finger idly caressing his chest. "You know, Jonah would be outraged to have Nils in his kitchen." She quietly laughed. "They'd butt heads, those two, for sure. Jonah was very laid back in other aspects, but he used to run his kitchen like a drill sergeant, while Nils thrives in dramatic chaos. Working with him is like being immersed in an opera. My father would have loved it. He'd have been appalled at the way Clint's behaving, though. And pissed at me for allowing it."

James's teeth clenched at the sound of that name. He was aching to tell her everything he knew about Clint, but it was too early, and they had nothing definitive that would tie him to Prince Charming. "You need to deal with Clint; you know that, don't you?"

She nodded.

He could easily enough deal with Clint, break all his teeth, and fire his sorry ass, but it was Tate who had to do that, at least the firing part. If he was the one sending the e-mails, though, or the one working behind the scene to run Tate out, James was going to do more than just break his teeth. He was going to obliterate him.

"I know Clint needs a wake-up call; his attitude frankly sucks. I just hoped it wouldn't come to that. Anyway, enough about that. It looks like I ruined your day."

He smiled. "Nope. Instead of working at the office, I spent all day in bed with you. What more could I want?"

She snorted. "Yeah right, like it must've been so fun to witness my crying jag."

He shrugged. "You go ahead and cry. I can deal with it." He didn't want her hurting, but going to her parents' house was something long overdue. And no matter how much she hated it, she needed to cry too.

"Well, thank you, but I think I'm done." Her eyes suddenly narrowed on him. "By the way, how did you know to come for me?"

"Elle called me." At her frown, he explained, "Mrs. Copernicus called her and she got my number from my dad."

Tate groaned. "Oh God."

"Yeah." He smiled. "Elle said she threatened him with unleashing your mom on him if he didn't give up my number."

Tate leaned her forehead on his chest. "Oh no, your dad has to be horrified. The three Cooper women in all their crazy neediness are falling upon his family; my mom stalks his cat, and Elle stalks him so that the Cooper woman left in Boston can ruin your life. What a disgrace!"

He chuckled. "Nils is not the drama queen here; you are." He reached for her face, lifting it to him and gazed lovingly at her. Her eyes were a bit red and swollen, her cheeks blotchy and her lips too. She was just breathtaking. For the longest moment, he just looked at her.

"A penny for your thoughts," she whispered.

"Do you really want to know what I'm thinking?"

She looked at him expectantly.

She was so beautiful, and he was so madly in love with her. Scared shitless to tell her too. So he did what any self-respecting man would: let his glands talk. "I want to fill you up with my cum."

She chuckled and reached down. "Is this your suave way to tell me you want a blowjob?"

He shook his head. He loved coming in her mouth, but that wasn't what he meant. "I want to take you bareback and come in you. I don't want any more condoms between us." It was something that hadn't bothered him before with any other girl. Now it did.

She froze, propped herself on her elbows, and looked at him, baffled. "I'm not baby-proofed, James. We can't risk it. I can't risk it. What if I get pregnant?"

"What about it?" he said. It was a slip of tongue that shocked the shit out of the girl and himself. What the fuck was he saying?

"What do you mean, what about it?" she shrieked, trying to push him away. He didn't budge, his hands clasped around her in a tight embrace. "This isn't the best of moments for me; my life is a wreck. A baby would sink me."

She was right. Of course she was right. He was an inconsiderate asshole. Still. "Sorry, princess. I don't want you unprotected, but I need to come in you more than I need my next breath."

She studied him for a second and then glanced around, shifting a tad uncomfortably. "I don't believe I'm going to say this. I was on the pill when I was with Aidan, but afterward...well, it felt kind of pointless, so I dropped them. I have a…um…diaphragm. I've never used it, but it's here somewhere. If you're serious about this, then—"

"Yes," he said with a rumble. "Go get it."

"Wait a minute, what do you mean go get it? We need to talk about this," she said, sounding outraged. "If we're going to start having unprotected sex, we need to agree about—"

"Yes. Sure."

"Yes? What do you mean yes? Yes to what?"

"Yes to all those questions you're about to ask me."

"Oh you're such an obnoxious smart-ass. Which questions might those be?"

He tilted her chin up and looked her in the eye. This was important, so she had to get the point. "Yes, I definitely want us to be exclusive. Yes, I want to have unprotected sex with you. Yes, you're mine. Yes, I won't have sex with anybody else. Hell yes, you won't have sex with anyone but me. Yes, I understand what all this means and the responsibility that entails. Yes, this brings our relationship to a new stage; we are a couple—not that we weren't before, but now even you will have to recognize it. And yes, I can't wait for it. Go. Get the thing in place," he said, shooing her out of the bed.

The breath whooshed out of her. She seemed too stunned for a comeback, too stunned even to move; she just looked incredulously at him while a nervous laugh bubbled up in her throat.

"Do you need help?" he said, rising to his feet and reaching for her. That snapped her out of her trance.

"Nope. Stay here," she said as she disappeared into the tiny bathroom.

He began undressing. He was dying to get her into his place. Into his bed, into his hot tub. Into his life, brothers, friends, and nosy neighbors included. But she was more comfortable in her territory, he knew. She'd start getting skittish if he forced her into accepting all he was going to give her, because there was no doubt in his mind he was keeping this woman. Nevertheless he understood the need to tread carefully; she looked so lost, she'd freak out if he told her he loved her. He himself was quite freaked out about it; he wasn't sure when he'd fallen in love with her, but it was a reality. His reality. She, on the other hand, was too scared to let herself love anyone, too frightened it'd be taken away from her. She definitely wouldn't react well to him loving her. And wasn't that a bitch? Because he wasn't sure how long he could keep it inside.

He began prowling the floor, butt naked and primed. Damn, she was taking too long. Thank God her tiny bathroom had no window, because he wouldn't put it past her to jump out and ditch him.

"Do you want me to come in and help?" he said toward the door.

He heard her harrumphing. "Stop bugging me. And get away from the door, you sex-crazed slug!"

There she had him. He was so hard he could barely think. Shaking his head, he went to sit on a chair. Man, he had it bad. He was getting way too easy; even her scorns made him hard.

"I must be mad for even considering this," she muttered as she left the bathroom naked, wrapped up in a towel. She looked at him and flushed. "This is embarrassing," she complained. "The moment's gone. Now what?"

The moment gone? In her dreams.

"Look at me, baby. Nothing's gone. It's burning brighter. Come here, let me get you in the mood."

"So you know, this is risky, mister. I don't have any experience putting diaphragms in. I may not have placed this thing properly, and at any second it could come down on you."

Laughter tore from him. "Okay, I'll be on the lookout for it. If we hear a plop, we're on red alert."

She rolled her eyes at him. "James..."

He placed his finger over her lips, silencing her. "I answered yes to all your questions, remember? Do we need to stop and have some more? Because I'm willing, but the answer is still the same. Yes to all of them."

She shook her head and let him drag her over until she stood between his thighs. She didn't flinch when he pulled the towel she'd wrapped herself in free, and then let out a low moan as he tugged at one of her nipples with his teeth.

"Ah, this is unfair. I can't stay mad at you when you do this."

"I know, princess. I know how much you like my mouth on your nipples, my tongue and my teeth abrading those tender tips." And then he proceeded to demonstrate.

"Oh God..." she said with a raspy breath as her hands sank into his hair, keeping him there.

After a short while, she was rolling her hips against him.

"Are you ready for me now, sweetheart?" He caressed her swollen folds, rubbed her ring, and probed at her entrance.

She nodded, turned around, bent over the nearby sofa, and presented him with her gorgeous behind. His mouth went dry, and his tongue stuck to the roof. He wanted her so much. He could just grab her by her hips and thrust in, claim her fast and furious to calm the raging need from deep inside his gut. But no, he had to rein in his instincts; this was too important.

"No way, princess," he admonished her and dragged her to sit on his lap.

She turned her face to him, perplexed. "But you love it from behind."

He ignored her and looked intently into the mirrored closet door in front of them. "Open your legs for me."

She turned to where his eyes were fixed and blushed. Nevertheless she obeyed him.

"Look into the mirror, baby; you're so beautiful," he whispered into her ear while he slid his hands over to her exposed core. "I love how your pussy looks when you're aroused, all red and puffy and glistening. How the gold of the piercing shines against your clit and your bare folds. It's so fucking pretty. Look at it, baby," he said while opening her core with his fingers. She was breathing hard. "Your clit is throbbing, princess. And so are you." He brushed the hard nub with his thumb, and she almost jumped from his lap.

"James, please, don't tease."

He tenderly caressed her slit and felt her legs tense further.

"Look at all this pussy juice dripping from you. You want me inside you, don't you? Yes, baby, just like that," he said as he slid one finger in and felt her walls clamp on it. "This is better, right? Watch how your pussy sucks greedily at me. You're such a greedy little thing."

"More," she whispered, and he slid another finger inside. She arched against him, her ass wickedly grinding against his cock. He watched in the mirror. He'd love to make her come this way before taking her, but he couldn't wait.

He removed his fingers from her core, and she whimpered. "Turn around and mount me."

"But you love it from behind." She repeated her earlier words, her eyes never leaving the mirror.

He turned her to face him. "Yes, but in this case, you want it too so that you can emotionally distance yourself from this, from us, and I won't allow it. The first time I come inside you, it will be with me looking into those wolf eyes of yours. We're going to make love face-to-face, where I can see the orgasm raising in your eyes as my seed claims you."

She snorted. "There's no claiming to be made, James. This is just sex."

She sat astride him while he pressed the tip of his cock against her hot lips, gliding it up and down through them, spreading her lube on himself.

"Keep saying that to yourself, princess," he said with a growl as he entered her. "You're fooling no one—not me and not you."

She was so wrong; this wasn't just sex, it wasn't even making love, it went beyond any of that. This was...soul mating; this was looking straight into Tate's eyes and getting lost in her, in her shudders, in her little moans. Every one of her gasps brought him higher, every glance from her heavy-lidded, smoky eyes made him pulse in need. She belonged to him, in his arms. Her body and her mind were so tuned to his that he wasn't sure where hers ended and his began. And by the looks of her and the way she trembled in his arms, she was feeling it too.

"James, this...us...is getting out of hand," she whispered in a barely audible voice, her little nails sinking into him, her body pulsing against him.

He fought a sigh of relief and a satisfied smile. "Why? Because I'm fucking you without a condom?"

She shook her head, her eyes never leaving his. She looked lost. As if she'd just realized the enormity of their connection. "It's not only that."

Finally, she noticed. "I know, babe, I know."

She was so hot and so tight, his whole body was throbbing so badly he was about to lose his mind. Unable to say a word, he just looked at her in awe as she tensed on top of him, threw her head backward, and, hugging him tighter than ever, went over. Fire was racing through his veins, burning him up, and the second her sweet pussy began clenching around him, the wave gathering in his balls overtook him. Furious jets of cum burst from him with such strength it felt like his head exploded.

After they came down, she rose slowly from him, and then she stopped, her pussy lips poised on the tip of his dick, kissing it, their contact barely there. Foreheads touching, they both looked down. Suddenly he felt how his crown was being bathed in something fiery hot. Fuck, his cum and her lube were trickling down her pussy and falling down onto his cock. It felt so intimate and so right. So damn hot. Just like that, he was ready to have her again.

FUCK, THE WHORE was mounting him, riding him as if he were a pony. Look at her, all wild and horny, opening her legs for that filth. Parading herself and offering him her ass. Inviting him to fuck her brains out. How dare she! He was much better than that asshole, had certainly been around longer, yet she continued to ignore him. And his messages.

She was clearly not taking him seriously, going about as if his warnings were nothing. Damn bitch, she was going to pay for this. For all of it. He was deeper in shit all the time because of her, because of her stubbornness. He wanted retribution. He'd given her enough opportunities to correct her ways, to listen to reason; now she was going to see what he was capable of.

CHAPTER ELEVEN

Watching James get ready in the mornings was a treat in itself.

Tate used to be a morning person, once upon a time, when she worked as a corporate secretary. She'd wake up two hours ahead of schedule to have time for a run, some tai chi to level her energy flux, a shower, and a leisurely breakfast reading the paper. Since stepping in to manage Rosita's, she invariably went to bed around two o'clock, and mornings were not such a fancy affair anymore. Mainly they consisted of her cracking an eye, cursing a blue streak, turning away from the window, and throwing the blanket over her head. These days, though, with James prowling around her apartment almost buck naked, fresh and wet from the shower, she had started seeing the appeal of mornings once again.

"Good morning, princess." He strode to her side and kissed her. "Sorry I woke you."

"Don't be. I like watching you in the mornings."

She knew he tried to be quiet, but his absence in her bed was a dead giveaway, so she'd wake up and follow him with her gaze. Normally Tate couldn't get away with more than three or four peeks before he'd notice. It was amazing how natural it felt having him around at all times, mornings included. She'd offered him a drawer, and little by little, he'd taken over. It wasn't that he'd brought a lot of things in, because he didn't, but his scent was all over the place and everywhere she looked, there was a reminder of James.

"What's today's plan?" he asked, nuzzling her throat.

She shrugged. "No plan. I'll sleep late, then go down to the restaurant to wait for the suppliers. Paige starts today, so I have to be there earlier in the evening to show her around."

"Mmm," he answered as his tongue flicked over her jaw.

"And Elle will be here tomorrow. To check you out mainly, I think." Since finding out about her involvement with James, she'd been calling Tate quite regularly. Fretting, Elle wouldn't say, but Tate figured her sis was worried about her. Nice turn of events.

"Good, finally I get to meet her in person," he said. "And don't worry, I'll warn all my tattooed, low-life buddies to stay away."

She smiled. "You'd better."

"Are we happy about it?" he asked, studying her.

She shrugged again, unable to sustain the smile on her face.

"If she gets her butt in Rosita's, then yes, we are. If not, it will just piss me off more." The truth was Elle's visits always left her sad and empty, especially since she wouldn't come to the restaurant.

"She'll come to Rosita's."

"How can you be so sure?"

"You say she's coming to check me out, right? Then she'll have to come to the restaurant because that's where I'll be."

She was going to say how much she appreciated all that he did for her, but James stopped her by placing his thumb on her lips and just smiled. It was such an easy, sexy smile that shudders raked over her body.

He lowered his mouth to hers, his tongue licking at her lips and then taking possession of her mouth with a tenderness that almost brought tears to her eyes. With a single word or a gesture, he made her feel so much it was damn scary. As his tongue invaded her, she encircled his neck with her arms and dragged him closer to her. "I got to go, baby," he mildly complained, but he just tightened his embrace, his thigh opening her legs, his lower body pressing against hers.

"And waste this wonderful morning wood?"

His quiet laughter rumbled through her. "So that's the reason you wake up every morning, no matter how quiet I am, huh? In hopes of abusing me?"

"What can I say? You look mouthwatering coming out of the shower all wet and slippery and with such a fine morning hard-on. Who could blame me?"

James's cell began buzzing, and he groaned in displeasure, leaning his forehead on hers. "Oh hell, I have to go, love. Zack is going to have a cow if I don't."

Reluctantly he got up and began dressing. His impressive morning hard-on had gotten even more impressive, and he winced while tucking himself inside the jeans. "Will you come by today to take me out to lunch? I very much enjoyed it when you came the other day."

Yeah, she bet he had. A couple of days ago she'd decided to make up for not getting to take him to eat waffles that day she ended up at her parents' place, so she passed by his office to take him out for lunch, or so she'd intended. James had dragged her to his office, turned the lock on the door, and proceeded to fuck the hell out of her on his desk. His secretary fantasy, he'd informed her as he'd pushed her skirt up, propped her on the table, and began licking and probing between her thighs.

It was so naughty that she'd had to fight not to come at his first lick. They were alone in the whole office, but at any second, anyone could have come in and come knocking at their door. Luckily no one had caught them. That possibility, though, had made her come explosively.

"*You don't have a secretary, right?*" she'd asked suspiciously afterward.

"*No.*"

"*Good. Don't even think about getting one,*" she warned him. "*I won't like it.*"

He'd chuckled, tipped her chin and gazed into her eyes. "*You don't have to worry; I won't.*"

After an hour, they'd left his office, her as limp as a noodle, her stomach empty, sure, but satisfied in the extreme. She was so limp and pleased that when on their way out she saw Zack and Tim carrying some boxes in, she couldn't find it in her to kick up a fuss for James hiring him. She narrowed her eyes on James, but he just shrugged.

"He's a great kid. I had to hire him. It was that or kick his lying butt every time he missed work in Rosita's, and you wouldn't want me manhandling your staff, would you? Besides, he is talented, and he can do better than sit around fixing up broken old computers."

Tate had harrumphed and let it go, mainly because her throat had swollen shut. If she attempted to talk, she'd have made a mess of herself and her feelings. She'd known Tim had been working at Technogeeks; what she hadn't known was that James had known too. Damn the guy, she liked him even when he was being arrogant and meddling.

Snapping out of her reverie, Cassie watched him get dressed. "Maybe I'll come take you out to lunch," she said. My, what was so sexy about a barefoot, naked man in jeans? It made her mouth water. "Although you shouldn't get used to getting your way that easily."

He chuckled. "Easy? I wouldn't call you easy. You're as difficult and complicated as they come, sweetheart."

As he grabbed his jacket from the sofa, something fell to the floor with a loud thud. A black velvet box.

Tate froze. If that was what it seemed, she was going to have a panic attack.

He saw that Tate's eyes were glued to the little box. He picked it up, and then rubbed the back of his neck. "Shit. I wanted to give it to you tonight, not now in a hurry. I guess there's no chance you'll wait until then, right?"

Was he kidding? "What is it?" Her panic must have been written all over her face, for he laughed.

"Breathe, Tate, breathe; you're going to pass out at this rate. It isn't what it looks like. Open it. If you don't like it, we can change it."

With shaky fingers, she opened it. Inside the box, there was a beautiful golden ring, a captive bead ring with a teardrop, and hanging from it was a gorgeous emerald stone. It was a clitoral piercing, dangle included.

"I thought that would look fantastic on you. The green of the emerald on your fair skin, dangling over those flushed pussy lips of yours. Nuzzling at it while I lick you is going to be heart-stopping. I can't wait to play with it."

As her mind conjured the scene, her womb convulsed and her clit throbbed. Jesus, the things he could do to her with just one word.

"Thanks, James. This is gorgeous." She was going to get an appointment in the beauty salon where she'd got the piercing and ask them to change the rings.

"You don't need any pussy piercing to hold my attention, princess, but if you insist on wearing one, it's going to be mine, not something you got to entice other guys." He kissed her and, with a wink, left.

She grazed that little piece of jewelry with her fingertips. Cute gesture, she thought, nothing more.

Why then did it feel as bonding as an engagement ring? And furthermore, why on earth couldn't she wait to put it on?

She knew the whole damn place smelled like a bakery but didn't care. The second James stepped in, he frowned. Clever boy.

"What's up?" James asked, hugging her from behind. For some weird reason, when Tate got really pissed, the only thing that seemed to calm her down was baking. By now, he knew her well enough not to ask how come there were more than six pies on the counter.

"I fired Clint," she muttered. "He was being a complete ass, as always. Sneering, undermining me, bullying the girls, and I finally had enough, so I took him into the kitchen, called him on it, and things got out of hand."

He tensed behind her. "Got out of hand, how?"

Noticing his sudden tension, she let out a snort. "No, nothing like that." She didn't doubt for a second James would mop the floor with him if he dared to do as much as touch her. Or scream at her, which of course he'd done, not that she was going to say anything to James. She could deal with her own disasters, or her own screaming matches, as was the case. "I ordered him to take a couple of days to cool off and not bother to come back without a complete attitude adjustment, and do you know what the asshole said to me? He said I'd be the same incompetent person in two days. That I was a stupid bitch, and he was tired of putting up with me. *He* was tired of putting up with me! Can you believe it? So I fired him."

"And?"

She snorted. "I feel great, obviously; can't you tell?"

"So why the pies?"

"I'm pissed at myself. I should've fired him months ago." How she'd been such a moron for such a long time when it came to the restaurant and especially to Clint annoyed her. She was the boss, and she was in charge, dammit! Enough of stupid sentimentalisms and second-guessing herself. From now on, it was her way or no way at all.

"Good for you," he whispered. "I knew sooner or later you'd get around to it. And it wasn't too late; I wouldn't have let it come to that. I would've intervened first. So don't worry, baby, you were just a bit behind schedule."

She frowned reprovingly at him, but it didn't have any effect on him; he just grinned and kissed the side of her neck. He knew she couldn't resist him, never mind how outrageous his words or behavior got. It put her at such a disadvantage.

"What are you doing?" He looked over her shoulders to the job applications in front of her. "Are you hiring someone?"

She nodded. "It's getting too busy to be understaffed. I already contacted a couple of interesting prospects. They're coming for interviews the day after tomorrow."

"Great. How was the new waitress, by the way? Is she still around or did Clint manage to scare her away?"

At that very moment, Paige came out of the kitchen, and as she approached them, she signaled to the pies on the counter. "What do you want me to do with those?"

It was time to take them to the kitchen; there were only a handful of diners left anyway. "Take a couple in, and I'll bring the rest myself. Paige, this is James. James, Paige, the new waitress."

"Nice to meet you, Paige," he greeted her.

She nodded, took one pie in each hand, and walked away and into the kitchen.

"So that's the new girl you hired?" James said, turning his amused gaze to Tate. "A Goth girl full of facial piercings and a two-inch leather choke collar around her neck?" Tate nodded. "In an Italian restaurant?"

"She's great. I like her. She's...colorful."

"Colorful? Tate, my love, she's dressed all in black. Even her lipstick is black."

She rolled her eyes at him. "You know what I mean. She's fine. And she makes one mean mojito."

"And that's relevant in an Italian restaurant?"

"Very. Fusion is in, haven't you heard?"

His shoulders shook with laughter, and he turned her in his arms, kissing her, a devastating kiss that left her dazzled and itching for more. "You taste so good, princess. I missed you today."

Sure she tasted good; she'd been sampling all her creations. Maybe it wasn't all the baking that relaxed her but all the extra sugar she wolfed down while she was at it.

"Me too. I couldn't come by; I've been in here the whole day. The suppliers brought some new samples, and Nils got inspired. We tried a couple of new dishes; there's still some left if you want to try. Go ask Tim; they must already be tidying up." There were only two tables occupied, and desserts had already been served. It looked like she and her staff were almost done for the night.

"Great, I'm starving. Coming?"

"In a sec. You go ahead."

He kissed her. "Okay, babe."

As he turned toward the kitchen, three women came in.

She wasn't expecting any more diners at this late hour, so when they headed for the cigarette vending machine, she wasn't surprised. She almost dropped dead, though, when the tits on a stick platinum blonde dressed in a tight business suit made a beeline for James and threw herself into his arms. James stepped back, caught off guard, his hands at his sides, not embracing her. It didn't seem to matter to her. She perched herself on him and went on her tiptoes to kiss him, but before her lips touched his, he swiftly grabbed her arms and broke the embrace, putting distance between them.

Oh God! Tate's legs buckled, and she had to grab the counter not to find herself on her ass. She was too far away to hear what they were saying, but the blonde was evidently flirting, her wandering hands tracing his chest, her wanton fingers playing with the buttons of his shirt. He stilled her hands several times, said something to her, and pulled them away from his chest. She just laughed and continued at the first opportunity.

"Tate," he said, walking toward her, tits on a stick on his heels. "This is Faith, a friend."

Faith threw him an amused look. "A friend? Is that what it's called nowadays?" Then she turned to Tate and to her friends near the vending machine and explained, "James is just being discreet; we screw each others' brains out every time we get together."

Fortunately Tate hadn't been holding anything, because it would have slipped from her hands. She felt as if she'd been run over by a tank. At this rate, not even her grabbing the counter with teeth and nails was going to prevent her ass from having a close encounter with the floor.

"We haven't seen each other in several months," James hurried to explain, his alarmed gaze intent on Tate. "Faith, this is Tate, my girlfriend. We are together."

"Together?" She looked astonished, turned her gaze to Tate in poorly masked disdain, and then laughed as if James had told the funniest of jokes. "James, James, you almost had me fooled." She slapped at his chest. James gave her a hard stare, and her smile faltered. "Are you serious?" Faith's mouth gaped, seeming genuinely confused. "But you don't have 'girlfriends.'"

"I do now."

She closed her mouth and narrowed her gaze on Tate like she was reassessing the situation. She must have come to the conclusion that she was no threat. "Really? Oops, sorry for that," she said while ironing James's pec. He took her hand and moved it away.

Faith plastered a seductive smile on her silicone-enhanced lips and turned her back on Tate. "Oh well, never mind, how have you been; how's everything?" She continued her chattering and her aggressive flirting, throwing herself at him like there was no tomorrow.

James answered her questions curtly, keeping his distance every time Faith moved to touch him, looking annoyed by her advances. That didn't derail her. Tits on a Stick was set on a course of action and wasn't ready to give up yet.

This was so great, the perfect ending to Tate's wonderful day. She did her best to ignore the scene, but she was so pissed that when the people from one of the tables left she could barely hold a smile for them. She was seeing red. What was she, a wallflower? She didn't need to see that. What she needed was a smoke, badly. Borrowing one from Tina, she marched to the front door. The last thing she wanted was to be in the same closed space with Tits on a Stick here, or she might end up throwing the rest of the pies at her.

James's first instinct was to go after Tate, but he forced himself to stay still. He should give her a couple of minutes to calm down. He knew she was pissed; he'd seen her muttering to herself while Faith had been talking to him. Although talking might not be the right word; fondling would be more accurate. Even after he'd told her he couldn't see her anymore, she'd kept flirting. The aggressiveness that he'd liked so much about her now made his skin crawl. Faith was gorgeous, no two ways about it, but she did nothing for him; her beauty bounced off him. He didn't want anyone but Tate touching him. And if her reaction was anything to go by, she agreed with that. And damn if that didn't fill him with satisfaction. But he was a wise man, so on his way out, he tried to stifle his emerging smile.

James found her outside, a few feet from the front door, no jacket, in the cold, smoking of all things. He leaned against the wall and crossed his arms. "What are you doing?"

She looked at him belligerently. "Smoking of course."

"You don't smoke, princess."

"I do sometimes," she said. "You don't know me as well as you think you do."

James took the cigarette and, despite her protests, put it out. "You're upset."

"Really? What was your first clue?" She glared at him, her arms crossed over her breasts.

"And you're jealous."

Tate shrugged. "Maybe."

Grinning like a damn fool, James cupped her face and brought his mouth down to her. He wasn't alone in this; she was as affected by him as he was by her. He ate at her mouth, licking and nibbling her lips, and when she opened for him, his tongue thrust into her in a wet caress, stroking her teeth and every corner of her mouth. He didn't release her until they were both panting.

"Listen to me. You don't need to be jealous, princess. Faith and I used to see each other sporadically—strictly physical. I haven't seen her since I met you. There's no reason to feel threatened by her. I won't see her again."

Tate snorted. "I don't think she got the memo the way she felt you up."

"Believe me, I made sure she got it. Loud and clear."

The second Tate had stepped outside, Faith had gotten even more daring, trying to perch herself on him to the point where he'd forsaken all formalities, had grabbed her by her upper arms, and jerked her away from him. He'd told her it was enough, that she was making a scene and was not only embarrassing herself but also disrespecting Tate, which he wouldn't tolerate. Faith had looked at him as if he'd lost his mind, but fortunately that went a long way to getting her to leave fast.

"You don't have to go out of your way for me." She waved at him. "You're free to pursue your little flings with whomever you want, pushy, heavily stacked, bottle blondes included. Just count me out."

James tipped her face up, holding her gaze. "No, I am not, and neither are you, sweetheart."

Unable to stop himself, he took her mouth again, one of his hands on the back of her head, the other pressing her against him. The way she trembled against him and held tight while they kissed got him every damn time; he could kiss her for hours and never get tired. Although he was pretty much the aggressor again, she also did her share of possessive kissing, and he loved it. When they reemerged, her lips were red and swollen and she was breathing hard.

"And just for the record, sweetheart, I know you very well, better than you might think. Better than you'd probably like. You aren't pissed at Faith. You're pissed at yourself because you don't want to care about me, yet you do, and that scares you."

She lowered her eyes. "I didn't like her touching you," she confessed. "It surprised me how much I didn't like it. I hated it, actually."

He smiled. "That's good, baby." More than good; this was the first time Tate was staking a claim on him. "I didn't like it either. Come on, it's freezing out here. Let's go inside."

She went along but let go of his hand as they reached the cash register. The last diners had already left; she had to take care of cash box closing. "Give me five minutes. Go tell Tim we'll need some food."

"You got it."

As he entered the kitchen, James saw Nils, Kelly, and Tim already preparing supper. His stomach rumbled. He'd been busy the whole day, consulting for one of their new clients, and then he'd been with Jack. It turned out the e-mails had been sent from different IP addresses, untraceable ones, although there were several that repeated. Internet cafés. That wasn't much, but it was a start. They could watch those and see who showed up. Between one thing and the other, he'd forgotten to eat.

"Just in time, man," Tim greeted him. "Do you want some food? We were thinking about staying for supper."

James leaned on the table and crossed his legs at his ankles. "Sure, count me and Tate in." Tate was going to be thrilled. She'd told him many times that before the troubles had begun in the restaurant, all the employees and her family used to eat dinner together. He knew how much that meant to her.

It seemed by getting rid of Clint, the work atmosphere had immediately improved. James was so happy that arrogant jackass was gone. He was one of those fairly violent, fairly dumb men that thought women were beneath him and there to serve him and do his bidding. He probably couldn't understand why Tate hadn't fallen at his feet and let him run the show and make the decisions for her. And wouldn't Vito have loved that. He'd have got his way, and Clint would have settled his debts. Win-win situation. It was a pity James had no proof of that arrangement.

Gradually everyone assembled in the kitchen, chattering and pitching in, except for Tina, who had to run home to her son. James was about to go get Tate when she appeared, bringing the pies, with that damn sweet smile of hers that went straight to his heart. And his groin.

Suddenly the alarm went off, and the sound of shattering glass and the squealing of tires made everyone jump. The pies she was carrying almost flew to the floor.

"Everyone, stay here! Tim, come with me!" he ordered and darted out of the kitchen, closely followed by the kid. And Tate, much to his aggravation.

James looked around, quickly locating the problem—the front door was on fire. But there was another problem too, the restaurant alarm wasn't on, yet an alarm had gone off. Something was going on in the apartment.

"Grab the extinguisher from the kitchen," he yelled to Tim as he was reaching for the one in the dining area. He had the feeling he was going to need it. "Take care of the fire. I'm going upstairs."

"James," Tate said as he passed by on his way to the back stairs that led to her place.

"Stay here, Tate, I mean it. And call the fire department and the police."

James ran upstairs, half hoping he wouldn't find a fire but an intruder. No such luck. The window was broken, and it looked like a gasoline-filled bottle had gone right through it and had landed on the bed, setting it on fire. The curtains too.

"Oh my God!" Tate cried out from behind him.

"Get out of here!" he screamed, but she grabbed a quilt from the sofa and began trying to help him. Damn stubborn woman didn't know how to follow orders.

As soon as that fire was out, he rushed her down to the restaurant, where the last flames had been extinguished.

"What the hell was that?" Nils croaked.

"A Molotov cocktail," Tim grunted, kicking some of the glass left on the floor. "Plenty of Molotov drive-bys where I live."

Nils wasn't familiar with skid row and didn't seem to understand, so James explained. "A glass bottle filled with fuel. You stick a burning cloth in it, and boom, you got yourself a fuel bomb. Is everyone okay?" he asked, reaching out to Tate.

She nodded and went to him. He encircled her with his arms, needing reassurance that she was unharmed. He hadn't wanted her near the fire, but she'd refused to listen to him and leave him alone in the apartment. She smelled like smoke, but she was fine, a bit in shock, but okay nevertheless. James was still pumped up with adrenaline and now that he was sure everyone was fine, fury was taking hold on him. Whoever had dared to pull this stunt was going to pay in blood. The material damage wasn't so big, especially in the restaurant, but her tiny cluttered apartment was surely fucked. The place was filled with smoke and shards of glass, the window had shattered on impact, her bed was scorched, and the ceiling and part of the walls were blackened. Plus there was foam over her curtains and the bed.

"Who would do something like this?" Kelly uttered.

"Someone's really pissed," Tim answered. "Mighty pissed."

Suddenly it dawned on Tate, and she reached for James. "Do you think Clint...?"

"I don't know, but I'm damn sure going to find out!" He did have his suspicions, but he wasn't going to share them until he was totally sure.

When Zack and Sean showed up, James was already checking the video footage. The camera they had installed pointing at the front door had caught a glimpse of the drive-by action through the window; a guy had jumped out of a vehicle and thrown the bottles while the car never completely stopped. It was too dark to recognize anyone, especially as the one throwing the bottles had a hood on and his face was hidden by a scarf. The car, though, was a dark Ford Taurus, the same model Clint drove.

James was burning with rage, his body totally wired up, ready to go hunting, but he willed himself to dampen his fury; he couldn't leave Tate alone now. The firemen came, the cops appeared too, and although dead tired by the time everything was sorted out, she was still pacing like a lioness—pissed and frustrated. He had to get her out of there before the adrenaline crash floored her.

"Let's go to my place. You can't sleep up there. There's smoke damage, and the bed is a goner."

"I won't let the bastard run me out of my place. I'll sleep on the couch."

Yeah right, the two-foot couch. No way. "You aren't being run out. Zack, Sean, and Tim will take care of everything here."

She stuck out her lower lip like a stubborn kid. "No!"

That did it; he was so not fighting with her over that anymore. He darted toward her, and without giving Tate a second to react, he threw her over his shoulder. "You are coming with me to my house. End of story. Are we clear?"

She whined and muttered and fumbled all the way to his place until, once in his house, he stopped her ranting by tipping her chin up and dropping his lips over hers, kissing her thoroughly.

"Enough. Let's put all that restless energy to use. Be naked when I get back from turning on the hot tub. Otherwise I'll rip your clothes off."

That statement effectively shut her up.

Once in the tub, he hauled her onto his lap, her back to his chest, and in between feathery kisses and caresses, he got her to calm down. He massaged her scalp, sinking his fingers into her luxuriously thick mane of hair. Then he massaged her neck, her shoulders, ran his hands along her arms, gently pressing each muscle. By the time he reached her hands, she was limp and her head was leaning into his shoulder, her sweet tits poking out of the water. She was so beautiful and giving. Delving his fingers down toward her core, he leisurely pleasured her and held her to him while she came in his arms. She didn't cry out her release this time, but whispered his name in a moan as she climaxed.

He'd been dying to have her in his place. She looked like she belonged.

Tate had been awake for a while. She had no clue what time it was, but she didn't care; she felt happy, content, and relaxed. The sun was coming up over the horizon, and James was breathing peacefully at her back, his arm protectively wrapped around her waist. The lake views from his bedroom window were so astounding, so captivating, she'd been staring in awe for an eternity already. No wonder James had insisted on them coming to spend time at his place. She'd only been there once before, when they came to pick up the alarms, but James had been so tense back then they had been out of there in a matter of seconds. After that, she'd always found a reason to stay away from Alden, afraid that staying at his place would make their relationship much more real and therefore dangerous. This time she'd had very little say. When one is being thrown over a man's broad shoulder and can't see shit but his yummy, hard butt, it was time to accept he's in charge.

His house was a work of art, magnificent and cozy at the same time, and the hot tub on the outer deck with views to the lake...well, that was beyond description. She was never going to look at her tiny bathroom in quite the same way again. She couldn't understand how he'd agreed to stay at her place night after night, especially on that shitty bed. The new one she'd bought was better, but it still couldn't compare with this one. This bed was huge and fluffy and smelled of him. No wonder she'd slept fantastically.

Thinking about her once-new, now scorched bed gave her goose bumps. What the hell was she doing lying here in contemplation, by the way? She should head to the city; she had a cleanup operation to mount. There were thousand of things to do at the restaurant; she needed to get a new front door and a new window, and Elle was coming today. She had to come up with a credible cover story for all the mess. When James had carried her away from Rosita's, he'd assured her Zack and Sean would take care of everything, that they'd be there first thing in the morning waiting for the insurance guys to assess the damage. The shutters would keep the restaurant closed in the night, and some firm he'd contacted would come and take the door and the frame out and bring a temporary replacement. For the window too. Everything was under control, he'd said, but she felt weird relying on him so entirely, not to mention that her stomach knotted in fear at the thought of how much worse all that could have been. What if she'd been in bed, alone, when the projectile had crashed through her window? Or if she'd been somewhere else, would she have found out in time that Rosita's was on fire?

Still. The day had many low points, no doubt about it, but seeing Faith throwing herself at James was a definite winner; not even the fire had come close to that. He'd marked the boundaries, but that hadn't stopped Faith from eating James up with her eyes. It wasn't so much the fact that she'd made her intentions clear; Tate knew women looked at James all the time. What scared her the most was her own reaction, those possessive instincts that had blazed out of her. She'd sizzled with fury, and fear, which proved that even the thought of losing him terrified her. Damn and double damn! She was building expectations, and that was the only thing she couldn't afford to do. She felt a pang of panic and a humongous urge to run away, but then the phone rang.

With a swift movement, James flipped his phone open and answered it in whispers, probably thinking she was still sleeping.

"Yeah?"

The arm he kept around her waist pressed slightly at her, his hand expanding on her stomach, soothing her, like it was willing her to continue sleeping. He assented with short replies and then, after some moments, his question froze her blood. "Did they check his place out? What about his computer? Is he our guy?"

He nodded some more and then cut the communication. She didn't move, but something gave her away. The fact that she'd stopped breathing and her heart was thudding madly might have been it.

James came even closer, nuzzling her ear.

"Who was that?"

"Jack."

"Not a social call, I suspect, right?" Jack didn't seem like the kind of guy inclined to make casual calls, much less at the crack of dawn.

He sighed. "No. He had news for us. Clint was brought in for questioning and is now under arrest pending further investigation. The police believe he's responsible for the incendiary bombs yesterday. Apparently he was too drunk to bother covering his tracks afterward. When they went to his house to question him, they noticed one of the bottles with gas in his car. The police are checking his computer now. It will take a while, but they're pretty sure he isn't only your arsonist but also your Prince Charming."

She turned around, her mouth gaping.

"Clint? You mean our Clint, the one I fired yesterday? There must be a mistake. It can't be. He's an asshole, I know, but he isn't that kind of asshole. He's harmless. He's been working for me for over a year!"

"I had Jack check Clint out. He isn't so harmless, honey. He's been arrested several times for being drunk and disorderly and for fighting. He also has a couple of restraining orders from previous girlfriends, and he's earned himself several mandatory anger management courses. He gets too intense."

"Yeah, but—" she tried to interrupt.

"He's also an unlucky gambler and owes a lot of money to Vito's son. We believe he's been using the hold he has on Clint to get him to aid in his campaign for you to sell. Clint might have expected you to grow close to him so he could convince you to sell out. The fire in the kitchen was probably his doing. He didn't want to burn the place down; he just wanted to send Aidan packing and scare you enough so that you'd turn to him for help and advice. When that didn't happen, he became more and more obsessed and erratic. Hence the worsening of the e-mails. Vito's son isn't known for tolerating failure or for being patient. And Clint isn't the most coolheaded guy. His frustration was showing in his attitude too."

She had trouble understanding it all. "And you guys think Vito put him up to it?"

"That's the general idea, yes."

She felt as if she'd fallen down the proverbial rabbit hole. "But...but Clint liked me. I thought he liked me and was pissed because I didn't reciprocate."

"I'm sure there's a lot of that too. And the more you ignored him, the more pissed he got. You were supposed to come crying to him, allow him to be the hero of the day."

"Wait, wait." She stopped him, remembering something he'd

said before. "You had Clint checked out behind my back?"

He nodded.

"And didn't it occur to you even once to let me in on that?"

"No."

"Damn, you're arrogant," she said with a grunt, slapping his chest.

"Ouch! What was that for?"

"You should have told me, James, I would have fired him."

"No, you needed to convince yourself that you run Rosita's, that you can make decisions, fire people regardless of whether they were hired by your dad or not. Besides, it's not against the law to be an asshole or to get drunk and rowdy or to have a couple of restraining orders from previous girlfriends and be an unlucky gambler. All we had until now was conjecture. The bottle in his car, though, is hard evidence."

"Has he confessed?" This was so surreal; she couldn't believe she was saying this.

"Didn't say anything intelligible. He was totally wasted and quite violent when the police arrived. Resisted arrest too. Today they'll know more. If he can be placed at any of the Internet cafés from where the e-mails were sent, he's going to be in deep shit."

Her brows furrowed.

"He might have sent a couple of e-mails from his computer, but Jack's friend found out Prince Charming has been using Internet cafés too," he explained. "There's also the possibility one of Vito's goons was taking care of the e-mails and Clint was just their inside guy in charge of working you and causing the fires, but the tone of those messages is so personal it's kind of unlikely."

She was stunned. This was too much information to process at such an early hour. All this time she'd had the source of all her problems under her nose and hadn't even realized it. She couldn't believe it. She turned around, nesting her back against James, and quietly observed the lake.

"Well, at least this time the insurance company won't be able to skip payment," she concluded after a while.

"No, they won't. And as soon as he confesses about the first fire, they'll have to pay for that one too."

"Good," she said. "God, every time I think of what could've happened yesterday if I'd been in bed alone, I get the shakes."

James hugged her tight. "You aren't alone anymore. Nothing would've happened because I would've been with you." She went quiet for a long time. She didn't want to talk about Rosita's anymore, or the fires, but James didn't lighten up. "Tell me, what are your plans now that Rosita's is off the hook? Diners are rolling in again, and soon the financial problems are going to be a thing of the past. Are you going to continue running it personally?"

She shrugged. "I don't know. Before I got derailed, I had been thinking about quitting being a secretary and going back to school to get a fancy degree. Maybe I'll hire a manager for the restaurant and do that. I really don't know. Although if I have to be honest with you, I like running the place. I'd miss it if I weren't there every day. What about you, James? What are your plans for the future?"

"I don't know. I've already earned enough money to live comfortably for the rest of my life. I might ask Zack and Sean to buy me out, or maybe I'll concentrate on the security consulting side of the business and leave the rest to them. That way I could have more free time to spend with you," he said, caressing her arm. "I like spending time with you, princess, and I like helping you out in the restaurant."

The implications of what he was saying hit her hard.

"This place is amazing. The views alone are breathtaking," she murmured after a second of silence.

He chuckled and traced her throat with his mouth. "You're breathtaking. And sneaky when you don't want to talk about something."

"I don't know what you mean."

"Yeah right! Just a hint; if you didn't want to speak about the future, sex would've been a much better distraction than mentioning the views. Come on, baby, distract me; turn around and come sit on my face. I want to lick your pretty pussy."

"Are you nuts?" She giggled. "I am not sitting on your face!"

"Come on, I've been dreaming about it for weeks now. Your bed doesn't have a headboard, but look at this one, baby, look at the metal bars. You could hold on to them as I pleasure you, as I stick my tongue deep inside you. I want to feel you coming on my tongue."

"I've come on your tongue plenty of times."

He ignored her. "And think about the possibilities of those bars. After you come on me, I could tie you down. Do you like that idea? I bet you do; your heart is racing, princess."

"Yeah, and how many girls have you had tied to this bed, huh?" Her chuckle died in her throat, not thrilled at all about that possibility. Then a question occurred to her. "Is this the place you shared with Elaine?"

"Why? Are you afraid I'm proposing oral sex to you in the same bed I shared with my wife?"

"Yes. No. Well, maybe." She shrugged. "The thought just crossed my mind."

"No, I didn't share this place with her. We lived in Boston, in an apartment. She thought Alden was too...provincial. I had just left my dad's company and taken up bounty hunting. I didn't have the means to build a house, let alone this one."

"What happened between you two?" she asked, turning around.

James groaned. "Do we really have to talk about this? I'd much rather have you sitting on my face. Are you sure I can't convince you?" he offered, his thumb caressing her lower lips.

As tempting as the offer was, she kept a cool head. "Nope, spill your guts."

He sighed, went on his back, obviously not thrilled with the way the conversation was going. "She got tired of being alone, basically. Being a bounty hunter involves many days on the road, tracking leads, people. There are no schedules, no hours. She said she felt lonely, neglected, so she started cheating on me behind my back. Until one of her lovers got a huge promotion and she decided she was done wasting time on me and traded me up for a hotshot with a fancy house and an expensive car who could give her a better life. So she upgraded husbands. But I don't want to talk about her."

"She was mistaken, James; she traded *down*."

"Did she? I'm not sure about that. I wasn't a good husband."

"You didn't ask her to cheat on you."

"No, but I did leave her alone very often. Not that it explained the whoring, but still. I don't love her, but for many years, I felt guilty about the way my marriage ended. Maybe she was right and I hadn't tried hard enough."

He'd gotten somber, his hazel eyes sad.

"No, she wasn't. And she did definitely trade down; take my word for it. Surely the sex couldn't be this great with that hotshot, never mind his fancy house and his expensive car."

He smiled. "Glad you think so."

"Or maybe she was crap in bed. Because face it, you need two to tango." Her hand slid from his chest down to his crotch, barely touching him. "And you have to admit, I am a great dancer."

He looked incredulously at her. "I saw you line dancing, baby. You were scary."

She giggled. "True, but you see, I'm a shy dancer. I need privacy for a top performance, alongside the right motivation," she said while intensifying her touch on him. "And I love to tango."

He quietly smiled and lifted his hips to her hand. "Miss Cooper, I believe you are a tease."

"Me? I think I made good on all my promises yesterday, Mr. Bowen. I don't recall you groaning and yelling in ecstasy because you didn't get to come." She'd been exhausted after the hot tub treat, and the second her body hit the bed, she'd fallen sleep, but she'd woken up in the middle of the night and kind of attacked him. Not that he'd complained or anything; on the contrary.

He covered her hand with his and lifted himself to her while her mouth fell upon his dragon. "And do you know what else I believe, Miss Cooper? I believe you are the one for me."

"Mmm," she answered a bit mockingly, her tongue tracing the ink. "Jeez, that I love nibbling your dragon. So sexy. Say, how many more tattoos are you going to get? How many pivotal moments in your life are you planning to have?"

"Don't know. I'm having one now, though."

Her heart skipped a beat.

He cupped her face. "I love you, Tate."

She froze. "James…"

"Shh, sweetheart, don't freak out on me. I know you don't want to hear it, but I won't keep it inside any longer. You don't have to say anything. I don't want you to feel obliged to answer anything back. I just needed to say it out loud. What I really want now is to make love to you until all you can see and feel is me. Would you let me do that?"

She closed her eyes and nodded, letting herself go. He turned her on her back, settling between her thighs. He eased the T-shirt he'd given her for the night up and over her head and trailed his mouth down from her throat to her breasts, nipping at her swollen nipples as she writhed.

"You are so beautiful, Tate." His hands expanded on her stomach, followed by his mouth kissing his way down her core. "Made for me."

He nuzzled the clit ring. "This isn't mine. I thought I made myself clear yesterday. I want my ring on your clit, sweetheart."

"Didn't have time to get to the beauty salon," she whispered, her body shuddering as his tongue circled her slit and lapped at her tender folds, licking each curve. "I'll go there first thing today, I promise."

"Good."

He lifted her legs up and bent them, leaving her totally exposed.

He brought her to a hard orgasm with his tongue and then moved upward. He brought her hands up and held them there in one of his while his mouth trailed down her breasts and his cock thrust inside her.

"I love having you in my bed, Tate, so you better get used to it, babe. No more avoiding Alden."

He made love to her with a clever combination of short and shallow thrusts and then long and deep ones, never letting her hands go. His other hand reached under her behind and lifted her to him, adding to the maelstrom already raging inside her. His mouth tormented her nipples, his teeth raking them.

"So sweet, Tate, so sweet and so tight. Do you like it, babe?"

She nodded, or she thought she did.

"Now I am going to let your hands go, I want you to hold on to the bars. Do not let go. If you let go, I stop, do you understand?"

She nodded and gripped the bars, her back arching at each of his plunges, her pussy on fire, the muscles fluttering with the need for release.

"Are you mine?" he asked as he hooked her legs over his elbows, forcing himself even deeper inside her core.

Her voice wouldn't come out; her throat was tight with emotion.

"Are you mine, Tate?" he asked again, thrusting into her deeply, the head of his dick slamming at her womb, her back arching at the tension gathering in her body.

"Yours," she whispered. "All yours." Body and soul. She couldn't lie; she was too raw for it. She needed too much.

He looked at her with such a fierce possessiveness and male pride it was shocking.

He began a hard rhythm that was going to kill her. His mouth and his tongue were tormenting her nipples, sending jolts to her clit and womb while his cock was claiming every inch of her.

"Oh hell, James, I'm coming."

"Give it to me, Tate." She heard his rough voice grating her senses. "I'm so close. Come for me, babe. Come for me while I fill you up with my cum."

His tongue took a hard swipe of her nipple, and then he bit it. She felt herself explode, her pussy convulsing, sucking James deeper and deeper.

She'd given herself to him without reservation, but she hadn't said the words. He'd seen the doubt and panic on her face when he'd told her, as if she couldn't or wouldn't let herself believe it. Clearly she was going to need some time to get used to the idea that he loved her. And that was nothing compared to the time it was going to take her to come to terms with the fact that she loved him, because she did, he knew, even if she refused to acknowledge it to herself. It was okay. His ego wasn't too happy about it, but he'd wait.

"I've got to go to the bathroom," she said.

The second she stood and he saw his cum trickling down from between her thighs, he got hard again. It must be some caveman instinct or some shit like that, because he couldn't control his reaction to it. It had been this way since that first time in her place, when they had made love bareback on that chair and as she'd risen from him his cum and her lube had trickled down from her pussy and onto his cock. It had been the most erotically charged experience of his life. He'd gone instantly hard again, thrown her onto the bed, and fucked her again. She'd laughed and squirmed but opened her legs for him and welcomed him inside her body again. But that had been then, before he'd dropped the big *L* bomb.

He was considering the benefits of giving it a go when, with Tate halfway to the bathroom, his door suddenly opened. Tate screamed and tried to cover herself with her hands while a surprised Max appeared in the doorway.

"Fuck, sorry," Max cursed, trying to keep his eyes on the ceiling and away from the girl. James had swiftly gotten up and placed his body in front of Tate, effectively covering her.

"Don't you know how to knock?" James barked at him.

"Sorry, I didn't know you had company." Max looked down at James's cock, standing naked in full salute, and smiled.

"What's going on?" James heard his brother Cole say before he appeared in the doorway. "Oh fuck!"

"Yeah man, exactly my thoughts," Max said with a grin. "It seems we're interrupting."

Tate was behind James, her nails digging into his arms. She pulled him backward, trying to reach the bed to grab the blanket. "Do you guys mind getting the fuck out of here?"

They didn't pay him any attention. "You haven't been sleeping here, so this morning when we saw your truck, we decided to come have breakfast with you," Cole explained.

"Good luck with that, the fridge is empty."

"Aren't you going to introduce us?" Max said. "I'd like a

name to go with that naked body that almost gave me a stroke."

James crossed his arms over his chest. "I find your eyes on that body again, and I'll rip them out, understand me?" He knew his brother was pulling his leg; from the moment he'd opened the door and Tate screamed, Max had tried very hard to keep his eyes off her. Good, otherwise he'd have kicked his ass. He still might if they didn't stop smirking and get the hell out of there fast enough.

Both his brothers crossed their arms over their chests. They were obviously going nowhere, so James breathed out hard and gave in. "Tate, these are my brothers, Cole and Max. Guys, this is Tate."

"Hi," she said from behind him. She'd managed to move him back enough to reach the blanket and wrap herself in it by now, but she was still hiding behind his back.

"Happy now?"

Both his brothers grinned.

"Now please get the fuck out of here!"

Nobody moved. "Do you realize this is the first time you have a woman here that you've allowed to stay until morning? Do we need to start shopping for tuxedos?"

"Enough!" James barked. "Everybody who's dressed, out of this room!"

"Fine, fine. But get down fast; we're going to breakfast at Aunt Maggie's. You too, Tate," Cole said. "You need to meet the in-laws. We're charming."

"Out!" James yelled. The last thing he needed now was his brothers scaring the hell out of her.

Once they were alone, he turned to Tate. Her face wasn't only a vivid red, but her eyes were huge and round.

"That was so embarrassing," she muttered.

Lifting her chin up, he forced her eyes to focus on him. "Sorry about that, princess. My brothers don't fully understand the meaning of privacy. I'll pound it into them, though; that won't happen again."

She let out a mortified smile. "Why is it that I always find myself in the weirdest situations with you? I was never caught, not even once with Aid—"

He cut off her words with a possessive kiss. "You're with me now, and I don't want you talking about other men, princess. I've discovered recently that I'm a very jealous man. Now let's get dressed; we have a family breakfast to face."

She looked panicked again. "James, I have lots of things to do. Plus, I should go to the police station, and I have a front door and an apartment to repair, and the insurance to deal with. And Elle is coming today. Maybe it's best if I meet them some other time." She was freaking out; he could see it.

"You have to meet my brothers sometime, and today is as good a day as any. And don't worry about the police; we'll go together later. I spoke with Zack. The temporary front door is already in place, and the insurance inspector has come already. Everything's under control."

She was going to complain, but he wasn't letting her.

"Please, baby, despite how they behaved just now, they are a very important part of my life. I want you to meet them."

The second she assented, he rushed her to get dressed and, grabbing her by her wrist, half dragged her to the diner. As she saw it she stopped dead on her tracks.

"A diner? I thought we were having breakfast at your aunt's. I meant at your dad's place. Didn't she move in with you guys to help out years ago?"

"Yeah."

"So why the hell are we going to have breakfast in a diner?"

"Aunt Maggie is temporarily helping out in the diner. She's great, and she's dying to meet you."

"Oh boy…"

CHAPTER TWELVE

It was eleven at night, and Rosita's was quite full. She'd made James promise he'd drag Zack and Sean along to dinner, and as always, he'd delivered. It was the least she could do seeing as how they'd gone out of their way to help her. However now that they were here, it seemed they preferred to wait until closing time and eat together with her and James, so after a detour to chat with Tim in the kitchen, James had left them on the far end table and had come to join her at the counter.

Regular patrons already knew him, and many greeted him while he passed by their tables. He looked so at ease there it gave her goose bumps. Although really, she'd been out of balance the whole day, starting with that trying morning with Jack's call about Clint, and then continuing with James telling her he loved her. Getting caught by his brothers butt naked and dripping cum down her inner thigh on her way to the bathroom hadn't helped matters, not to mention the family breakfast with their aunt while half the town watched. Oh, they were all nice to her and smiled approvingly the whole time. There was nothing wrong with his family. It was her. She was wrong; she didn't have a family nowadays, family breakfasts were very much out of the picture, and she had no business having those. Nevertheless she'd loved it, absolutely loved it, sibling banter included. Max and Cole were funny and charming and had teased James to no end. Aunt Maggie had hugged and smooched her to death. By how thrilled she'd looked, it was plenty obvious those boys weren't big on bringing girls to her. Tate could have done without the groupies around, stupidly smiling at James and his brothers, but all in all, Alden had turned out to be a lovely place full of people that seemed to know and respect the Bowen family.

"Where's Elle?" James asked, leaning at the counter and looking around.

"On her way, last I heard."

She really hoped that was the case. After a short visit to the police and helping her with the cleanup, James had accompanied her to pick Elle up from Logan Airport, dropped her at one of her friend's, and then had gone to work. Tate hadn't been surprised about her sister's choice of accommodation; she knew Elle wouldn't want to stay at their parents' house, alone on top of everything. Although Tate had gone there with James twice after that first time, she didn't feel ready to sleep over yet. She asked Elle to stay in Jonah's apartment, but she'd refused, claimed the place was barely big enough for one, let alone two people. They could have roughed it, no problem, but too much immersion in the life scraps of the Coopers was too painful for Elle, or at least it had been for all her other visits, so Tate hadn't insisted. This time, though, Elle had quickly agreed to come to Rosita's, probably just to get the chance to check James out some more and hear the whole version about the fires and Clint, but whatever the reason, Tate was happy. Elle was as much a part of the restaurant as she was; it was past time she got herself involved in it, even if it was only for a night.

James smiled at her. "She'll be here, princess, you'll see."

She surely hoped so. If she could go to their home, as sure as hell Elle could get her ass to Rosita's. Lifting her eyes to the door, she realized she wouldn't have to hunt her down and drag her in. Elle was there. Smiling. A bit shaky, but smiling. Tate's eyes filled, and she blinked to stop herself from crying, Elle didn't like touchy-feely scenes; it would freak her out.

She blew a kiss to Tate and leaned on the counter. "So," she began pointing at the front door. "Are you taking suggestions for the new door? Because if so, I vote for a modern glass door instead of the old-fashioned wooden one. You know, to go with that Gothic girl you have waiting tables."

James and Tate looked at each other, jaws slack. Elle seemed so relaxed it surprised Tate.

"Now, is the food still any good in this joint?"

Tate smiled. "Sure, but you need to wait some tables first if you want to earn dinner."

"Deal," she said, rubbing her hands. "Let me drop by the kitchen to say hi first." And she strode away, stopping several times to greet regular patrons as if she'd never been away.

"Well, that wasn't so hard," James whispered to Tate.

No it hadn't been. With Elle the most difficult thing was to get her to take the first step; after that and once she'd made up her mind, she'd waltz through anything.

"And she hasn't been so hard on me either," James said.

That was also true, but only because she hadn't got up to speed yet. From the second Tate had introduced them, Elle had narrowed her gaze on him, and for the fifteen-minute ride from the airport, she'd studied each of his words and gestures. She wasn't done with him, oh no, not yet. Soon she'd cross her arms over her chest, cock her eyebrow, and start with the hard questions, the ones she always failed to ask her wannabe loser boyfriends.

"She's just waiting for you to let your guard down. Tonight, when you least expect it, you'll get the third degree."

James looked weirdly at her, clearly amused. "Bring it on; it can't be worse than Max and Cole, right?"

"And speaking of the devil," she said, pointing toward the door. Max and Cole were there, Max grinning devilishly, Cole nodding, a bit more dignified. "It seems we have a full house."

"Told you not to invite them."

While running away—literally—after breakfast, she'd politely invited them to pass by whenever, she just didn't think whenever meant right away that same night. She was probably a bit rusty as far as family matters were concerned, because James didn't seem at all surprised.

"Cool place you've got here," Max stated, looking around. She wasn't sure he meant the place or the cuties that were all smiling back at him. Like it wasn't enough to have chicks drooling over James, now she had the whole Bowen male panty-creamer clan parading through Rosita's. She should be charging for entrance.

"Nice job my men did with the temporary door. You like it?"

Tate looked at Cole. What was he talking about?

"Didn't James tell you he sent my guys to do it?"

"Cole runs my dad's construction company," James said.

Yeah, Tate remembered vaguely he'd mentioned working as a carpenter for his father. What he didn't mention, though, was that now she was in debt not only to James, but to his brother too. She doubted it was in their modus operandi to leave whatever it was they were doing to come early in the morning to take measurements to put in a temporary door for a stranger.

"Window too?" she asked, staring at James. He nodded, and her nostrils flared. To Cole she just smiled.

"Thank you, Cole. It's great. Be sure to send me the bill."

"Anytime, sweetie. And no, you don't get bills from me. When you decide which kind of door you want, just come see me, and I'll fix you up."

She pursed her lips. "Yes, I get bills from you." He was going to complain, but she stopped him. "Especially bills I'm going to pass along to the insurance company for them to pay, so hit me hard; the insurance company deserves it for stiffing me the first time around."

Cole grinned and turned to his brother. "She's frisky!"

"That she is," James said, and as Tate frowned at him, he just winked at her.

"I'll take you up on the new door, Cole. Although I'm not sure which kind we want. My sister, Elle, came for a visit, and we may want to change the look of this place."

"Your sister's here?" Max asked. "Great. I'm dying to meet her. I bet she's as beautiful as you."

She laughed. "Oh no, she's way prettier than me. But you need to be a mean asshole full of tattoos to catch her eye."

"I like her already." He grinned.

"Go with them," she said to James as his brothers moved to the table occupied by Zack and Sean.

"Are you sure? If you need help—"

"Go!" she insisted, laughing. She had everything under

control there.

After several minutes, Jack came in and joined them, bringing the total amount of hunks at that table to six. There was not a single woman in Rosita's that was not sneaking peeks at them.

With Elle pitching in, everything was running smoothly. She felt...happy. Until she saw Faith coming in. She went straight to the cigarette vending machine, as she'd done the night before. On her way out, she approached Tate at the counter.

"Don't get used to him. He isn't yours to keep. I've known James for years; he doesn't give himself totally to anyone. And he doesn't do the girlfriend scene, no matter how much he'll try to convince himself otherwise."

Before Tate could answer, Faith had already turned around and left.

James hadn't wanted his brothers to know about Tate's stalker or any specifics about the problems with the restaurant, but with them sitting at the same table along with Zack, Sean, and Jack, there was no chance of that happening, especially as everyone else assumed they were in on it. In three minutes flat, Cole and Max were up to speed and glaring at him for leaving them out of the loop.

James hadn't elaborated on the need for a new door and window further than pinning it on vandalism, mainly because meddling in other family members' affairs was not only a pastime for Aunt Maggie but some kind of frigging genetic condition all Bowens shared. His brothers had proven time and again that they didn't know when to butt out of his business, so clueing them in would have been carte blanche for full frontal assault. They would have gone all protective on Tate and scared her shitless with their intensity, because although she didn't fully understand the ramifications of him taking her to breakfast with them, Cole and Max did. She was very important to him, which according to them meant her well-being was also their responsibility. And Tate was definitely not ready for that; it would freak her out big-time. Hell, she'd been looking badly off balance since this morning when he'd gone and blurted he loved her—no need to go for a home run and knock the poor girl down on her ass.

As Elle came by and they ordered drinks, James introduced her to everybody. She had a bright smile ready for everyone except him. Him she regarded with wariness. Tate thought her sister hadn't yet given him the third degree, but she was wrong; while he'd been taking care of the parking ticket at the airport, Elle had approached him.

"*You get the benefit of the doubt because according to the Eternal Sun gossip committee, you're good as gold. They better be right, or I'll stick my boot up your ass so far it'll set up residency in your throat.*" Those had been Elle's first words to James, accompanied by a wide smile that had left him speechless. Now if Max or Cole had said that to him, it would have been another story altogether, but he wasn't used to dealing with brassy girls with angelical smiles.

"Was Clint sober enough today to answer questions?" Zack asked after she'd walked away. He was appreciatively watching her, and James smiled inwardly. Zack was an easygoing, laid-back guy; Elle would chew him up and spit him out in a second.

"The police are still holding him, but he insists he spent the night getting plastered and then went home. No one at the bars he visited can account for his whereabouts at the time the bottles were thrown, including him. He admits to having an agreement with Andrew Vito to get Tate to sell, but Clint says he had nothing to do with the e-mails or fires. He insists someone broke into his car and planted the gasoline-filled bottle there. He says he's done nothing illegal, that he only tried to be a good friend and convince Tate she'd be better off without the restaurant on her shoulders. But she wouldn't let him get close or see reason, so he grew more exasperated every day until not even the ten thousand that he owes Vito could justify putting up with her. He of course blames Vito, saying he must be the one behind the arson trick and the threatening messages."

"And what does this Andrew say?" Cole asked, still looking furiously at him, making him feel guilty. At least Max wasn't glaring and just seemed happy he got there in time to get a piece of the action. "Have the police interrogated him?"

"Yep, but he denied even knowing the guy, let alone having

any agreements with him or having anything to do with the gasoline-filled bottles or the e-mails."

"And they bought it?"

James shrugged. "The police have a solid case; their suspect is a scumbag with a long rap sheet, and they have nothing substantial to tie Rosita's to Andrew Vito, who as far as they're concerned is a straight enough businessman. They aren't interested in a wild-goose chase. That's why Jack and I paid him a visit this afternoon."

"You had us replacing doors and windows while you were confronting thugs?" Now Max was pissed too. "Very smart, bro."

"There was no need for backup; it was all very civilized." Besides, Jack was intimidating enough. It was amazing what he could accomplish just by staring at someone and saying, "*I want to see your boss*." It had something to do with his ice-cold demeanor and dangerous stillness.

"We told him we knew about the suppliers and his interest in buying Rosita's, and about Clint's debt to one of his bookies. The asshole laughed, said the suppliers' trick was his father's crooked sense of humor. He said his dad had always had a soft spot for Rosita's, but he wasn't ready to resort to illegal measures, that the joint wasn't worth it and that they had already acquired a restaurant downtown. Concerning Clint, he admitted seeing the guy once and suggesting that it would be mutually beneficial if he could remind Tate from time to time how he'd pay a fair price for the restaurant and how selling could be a great option. In exchange he'd consider settling his debt. He denies ordering Clint or anybody else for that matter to threaten her or set fire to the place, of course."

"Do we believe him?" Max asked.

"We believe no one," Jack said. "We'll check with the Internet cafés where the e-mails were sent, and let's see if anyone there recognizes Clint's picture or any of Andrew's thugs. Let's also test how loyal the guys are in Andrew's inner circle. Maybe there's someone with a weakness we can exploit or a deal we can make to get some reliable info."

At that point, someone cleared her throat. Their eyes lifted to see a wide-eyed Elle holding a tray with their drinks. How long had she been there listening? By the looks of her, James figured she'd heard more than her fair share.

"Can I talk to you in private?" That wasn't a question but a demand, so without waiting for James's reply, she left the tray on the table and moved to a far corner, away from prying eyes.

James reluctantly followed her. This was a conversation he so didn't want to have. Tate had diminished the whole Clint thing while talking to Elle in the car; an unhappy employee, she'd said. There had been no mention about the threatening messages or Vito's early attempts at boycotting the restaurant. No wonder she was pissed now.

"What the fuck were you guys talking about back there?" she asked as soon as they were out of earshot.

James frowned, his lips pursed into a tight line. "You really should talk with Tate. It isn't my place to—"

"Start talking or I'll go get it from them," she threatened, pointing at the table where the others were. "How long do you honestly think it's going to take me to get the truth out of them?" Not long, that was for sure. They were all half taken with her; she'd bat her eyes and they'd all cave in. Except for Jack—he was immune to any and all women's tricks, no matter how sweet or how brassy. But the rest? Ha! Give her three seconds with them and they'd all be spilling the beans.

Letting out a slow breath, James ran an aggravated hand through his hair. Okay, time to engage in some damage control; he'd tell the story as clipped and short as possible.

She was flabbergasted by the end of it.

"How come I didn't know anything about it?" she said.

He eyed Tate. It was a good thing she was busy and hadn't noticed them talking. Yet. "I guess she didn't want to worry you."

"Damn her! She shouldn't have kept all that to herself. I would have—"

"Yeah, well, you weren't available," he defiantly added, crossing his arms over his chest.

Elle shot him a furious look. "You don't get to judge me. This," she said and gestured to the restaurant, "is none of your business, Mr. Wonder Boy."

"True, it isn't my business, it's *yours*. Your business, your responsibility. Maybe it's time you get your ass into gear and act upon it. Tate lost as much as you did in that accident, not any less."

That last sentence seemed to get to her. She still stared defiantly at him, but her tone softened a bit. "I know."

His tone didn't soften. "Yet you've been letting your baby sister deal with everything." He knew that was a cheap shot; Elle was barely a year older than Tate, but still.

"She's the one that wanted to keep Rosita's in the first place, not me!"

"She's doing it for you and your mother as much as for herself. Or are you truly telling me in time you won't feel sorry you gave up a restaurant that had been in your family for more than fifty years just because for a while after the death of your dad and brother, being there was too painful to bear?"

She didn't answer right away. "I might have been a bit out of it, I recognize that, but I'm here now, am I not?"

"Yes, you are. And now that you got your shit together, you don't really have any reason to continue to bail out on her."

The glint of annoyance in her eyes grew stronger. She might be down, but she was by no means beaten. "You don't beat around bush, do you?"

"No, but neither do you."

She quirked her lips up slightly at that. Yeah, she gave as good as she got. "True." She sighed. "We're going window-shopping tomorrow. I'll speak to Tate then."

James nodded to her, and as he threw another glance in Tate's direction, he noticed someone very much resembling Faith walking to the door. A frown marred his face. Tate was standing very still at the counter. Too still. Was that Faith? He'd got only a glimpse, but the clothes and the way she walked looked like Faith. And the platinum hair.

"I'm sure you'll work everything out," he added without looking at Elle, and after excusing himself, he headed for the counter and leaned on it in front of Tate. "Hi, princess." She offered him a short smile. "Who was that?"

"Who was who?" she asked, averting her eyes. She moved a bit to the side and pretended to busy herself.

"The girl that just left. Was that Faith?"

"Nope," she replied in a clipped tone. She looked a bit tense, and she was so lying.

"Come here," he said. As she raised a questioning eyebrow at him, he wiggled his finger for her to approach. She rolled her eyes at that presumptuous gesture but humored him nevertheless. And damn if he didn't love her for it. When she was within reach, he grasped her hands and, after pulling her to him, kissed her softly over the counter. There were still many diners, so he just brushed her lips.

"Who was that, huh?" he whispered to her before kissing her again.

"No one." She pouted stubbornly.

"You're lying, and you're tense," he said between feathery kisses.

"That's because you're kissing me in front of God and everyone," she muttered in spite of his best efforts.

He grinned. "Don't worry; they all know I'm crazy about you." Damn she was so beautiful when annoyed. And she was losing the battle; he could see a small smile forming.

Unable to help himself, he cupped her face and kissed her thoroughly.

"Okay, you lovebirds, cut it out," someone said.

As James turned around, he saw old Mr. Ryan with a credit card in hand. "I haven't had any action since the late seventies, so don't make me jealous. I don't think my heart can handle an erection."

Tate blushed as red as a traffic light, mumbled an apology, took the card, and charged it. Mr. Ryan, a gentleman that came to Rosita's quite regularly, just looked at her, amused.

"Jonah and Thomas would have given you hell for getting close to her," he warned James with an admonishing finger, then turned to Tate with a wide smile. "But I'm sure they'd have loved him."

After closing time, Tate approached James's table, and he pulled her into his lap while he talked to his brothers, Jack, Zack, and Sean. Then Elle came and sat down, chattering and joking like she used to before her year away from Rosita's. As Tim joined them, all the kitchen personnel and the waitresses did the same. One thing led to another, and they were all having dinner.

The table was full of people and laughter. Tim, Zack, and Sean were animatedly talking with Tina and Kelly, laughing and discussing something about the last concert they'd sent bodyguards to. Paige was serving everyone another round of mojitos. Nils, Jack, and Kelly were talking about Mexican food. Elle was laughing at something Cole had said, and Max and James were talking about Aunt Maggie. Everyone was happy and relaxed, except for Tate; her heart was stampeding, and she could hardly breathe. Yep, this must be what people called panic attacks.

She looked around; it was like the old days, when most of Rosita's employees would stay for supper, comment on the night's events, sometimes fight, but most times joked and laughed with each other about anything. She could almost hear her father and Jonah and her mom. Jeez, wrong turn there. The whole place was now spinning, and all she could hear were Faith's words: "*Don't get used to him. He isn't yours to keep.*" And Mr. Ryan's: "*They would have loved him.*"

She loved him. She really did. Boy was she screwed. A huge lump knotted her throat, and she felt sick to her stomach. Panic spread over her like wildfire. What the fuck was she doing? Letting herself go like this, being happy like this? She must be nuts for allowing this to go so far. Hadn't she learned anything from all that happened last year? From all that pain and misery she'd endured? All this could be taken away from her at any given second, as it had been taken away from her once before already. All that happiness, *poof*, gone with the wind. Dread began to take form inside her, dread for the pain to come.

She felt like laughing at her naïveté. She'd been deluding herself. Despite her better judgment, James had gotten under her defenses, convinced her she could trust him, that it was safe to love him. What had she been thinking giving in like this? What the hell was she to do when he dumped her? It'd rip her heart out. He'd take all this happiness with him, all this...rightness, and she'd be alone in the hell pit she'd been in before. She'd be broken, empty. Again. She couldn't risk it, having all her well-being in a man's hands. He'd walk like Aidan, like her father and brother, and then what? This, all those laughs in there were a mirage, something that would disappear as easily as it had come, leaving her to face the music all by herself. Suddenly she resented James for giving her that sense of belonging again. All her life now revolved around him; he was part of everything, from the restaurant to her nights to, God forbid, her dreams. This was bad; this was very bad. She had to stop this, get off this train now because she sure as hell wasn't strong enough to endure the crash, and the longer she allowed the situation to continue, the worse the fallout would be. Mainly for her.

James turned to her and stroked her back, but she stood, jerking away, and all but ran to the front door. She needed fresh air; she was going to pass out.

James was too tuned to her, and he came after her. She was bent over, her hands on her knees, her eyes shut tight, trying to get her head to stop spinning. Her breath was choppy, and no matter how hard she tried to breathe, she wasn't getting enough air.

He reached for her. "What's wrong, sweetheart?"

She straightened, fighting to get herself together.

"You and I are through." She hadn't planned to come out and say it like that, but there it was. She kept her eyes glued to the wall on her right; her resolve would falter if she looked at him. He had that much power over her.

"What are you talking about? Look at me, princess," he said, grabbing her and forcing her to face him. She did her best to look at him and not see him. "You are joking, right?"

"No, I am not joking." The air she was getting was barely enough to let her talk. She needed to finish this conversation now, before she choked, or worse, broke into tears.

"This is because of Faith? Whatever she told you, ignore it. I made it clear to her I was with you."

She shook her head, afraid to even give his words consideration, or she'd falter. "Give your keys to Elle."

Tim came out. "Is everything all right?"

Tate nodded, but James ignored him, his gaze never leaving her. "Talk to me."

She disentangled herself from him. Time to be strong. "Good-bye, James."

"Don't do this, Tate."

She hurried back in, whispered to Elle to close for her, and avoiding questioning glances and without stopping to explain anything, she ran to her apartment. Walking would have been more dignified, but she was past caring about saving face. And running away was more important at this moment. She needed to be alone, pull herself together. It had been nice as long as it lasted, but now it was time to get off the ride before it derailed, crashed, and burned with her in it.

Once in her apartment, she barely managed to sit before the door opened. It was James; the man didn't know when to quit. Although she had to recognize it; she'd been surprised he'd let her run away down there.

She sighed, her voice coming out like a broken string of sound. "What are you doing here? I asked you to give your keys to Elle." She felt dead tired, drained, but she had to stand, show him she meant business.

"What the fuck is wrong with you?" He widened his stance. Clearly she wasn't going to drive him away that easily.

"Language," she reprimanded him.

He remained silent, his eyes flaring. He was pissed.

"Please don't make this more difficult. Just go."

"What's gotten into you?" She kept quiet, her arms also crossed. "Talk to me, dammit. I deserve at least that much!"

"There's nothing to talk about. This thing between us is history. We are history."

"Not so fast, sweetheart. I want to know why you are freezing me out. This is about Faith, right? What did she tell you?"

She shrugged. Yeah, this was about Faith, but then again,

it wasn't. "Faith just sped thing up. I knew you weren't the kind I could trust in the long run."

"My kind?" he said, his eyes glittering furiously. "Are we back to that shit again?"

"As far as I'm concerned, we never left it behind."

He laughed bitterly. "You're such a bitch; I tell I love you, and what do you do next? You drop me like a bad habit. Hasn't it occurred to you I may deserve better than a coldhearted hypocrite so full of fears and prejudices she can't tell her head from her ass? I won't beg for anyone's love, and yours is no exception. I deserve a woman that doesn't have to be talked into showing that she cares. Someone who'd trust my commitment to her."

"Good luck finding her," she said, trying to keep her expression blank. Lord help her, the mere thought of James with someone else made her physically ill.

Cursing, he strode toward her, pulling her against him. "Who the fuck am I to you, uh? A stray dog to be returned to the kennel when it pleases you? I've been bending myself backward and forward like a damn pretzel for you, accommodating you, giving you all the control in the speed of our relationship so you wouldn't feel pushed! So you wouldn't flip out!"

"Accommodating me? Fuck off, you asshole! I am not your project! Or your damn rescue operation! No one asked you to go to such trouble! I just wanted a fuck! You get it? A fuck! I made it crystal clear from the beginning that this was sex. You were the one obscuring everything, pushing again and again for a relationship I didn't want. Don't blame me if you aren't getting what you think you deserve! Now get the fuck away from here!"

He fell upon her lips, kissing her with an intensity that bordered on pain.

"Why should I?" He breathed into her lips, his gaze boring a hole in her. "I'm always up for a fuck myself. And don't give me that look. You want me. I can feel your heart speeding up; I can sense your need for me."

Damn, he was as arrogant as ever. And twice as right.

"We've established you can turn me on." She shrugged dismissively. "That just proves my point. Now leave." She kept going for indifferent, but her breath was labored.

Suddenly her back was against the wall, James pressing at her front, his hard cock forcibly grinding at her lower belly. "I don't think so, babe; you don't get to dismiss me. Not yet," he said, nuzzling her ear, his hands gripping her hips. "Stop pretending you are not interested. We both know you are wet for me. And I can give it to you the way you like it."

Her breath caught in her throat, and she shivered. Her felt so right against her. Damn, she wanted him. She wanted this, for the last time. If this was the end of it, she wanted to feel him inside her once more. He noticed right away the sexual tension flowing through her, grabbed her buttocks, lifting her to him, nudging his erection against her core. She gasped, her nails sinking into his shoulders, her eyes closing.

He looked furious and very aroused. "Yeah, you want me to fuck you. Let's get to it, shall we? That's at least one we've been able to agree on without any problems since the beginning. And I deserve to fuck you one last time too, if for nothing else than for all my troubles."

"You asshole." She slapped at him, but he didn't budge.

Unbuckling his pants, he lifted her skirt and tore her panties aside. He parted her legs with his thigh and roughly probed her with his finger. It was totally unnecessary; he could make her wet with his voice alone. Her muscles greedily sucked him in.

Covering her with his body, James entered her. She was wet but not ready for him, and as he filled her to the hilt, she cried out. James stilled and looked her in the eye. Such a cold stare. So aroused yet so hard. This wasn't the attentive lover she knew, but her body was so tuned to him it wouldn't deny him anything.

She held him tight against her, willing her muscles to accommodate him; she hadn't been planning on having sex with him, but now she wanted it, wanted it badly.

There was nothing tender in the way James took her. He pumped into her hard until she came, and then he used her body even harder until he found his release and his semen spurted into her. He didn't look at her. No tender words, no wicked comments, no caresses. No intimacy. Just heavy breathing, heavy fucking, and the sound of slapping bodies.

Still panting, she looked at him. "I love to get fucked by you; I won't deny it. But that's all." Her voice trembled with a lack of conviction she found difficult to hide.

"Don't insult me with your bullshit. You're scared of giving yourself to me, scared shitless of investing yourself in this relationship. At least recognize that much."

He was so right. Not that it made a difference. She closed her eyes, steeling herself for the hurt she was going to inflict upon him. "I don't want a relationship with you, and I don't love you, so get that through your thick skull. To me, you're nothing more than a good fuck. And a temporary one at that."

His stormy eyes, always so expressive, turned glacial, and she inwardly winced at the sharp change in him.

"Fuck you too, Tate." He didn't scream, he didn't look mad, he was just icy cold. He pulled out of her, buckled up, and left her apartment. On his way out, he left the keys on the table. "Have a nice life," he said without looking back.

Mission accomplished. He was gone. For good. Her legs gave out, and she fell to the floor. The pain she'd been feeling before James came up to her place had been inconsequential. This was so much worse, so much more real. The world was crashing down around her. She opened her mouth to gasp for air, but nothing came in. She wrapped her arms around her stomach, pressing it, the knot at the pit of it tightening and tightening. It was done; she was alone. Although she knew this was the right thing to do, that didn't make it less painful.

Madly panting for air, she closed her eyes, but then she opened them again, for all she saw was James's warm hazel eyes turning ice-cold. She curled into herself like a baby.

Come on, Tate, get your shit together, she reprimanded herself while getting up. *You knew this was coming, nothing new about it, just business as usual. You've survived much worse things.*

But no matter how hard she tried to pull her shit together, all she could see was James walking away.

CHAPTER THIRTEEN

His cell was ringing, but hell if James was interested in answering it.

After a long night getting acquainted with his old friend Jack Daniels, James was feeling weirdly numb, finally; he didn't want anything or anybody bringing him back to a shitty reality he didn't feel like facing yet.

Tate.

He was pissed and hurt. He'd thought he could work around any shit Tate threw at him, but apparently he couldn't. Yesterday he saw a glint in her eyes, a resolve that hadn't been there before, not even once in all their clashes, every time she said no to him and he ignored her. She was letting him go, with or without his consent. He knew he couldn't fight against that; if she didn't want him, he couldn't hold her. The sad part was that he thought she did want him, but not even then could he hold her; she'd decided he wasn't worth the effort, and nothing he said would have mattered.

Ah hell, he was so fucked. Dumb shit that he was, he'd fallen in love with her hard, in a way he'd never fallen in love before. But he was done banging his head against the wall; he couldn't keep fighting for the both of them—wouldn't, actually. Life was too short and he had too much respect for himself to destroy his life chasing after her.

Shit happened; it hurt, yeah, but he'd get over it. Eventually.

He had trouble remembering what he used to do before she

entered his life, how he'd occupied his time. He figured he should head to the office and get on with his life or go to the gym, sweat off all this crap clenching his chest, but he felt empty. Gutted. Every instinct inside him yelled to go to Tate and shake some sense into her—which, taking into consideration her lovely farewell words to him, could only mean he was completely deranged, but fuck if he would perform tricks for peanuts; he wasn't a pathetic chump ready to settle for scraps. There was a limit to everything, and he'd reached it. He was done. He didn't want to have to convince Tate she loved him or force her into seeing something she didn't want to; he had too much pride for that. He deserved a woman that would fight for him too, not one that would run scared in the other direction.

The constant beeping of the phone was driving him mad, so he reached for it and checked the caller ID. Elle.

"What do you want?"

"Hi. Is Tate there with you?"

"Why?"

"Listen, I know you had a fight yesterday, but I figured you'd made up by now. I need to talk to her, and since she's not answering her cell, could you please get your hands away from her long enough to put her on the phone?"

He went on alert right away. "She isn't here. What do you mean she's not answering?"

"She was supposed to meet me at Heaven for coffee and then some shopping. She hasn't showed up, and nobody's picking up the phone at Rosita's. I thought about going there, but I don't have the keys and I'm already downtown."

The hairs on the back of his neck were standing straight up. Damn, he had a bad feeling about this. Tate was too thrilled her sister was finally coming around; she wouldn't voluntarily miss a date with her.

"No, stay where you are, I'll take care of this. As soon as I contact her, I'll ask her to give you a call."

As he was getting dressed and dialing Tate's number all at once, another call came in.

"What?" he barked at the cell.

"Clint is out on bail," Jack answered. "I just got a call about it."

"How the fuck did that happen?" They'd been in the police station yesterday afternoon giving a statement, and the case against him seemed solid.

"Not sure yet how that happened, but someone bailed him out. You better call Tate and let her know, just in case."

"Tate isn't answering. Elle just called me because she was supposed to meet her and she hasn't shown up. I was trying to reach her when you called. I'm on my way now."

"I'm almost an hour away from Rosita's. Wait for me."

Yeah right. "Whatever."

"There's another thing. I've been checking the Internet cafés where some of the e-mails came from. You aren't going to like this."

His blood was boiling; it had been boiling since yesterday. That he had spent the worst night ever didn't help a shit. Sleeping had been out of the question of course, and he was still wearing the same clothes as yesterday, before his world had been tilted on its axis. All his plans ruined. Now he was out of patience. Enough. He'd lost enough time, enough money, enough sleep over that bitch.

The metal shutters were halfway down, and there was a temporary door instead of the front door he had a key for, so he knocked. Snooping through the glass of a window, he saw Tate at the counter, the receipts from last night in front of her. He'd figured she'd be there this morning doing the paperwork for the restaurant. Tate was a creature of habit, stubborn in her ways. For once this was going to serve him.

She looked warily at him, but he smiled and waved at her, signaling for her to open the door.

Tate frowned but opened the door. "What are you doing here?"

"Hello to you too," he said, his smile all teeth as he punched her in the face.

The pain in her jaw woke her up just as she was being tied to a chair. By Aidan, of all people.

"Aidan? What the hell…?"

"You couldn't let it go; you had to push and push, mock me at every step! Why the fuck is it that you can never do as you're told?"

Tate was at total loss for words. Was she having a hallucination?

"Is it that difficult? How stupid are you, really?"

"What? What the hell are you talking about? You're hurting me. Please let me go!"

He ignored her, finished tightening her wrists together at her back with the duct tape, and faced her. "You stupid little bitch, how difficult was it to do the right thing? Tell me, I'd like to know."

"What are you saying? What right thing? This is insane, Aidan. You left me, remember?"

"You chose this stinky place over me! You were supposed to close this joint or sell it to that Italian, and crawl back begging for me to take you back. I'd have done that, allowed you to be part of my life again. Given you a sense of belonging, a purpose. But no, what does Tate do? She sticks to this hellhole no matter what, come hell or high water, through debts, fires, and threats. All just to show me you can do it without me. To spit in my face!" he yelled.

Tate was having difficulty following him; her face throbbed, and she felt queasy, panicked, and as frantic as she was, she found it extremely difficult to focus her attention on finding a way out of this mess. On top of that, Aidan angrily pacing up and down in front of her with that damn gun pointed at her was triggering her gag reflex. She was so going to lose her breakfast—not very ladylike, or effective for that matter, but still. From the little she understood, it was clear the guy was nuts. Aidan, the well-adapted, successful, handsome, clean-cut top lawyer, was one nut short of a fruitcake, to put it mildly, and she was alone, unprotected, and at his mercy tied to a chair. She pulled at her wrists, but the tape had been wound tightly. She needed to get her hands free, find a way to get some help. That gun and the big canister of gasoline in front of her were quite telling; she was going to die, one way or the other. If it was all up to Aidan, she was checking out today.

What she wouldn't give now to have the panic button James had given her. He was an honorable guy; in spite of her despicable behavior yesterday, she was sure he'd answer her distress call. But the watch with the damn button was somewhere upstairs, lying around, forgotten. He'd lectured her again and again on the need of wearing it, but she hadn't listened. She never did. Maybe she did deserve to die after all, if nothing else, then just for her sheer stupidity. And for the way she'd treated James too; that alone should grant her a one-way ticket to the depths of hell.

"Look at me, you whore! I am talking to you!" he said with a snarl, waving the gun in her face, obviously still hating when he wasn't the center of attention.

She tried to placate him. "Aidan, I don't know what it is you think I did to you, but—"

"What you did to me?" A creepy, crazy laugh tore from his throat. "You made me look like a moron, that's what you did! You and this stupid place, mocking me at every turn!" He darted toward her and gave her face a fierce slap that made her tumble and fall to the floor with the chair, bringing the nearby table down. The sound of breaking glass and falling plates and cutlery clattered around her. "Everyone, from my boss to my colleagues, all saw and understood how you disrespected me! You looked down at all my attempts to help you see the error of your ways. But I'm done playing nice with you."

He wasn't making any sense, she thought, terrified, looking at him from the floor. There were pieces of glass everywhere, and she wasn't sure whether she'd hurt herself in the fall; all she could feel was her throbbing face. Realizing a fairly big piece of glass was within her reach, she grabbed it and hid it in between her hands. If Aidan didn't notice, she could use it to try to saw the duct tape.

"Get up, you worthless imbecile!" he said, jerking her up with one of her arms. She yelped in pain from the sudden movement, but she kept her hands fisted.

He got her chair standing upright again and continued yelling into her face. "Was it too much to ask to sell out as I suggested at the beginning? Even your mother and that moron Elle agreed with me. But no, you had to prove everyone wrong! I was the one who orchestrated that first fire; I sneaked in, set the rag on fire, and later called in a tip to the fire department about seeing smoke. It was my present to you, ungrateful bitch, so it'd be easier for you to give up the place. I was sure the mounting debts from the fire would make you see what a money pit Rosita's was, but no, you wouldn't listen to reason, you kept going! I really hoped the e-mails would eventually change your mind and scare you enough. Even when I left you, I thought you'd eventually come back to me, where you belong. And maybe you would have if your boyfriend hadn't appeared on the scene. After all the time I spent on you, and you had to go opening your legs for that thug." He paced some more, shaking his head at the same time. "I was feeling magnanimous, ready to take you back that night I came to invite you for a drink, but you dared to turn me down. Even after that slap to the face, I still tried to be understanding and forgiving. I thought if I gave you time, you'd come to your senses and break things up with him, but no, of course not. You defied me at every step; you get off on it. Two nights ago, when I saw him kissing you in the entrance of the restaurant as if he owned you, I knew that was it. I'm through playing games with you. Now I wouldn't want you even if you came crawling back to me on your hands and knees."

"You were the one sending those e-mails?" She needed him talking—sawing her way though the wide tape was going to take some time, especially as her pulse was so frantic and erratic. She suspected her wrist was the part getting the more damage.

"Of course I sent them. Did you really think Clint was smart enough to cover his tracks in the cyber world? Please! He's an asshole, I give you that, but that's all. He isn't in any way a mastermind. Although he is going to come in handy; he's going to get blamed for all this. It was such a lucky stroke to find out about his debts and his connection to Old Vito. I decided on the spot he was going to be my scapegoat. You see, one of the sucky parts of being a partner is to have to take several pro bono cases. Those have granted me access to certain acquaintances of doubtful reputation that are more than happy to throw incendiary bombs and frame another for it."

"You framed Clint?" No matter how important it was to free her hands, she could not help but stop and look at Aidan, flabbergasted. My God, who was this man? She didn't know him, not at all. "You're responsible for the gasoline-filled bottles too?"

"Of course, you brainless twerp. The day you fired him, I'd been watching this place. After leaving here totally pissed, he went to a bar and got smashed. He's such a sour drunk, whining and bitching at you for firing him. When he went home to sleep it off, I came back here, just in time to see you kissing *him* out there. I couldn't let you get away with that anymore, so I decided then and there I was going to end it and let Clint take the fall. I'm going to burn down this shithole with you in it, and Clint is going to go to jail for it. I got a bail bondsman to get him out, and I made sure he went home, where those acquaintances of mine will make sure he stays, drugged up to his ears with sleeping pills. He's going to have no alibi."

"Neither will you."

"Oh, but I do. I'm at the moment traveling downtown to see one of my clients from the pro bono cases. One of the guys watching out for poor sleepy Clint, as a matter of fact."

At that moment, she heard the door, lifted her eyes and saw James standing there. Her breath caught in her throat.

"How nice of you to come through the front door!" Aidan chuckled while turning toward James with the gun pointing at him.

James ignored him and sought Tate with his eyes. "Are you all right?" When she nodded, he turned to look at Aidan and shrugged. "You're in the middle of the dining area, your back to the wall, so there's no way to surprise you, not through the front door, not through the back door. So no need for theatrics. I thought I'd take the direct approach and come in so we could have a chat, man-to-man. Tate doesn't really need to be here; your problem is with this place and with me. I forced Tate to keep going despite the e-mails and the threats, while all she wanted was to close it down," he lied.

Tate was shaking her head, but her throat was shut tight, and she couldn't get a word out. All she could see was James and that gun pointing at him, threatening his life. She couldn't allow that; she loved him too much.

Aidan laughed. "How cavalier of you to come to her rescue. Sorry, but no can do. Keep your hands up where I can see them, and come in slowly. Now that you're here, you'll have to burn down with the place."

"Very smooth move trying to frame Clint for your doings, especially because of his involvement with Vito. I have to say, you had us fooled for a while. You won't get away with this, though. We followed you for a while at the beginning, and we have some surveillance footage of you. Luckily one of my associates happened to have it with him while interviewing the employees of the Internet cafés you used to send the e-mails. They all recognized you from the pictures; they didn't recognize Clint or any of Vito's employees. I'm not the only one that knows that; you're going down, man. And the guys you used to try to burn this place down yesterday will be found, and they will talk."

As James closed in, Tate kept cutting the tape. The canister of gasoline Aidan had at his feet was a precursor of things to come, and it scared her to death. James didn't seem scared, though, his gaze on Aidan, his moves controlled.

Aidan laughed, his crazy eyes narrowing. "I'm a good lawyer, James, and the connection with the Internet cafés is flimsy at best. You got nothing on me, no evidence. And those guys, if they are ever found, they won't talk; I'm the only thing keeping them out of jail. Besides, no one would believe them over me."

James reached Tate and tried to stand in front of her.

"Nuh-uh, move to stand by her side."

The tape finally gave, and Tate's hands were free. Damn, she should have taken a knife instead of a piece of glass; it would have been more effective as a weapon.

"So what's your plan? Because the police are on their way. I called it in before I came," James said.

"No, you didn't; you had no reason to. The plan is to put a bullet in you both and then burn this place down. As you've been a particularly painful thorn in my side, I'll shoot you first, let Tate see how you bleed to death," he said, pointing his gun at James.

Oh no, she couldn't allow this. James was in this mess because of her. "James has nothing to do with this. Your quarrel is with me," she said, and before thinking it through, she stood and swung her chair toward Aidan, who turned his gun on her right away.

"No!" she heard James yelling. Two shots rang in her ears at the same time that James tackled her and covered her with his body.

From under James, she saw Aidan falling on his knees, surprise on his face, blood seeping from his chest from the same spot where seconds before had beaten the heart of a madman.

Jack was approaching them, holding a sniper rifle, his finger still on the trigger. He'd come through the back door.

Jack was talking, and James was asking her something while checking her over, but she didn't understand either one of them. She heard them from far away.

Finally they got through to her. "Are you hurt? Answer, princess!"

She looked at herself, not totally sure. She felt nothing, absolutely nothing.

"What were you thinking swinging that chair at him? You almost gave me a heart attack."

What had she been thinking? She wasn't sure of that one either. "I was trying to help."

"Baby, Jack and me had everything under control."

She heard the police sirens, and as she felt James scooping her up in his arms, she snorted and passed out.

CHAPTER FOURTEEN

Tate turned off the engine and, taking a fortifying breath, stepped out of the car. Time to man up and bite the bullet. What was the worst that could happen really? He could send her to hell, but that's where she was now, so no biggie.

It had been a week since the whole mess with Aidan. Seven days since James had disappeared on her—after coming so bravely to her rescue, of course. He'd taken her to the hospital, made sure she was all right, and gotten Elle to come to stay with her. Then he'd vanished. And rightfully so. She'd been such a bitch to him. No wonder he'd run like hell and hadn't tried to contact her.

She'd woken up in the hospital with James by her side looking shaken and worried. She'd wanted to apologize so badly, but she'd been pumped up with tranquilizers, her mind fuzzy, and she hadn't known where to start. He'd seemed strained and distant, as if a wall had been erected between them. She'd hated it.

"*Sorry...*" she barely got out. "*For this and—*"

He hadn't acknowledged her words in any way. "*Elle is probably already here. I'll go get her,*" he'd said, heading for the door and opening it.

He was going for Elle and not coming back, she'd been sure of it; it was written all over him. A sense of urgency had gripped her; she couldn't let him go, she had to clear this thing between them, she'd made a horrible mistake. "*Stay,*" she'd whispered to him. "*Stay, please.*"

He had turned to look at her and shook his head. She hadn't been able to breathe. His stare was so hard, so cold. Sad but resolute. He was done with her. She'd needed him close, his scent surrounding her, but all she could smell was the sickening stench of disinfectant. And her fear.

"*Better not. I got to go. Take care, Tate.*"

And she hadn't seen him since.

She'd fucked up big-time, she knew, and after getting discharged from the hospital, Elle hadn't wasted an opportunity to remind her of it.

The ball was in her court; she had to suck it up, swallow each and every one of those stupid, hurtful words she'd spat at him, hope he could see past them, and beg him for forgiveness.

She'd been without James for seven days, and that was frankly seven days too many. The restaurant was doing fine; she was physically okay. Elle had told her she was coming back to Boston permanently, so things were really looking up. Without James, though, none of that mattered. She was lost without him. He may not want her back, but she had to give it a try. She'd say her piece and then pray really hard he'd still want her and wouldn't send her packing.

After ringing the doorbell twice without any success, she decided to go around the back. As she turned the corner, she saw him working in the garden. Suddenly she couldn't breath. He was so beautiful, even with his back to her, he was the most breathtaking male she'd ever laid eyes on. And it wasn't only his physique; on the inside, James was the most caring, loving man she'd ever met. She winced as she remembered how she'd pushed him away, how she'd insulted him. Punished him for caring. She'd used Elle's bad experiences as an excuse to drive him away and justify her behavior when the truth was she was scared. Scared to be happy, scared things would work out. Despite his looks, James wasn't a "type"; he was the man she was in love with, her hero, the man of her dreams, the one she'd treated so badly.

As she gathered her strength to call him out, she noticed Max coming her way.

"You're here. Good," he said, reaching for her and hugging her, lifting her off the ground. "He's being unbearable. Grunting and moping all over the place."

"Put her down," James said with a deep, dark voice that gave her shivers.

Max didn't flinch at the hard tone; he smiled knowingly, kissed her loudly on the cheek, and whispered into her ear. "He's been driving to your place almost every day, never having the guts to stop and knock on your door. Please take him back and put him out of his misery—and ours."

She smiled sadly. "I'll try. I don't know if he's going to let me." Besides, he was the one who had to take *her* back. And he would be within his rights not to. She didn't deserve him, not the way she'd behaved. She'd have to do much better.

Max put her down and then glared at his brother. "You fuck this one up, man, and I won't stand down, you hear me?"

James didn't answer, but his growl was menacing enough that Max lifted his hands and left.

Once alone, the uneasy silence weighed between them.

She glanced around nervously. "Hi, James."

"Hello," James answered, not moving a muscle in her direction.

She breathed out and began walking his way. When she was close enough, she lifted her eyes to him and noticed the husky eyes he'd gotten tattooed where his collarbone met his sternum.

"Is this...?"

"Yes, more ink."

He'd talked about getting another tattoo. That had, of course, been before she'd lost all her marbles and dumped him. "I thought you wouldn't want to..."

He ran his hand through his hair and grabbed his neck. "You thought wrong. What do you want, Tate? Are you here to bitch at me about my ways?"

"No," she answered quietly. Despite what Max had said to her, he wasn't going to make it easy for her. She was going to have to work for each crumb. And it was only fair; she'd been an ass, maybe even caused irreparable damage. She deserved all that and much more. First things first, though. "Thank you for coming to my rescue."

He didn't answer, just stared at her. "How are your wrists?"

She shrugged. Her wrists were still angry red, her face felt weird, and she was having nightmares. In no way could that compare with the state of her heart. That one was smashed. "I'm okay; I was discharged from the hospital after twenty-four hours of observation for the concussion."

"I know. Elle kept me informed."

She tried to hide her surprise; Elle hadn't said a word to her about that. She'd said plenty though about how Tate had been an idiot to push James away and how she needed to get her ass kicked for such a stunt.

"What are you doing here, Tate?"

Ouch, he was really going for glacial cold. "You didn't come to see me. Why?"

He chuckled humorlessly. "You didn't want me, remember?"

Tate looked at the ground, her voice barely audible. "I see. And am I so easy to walk away from?"

"No, you aren't." Pain seeped through his hard tone. "Happy now? Is that what you came here for? Because you can forget it if you think I'm going to grovel. You made yourself clear the last time we spoke."

She shook her head and reached for him, but he didn't move. "No, I'm not happy. I've realized I can't be happy without you." She lowered her eyes and went for broke. "I've been a total bitch, and I'd understand if you don't want to have anything to do with me again. That said, I want very much for you to forgive me. You were right. I was running scared shitless, and it was much easier to drive you away than to face what you mean to me. I was mean and hurtful, and I'm so very sorry."

He lifted his eyes to hers, but he remained silent, his hard stare boring a hole through her.

Here it went, the leap into the dark; hopefully he'd catch her. Otherwise she'd crash hard. "I love you, James. I did love you when you said it to me, I loved you way before that, probably in Florida, but I was just too stubborn to recognize it. You're by far the most important thing that has ever happened to me. I've been an idiot and a coward. I had a great guy, the best, and I threw it all away and now I'm scared out of my mind that I blew things off beyond any possible reparation. Please believe I never meant to hurt you. I just panicked and wanted you away so that I wouldn't have to face all that you make me feel. You scare me. When I'm with you, you make me feel so loved, so protected, the thought of you taking that from me made me freak out."

"I would never have taken that from you." His tone was hard, and she winced at it.

"Yeah, I know that. Now. Is now too late?" she asked hopefully.

James didn't say anything, his face impassive.

He didn't believe her. Or maybe he did but wasn't giving her another chance.

She tried to breathe through the lump in her throat and blinked a couple of times, trying to avoid the tears that were welling in her eyes. Yeah, it was too late; she'd lost him.

"I see. I-I'm...I'm going to go now," she said, taking a step back. "I want you to know that all I said that day, about you being good only for a fuck, it was all a big lie. It's impossible to trade up, James; you're as good as it gets, and I didn't know how to deal with that. I was too messed up to see it, and I screwed it up. I'm sorry."

She turned around, furiously blinking. She needed to get out of there before she made a bigger ass of herself and threw herself at him.

HE COULDN'T BELIEVE Tate was in front of him, fidgeting and on the verge of tears, telling him she loved him. And trying to run out on him again.

"Oh no, you aren't walking out on me."

He grabbed her, and before she could react, he had her pinned against the table, his arms on either side of her, his face a millimeter from hers. Tate's silver eyes glittered with unshed tears.

"You don't get to come here to tell me you love me and then walk away." He was looming over her menacingly; he should back down a bit, but he couldn't get himself to. "That's not the way it works."

Her voice trembled. "I don't want to walk away." Then she closed her eyes, like she was afraid of his reaction, and continued, "I want you to tell me you still love me, that although I don't deserve it—and I know I don't—you'll give me another chance. I promise I won't ever let you down again, I—"

She opened her mouth to say something more, but he couldn't deny himself any longer and fell upon her. He held her head with both hands and ruthlessly took her lips. Jesus, she tasted so good, like heaven. It felt like coming home again. She belonged there, with him, in his arms, her small hands wrapped around his neck. Her heart beating against his chest.

"I'm so sorry, James," she whispered, her lips quivering, her tears running freely down her cheeks now. "Please forgive me. I—"

"Shh, love," he interrupted her and kissed her again. She was clinging so hard to him, her small body holding to him so tight his heart swelled.

He'd been cold and numb without her. First he'd been pissed at her for dumping him, hurt by her words, then scared to death when he saw Aidan pointing a gun at her. The mere thought he could lose her, that Tate wouldn't be in this world anymore, robbed him of breath. He couldn't live without her. The bitch of it was as long as she didn't acknowledge she wanted him in her life, without conditions, reservations, or doubts, he couldn't live with her either. That had been exactly the reason why he'd forced himself to leave her bedside at the hospital. She'd looked so small and so white in that bed, so lost. And then she'd asked him to stay, twice, and he'd wanted so much to do just that: stay, protect her, take over. It had ripped his heart out to leave her there, but he had to; he'd meet her halfway, but he wouldn't carry the weight of their relationship all on his shoulders. She'd needed to decide by herself if he was what she wanted, and if so, take a stand. It was just his good fortune she did, because he didn't know what he'd have done if she hadn't.

"I'm so sorry I hurt you. Please forgive me," she ranted while he peppered kisses all over her face.

He stared at her while he lovingly dried her tears with his thumbs. "I love you, Tate. I should have never let you push me away. I won't ever let you do that again. I can't live without you."

"I thought you didn't want to have anything to do with me anymore." He snorted in disbelief, and she cupped his face, asking, "Why didn't you come to me?"

"In short? I've been an idiot, scared shitless you'd reject me again."

"You aren't the idiot," Tate mumbled. "The second you left my apartment, I knew deep inside I'd made the biggest mistake of my life. Even Elle told me so every chance she got. I was so afraid you'd send me packing, though, that it took me seven days to make it here."

"I'm happy you made it here." If she hadn't, it wouldn't have mattered; it was just a question of when he'd have broken down and gone to her. "But I would have come for you, princess; you can be sure of that. You're too important for me. I've been dying without you."

"Your new tattoo."

He stiffened a bit. "What about it?"

She passed her fingers over it lightly. "I love it."

"Your eyes. The most beautiful, captivating, and wicked eyes of all. The only eyes I want by my side when I wake up."

She smiled at him, that damn sweet smile that got him every time. He plastered her to his chest, hugging her. "Something of mine marking you. Very sexy. This says you're mine."

She had no clue, but she'd marked him down to his soul. "I am yours, princess. Always have been, since the beginning." James tilted her chin up with one hand, wrapped the other around her waist and he kissed her, caressing her lips with his tongue, rocking his hips against her.

She looked at him, her eyes smoky. "I want you. Can I have you?"

He narrowed his gaze on her; she was repeating the same words he'd said to her long ago in Eternal Sun.

"Just sex, right?" he asked, also borrowing her words. "Because if that's the only thing you want from me, then no, you can't have me. I won't do this anymore. Have you ever heard about not buying the cow if you get the milk for free?"

"What?"

"You're marrying me."

"Am I?"

He caressed her jaw. "Yes, you are. No more free milk. If you want the milk, you'll have to buy the cow first. If you want sex, you'll have to wear my ring and marry me."

"Yes, I will marry you," she said, hugging and kissing him, new tears running down her cheeks. "Of course I'll marry you."

"And you'll move into my house and you won't complain. I want to give you babies, now or later, whenever you want them, and they're going to need space to run around. And don't say the apartment on top of Rosita's is big enough."

She was nodding and mopping her eyes with the back of her hand. "Yes. No, I won't complain. Much."

He chuckled, lifting her, and she wrapped her legs around his waist. "I love you, princess. I love you so much I've been lost without you. Just try to push me away again, see how far it gets you. I'll spank your pretty ass so hard you won't be able to sit for a week."

"You can try." She smiled wickedly at him, and nipped at his chin with her mouth.

"Now I'm taking you ring hunting. I won't let you go back on your word. And once my ring is on you, I'm going to take you to my room and fuck you senseless."

"I'm already wearing your ring, James," she whispered to him, her little pink tongue lightly caressing his ear. "You were right; green suits me. Do you want to see it?"

"Oh yes, please," he said with a groan. He wanted her more than he wanted to take his next breath.

"I promise the cow is as good as sold. We'll get the official ring afterward. Make love to me, James, please, now. I've been dying without you too." Her sexy tongue flicked over his lips, and she bit his lower lip while grinding her core against his erection. James groaned and pressed her against him, engulfing her, taking charge of the kiss.

When they resurfaced, they were both flushed and panting. "Let's get into the house, princess, before I lose my mind and take you here in the grass."

As he carried her upstairs, his lips never leaving her mouth, his hands never leaving her body, he heard his brother laugh.

"So I gather everything's well, huh?" Max said from the hallway.

"Start shopping for the tuxedo, bro."

Elle Aycart

After a colorful array of jobs all over Europe ranging from translator to chocolatier to travel agent to sushi chef to flight dispatcher, Elle Aycart is certain of one thing and one thing only: aside from writing romances, she has abso-frigging-lutely no clue what she wants to do when she grows up. Not that it stops her from trying all sorts of crazy stuff. While she is probably now thinking of a new profession, her head never stops churning new plots for her romances.

Visit Elle at http://elleaycart.blogspot.com.

Loose Id® Titles by Elle Aycart

Available in digital format at http://www.loose-id.com
or your favorite online retailer

Heavy Issues
Inked Ever After
More than Meets the Ink

The OGs Series
Deep Down

In addition to digital format, the following titles
are also available in print at your favorite bookseller:

Heavy Issues
More than Meets the Ink

CPSIA information can be obtained at www.ICGtesting.com
Printed in the USA
LVOW11s1625110116

470117LV00001B/285/P